New York Times bestseller Jill Shalvis
novels including her ... ... Luck
and Cedar Ridge series. ...
Readers Choice winner makes her home ...

Visit her website at www.jillshalvis.com for a complete book list
and daily blog, and www.facebook.com/JillShalvis for other news,
or follow her on Twitter @JillShalvis.

Jill Shalvis. Delightfully addictive:

'Packed with the trademark Shalvis humor and intense intimacy,
it is definitely a must-read . . . If love, laughter and passion are the
keys to any great romance, then this novel hits every note'
Romantic Times

'Heart-warming and sexy . . . an abundance of chemistry,
smoldering romance, and hilarious antics' *Publishers Weekly*

'[Shalvis] has quickly become one of my go-to authors of contemporary
romance. Her writing is smart, fun, and sexy, and her books never fail to
leave a smile on my face long after I've closed the last page . . .
Jill Shalvis is an author not to be missed!' *The Romance Dish*

'Jill Shalvis is such a talented author that she brings to life
characters who make you laugh, cry, and are a joy to read'
Romance Reviews Today

'What I love about Jill Shalvis's books is that she writes sexy,
adorable heroes . . . the sexual tension is out of this world. And of
course, in true Shalvis fashion, she expertly mixes in humor that has
you laughing out loud' *Heroes and Heartbreakers*

'I always enjoy reading a Jill Shalvis book. She's a consistently
elegant, bold, clever writer . . . Very witty – I laughed out loud
countless times and these scenes are sizzling' *All About Romance*

'If you have not read a Jill Shalvis novel yet, then you really have
not read a real romance yet either!' *Book Cove Reviews*

'Engagin ... ...eart,

JILL SHALVIS
the trouble with mistletoe

headline
ETERNAL

Published by arrangement with Avon Books,
an imprint of HarperCollins Publishers

First published in Great Britain in 2016
by HEADLINE ETERNAL
An imprint of HEADLINE PUBLISHING GROUP

2

Cataloguing in Publication Data is available from the British Library

ISBN 978 1 4722 4293 8

Offset in 12.65/15 pt Times LT Std by Jouve (UK), Milton Keynes

Printed and bound in Great Britain by CPI Group (UK) Ltd, Croydon, CR0 4YY

Headline's policy is to use papers that are natural, renewable and recyclable
products and made from wood grown in well-managed forests and other
controlled sources. The logging and manufacturing processes are expected to
conform to the environmental regulations of the country of origin.

HEADLINE PUBLISHING GROUP
An Hachette UK Company
Carmelite House
50 Victoria Embankment
London EC4Y 0DZ

www.headlineeternal.com
www.headline.co.uk
www.hachette.co.uk

To my Oldest, who isn't that old—
and let's not forget I had her when I was twelve,
so I'm not that old either—
for tirelessly walking me around San Francisco
every time I needed to see
something for this book.
I'm so proud of you.
XOXO forever.

Chapter 1

#TheTroubleWithMistletoe

The sun had barely come up and Willa Davis was already elbow deep in puppies and poo—a typical day for her. As owner of the South Bark Mutt Shop, she spent much of her time scrubbing, cajoling, primping, hoisting—and more cajoling. She wasn't above bribing either.

Which meant she kept pet treats in her pockets, making her irresistible to any and all four-legged creatures within scent range. A shame though that a treat hadn't yet been invented to make her irresistible to *two*-legged male creatures as well. Now *that* would've been handy.

But then again, she'd put herself on a Man-Time-Out so she didn't need such a thing.

"Wuff!"

This from one of the pups she was bathing. The little guy wobbled in close and licked her chin.

"That's not going to butter me up," she said, but it totally did and unable to resist that face she returned the kiss on the top of his cute little nose.

One of Willa's regular grooming clients had brought in her eight-week-old heathens—er, golden retriever puppies.

Six of them.

It was over an hour before the shop would open at nine a.m. but her client had called in a panic because the pups had rolled in horse poo. God knew where they'd found horse poo in the Cow Hollow district of San Francisco—maybe a policeman's horse had left an undignified pile in the street—but they were a mess.

And now so was Willa.

Two puppies, even three, were manageable, but handling six by herself bordered on insanity. "Okay, listen up," she said to the squirming, happily panting puppies in the large tub in her grooming room. "Everyone sit."

One and Two sat. Three climbed up on top of the both of them and shook his tubby little body, drenching Willa in the process.

Meanwhile, Four, Five, and Six made a break for it, paws pumping, ears flopping over their eyes, tails wagging wildly as they scrabbled, climbing over each other like circus tumblers to get out of the tub.

"Rory?" Willa called out. "Could use another set of hands back here." Or three . . .

No answer. Either her twenty-three-year-old employee had her headphones cranked up to make-me-deaf-please or she was on Instagram and didn't want to lose her place. *"Rory!"*

The girl finally poked her head around the corner, phone in hand, screen lit.

Yep. Instagram.

"Holy crap," Rory said, eyes wide. "Literally."

Willa looked down at herself. Yep, her apron and clothes were splattered with suds and water and a few other questionable stains that might or might not be related to the horse poo. She'd lay money down on the fact that her layered strawberry blonde hair had rioted, resembling an explosion in a down-pillow factory. Good thing she'd forgone makeup at the early emergency call so at least she didn't have mascara running down her face. "Help."

Rory cheerfully dug right in, not shying from getting wet or dirty. Dividing and conquering, they got all the pups out of the tub, dried, and back in their baby pen in twenty minutes. One through Five fell into the instant slumber that only babies and the very drunk could achieve, but Six remained stubbornly awake, climbing over his siblings determined to get back into Willa's arms.

Laughing, she scooped the little guy up. His legs bicycled in the air, tail wagging faster than the speed of light, taking his entire hind end with it.

"Not sleepy, huh?" Willa asked.

He strained toward her, clearly wanting to lick her face.

"Oh no you don't. I know where that tongue's been." Tucking him under her arm, she carted him out front to the retail portion of her shop, setting him into another baby pen with some puppy toys, one that was visible to street traffic. "Now sit there and look pretty and bring in some customers, would you?"

Panting with happiness, the puppy pounced on a toy and got busy playing as Willa went through her opening routine, flipping on the lights throughout the retail area. The shop came to life, mostly thanks to the insane amount of holiday decorations she'd put up the week before, including the seven-foot tree in the front corner—lit to within an inch of its life.

"It's only the first of December and it looks like Christmas threw up in here," Rory said from the doorway.

Willa looked around at her dream-come-true shop, the one finally operating in the black. Well, most of the time. "But in a classy way, right?"

Rory eyed the one hundred miles of strung lights and more boughs of holly than even the North Pole should have. "Um . . . right."

Willa ignored the doubtful sarcasm. One, Rory hadn't grown up in a stable home. And two, neither had she. For the both of them Christmas had always been a luxury that, like three squares and a roof, had been out of their reach more than not. They'd each dealt with that differently. Rory didn't need the pomp and circumstance of the holidays.

Willa did, desperately. So yeah, she was twenty-seven years old and still went overboard for the holidays.

"Ohmigod," Rory said, staring at their newest cash register display. "Is that a rack of penis headbands?"

"No!" Willa laughed. "It's reindeer-antler headbands for dogs."

Rory stared at her.

Willa grimaced. "Okay, so maybe I went a little crazy—"

"A *little*?"

"Ha-ha," Willa said, picking up a reindeer-antler headband. It didn't look like a penis to her, but then again it'd been a while since she'd seen one up close and personal. "These are going to sell like hotcakes, mark my words."

"Ohmigod—don't put it on!" Rory said in sheer horror as Willa did just that.

"It's called marketing." Willa rolled her eyes upward to take in the antlers jutting up above her head. "Shit."

Rory grinned and pointed to the swear jar that Willa had set up to keep them all in line. Mostly her, actually. They used the gained cash for their muffins and coffee fix.

Willa slapped a dollar into it. "I guess the antlers do look a little like penises," she admitted. "Or is it peni? What's the plural of penis?"

"Pene?" Rory asked and they both cracked up.

Willa got a hold of herself. "Clearly I'm in need of Tina's caffeine, *bad*."

"I'll go," Rory said. "I caught sight of her coming through the courtyard at the crack of dawn wearing six-inch wedge sneakers, her hair teased to the North Pole, making her look, like, eight feet tall."

Tina used to be Tim and everyone in the five-story, offbeat historical Pacific Pier Building had enjoyed Tim—but they *loved* Tina. Tina rocked.

"What's your order?" Rory asked.

Tina's coffees came in themes and Willa knew just what she needed for the day ahead. "One of her It's Way Too Early for Life's Nonsense." She pulled some more cash from her pocket and this time a handful of puppy treats came out too, bouncing all over the floor.

"And to think, you can't get a date," Rory said dryly.

"Not *can't* get a date," Willa corrected. "Don't want a date. I pick the wrong men, something I'm not alone in . . ."

Rory blew out a sigh at the truth of that statement and then went brows up when Willa's stomach growled like a roll of thunder.

"Okay, so grab me a muffin as well." Tina made the best muffins on the planet. "Make it two. Or better yet, three. No, wait." Her jeans had been hard to button that morning. "Crap, three muffins would be my entire day's calories. One," she said firmly. "One muffin for me and make it a blueberry so it counts as a serving of fruit."

"Got it," Rory said. "A coffee, a blueberry muffin, and a straitjacket on the side."

"Ha-ha. Now get out of here before I change my order again."

South Bark had two doors, one that opened to the street, the other to the building's courtyard with its beautiful cobblestones and the historical old fountain that Willa could never resist tossing a coin into and wishing for true love as she passed.

Rory headed out the courtyard door.

"Hey," Willa said. "If there's any change, throw a coin into the fountain for me?"

"So you're on a self-imposed man embargo but you still want to wish on true love?"

"Yes, please."

Rory shook her head. "It's your dime." She didn't believe in wishes or wasting even a quarter, but she obediently headed out.

When she was gone, Willa's smile faded. Each of her three part-time employees was young and they all had one thing in common.

Life had churned them up and spit them out at a young age, leaving them out there in the big, bad world all alone.

Since Willa had been one of those lost girls herself, she collected them. She gave them jobs and advice that they only listened to about half the time.

But she figured fifty percent was better than zero percent.

Her most recent hire was nineteen-year-old Lyndie, who was still a little feral but they were working on that. Then there was Cara, who'd come a long way. Rory had been with Willa the longest. The girl put up a strong front but she still struggled. Proof positive was the fading markings of a bruise on her jaw where her ex-boyfriend had knocked her into a doorjamb.

Just the thought had Willa clenching her fists. Sometimes at night she dreamed about what she'd like to do to the guy. High on the list was cutting off his twig and berries with a dull knife but she had an aversion to jail.

Rory deserved better. Tough as nails on the outside, she was a tender marshmallow on the inside, and she'd do anything for Willa. It was sweet, but also a huge responsibility because Rory looked to Willa for her normal.

A daunting prospect on the best of days.

She checked on Six and found the puppy finally fast asleep sprawled on his back, feet spread wide to show the world his most prized possessions.

Just like a man for you.

Next she checked on his siblings. Also asleep. Feeling like the mother of sextuplets, she tiptoed back out to the front and opened her laptop, planning to inventory the new boxes of supplies she'd received late the night before.

She'd just gotten knee-deep in four different twenty-five-pound sacks of bird feed—she still couldn't believe how many people in San Francisco had birds—when someone knocked on the front glass door.

Damn. It was only a quarter after eight but it went against the grain to turn away a paying customer. Straightening, she swiped her hands on her apron and looked up.

A guy stood on the other side of the glass, mouth grim, expression dialed to Tall, Dark, and Attitude-ridden. He was something too, all gorgeous and broody and—hold up. There was something familiar about him, enough that her feet propelled her forward out of pure curiosity. When it hit her halfway to the door, she froze, her heart just about skidding to a stop.

"Keane Winters," she murmured, lip curling like she'd just eaten a black licorice. She hated black licorice. But she was looking at the only man on the planet who could make her feel all puckered up as well as good about her decision to give up men.

In fact, if she'd only given them up sooner, say back on the day of the Sadie Hawkins dance in her freshman year of high school when he'd stood her up, she'd have saved herself a lot of heartache in the years since.

On the other side of the door, Keane shoved his mirrored sunglasses to the top of his head, revealing dark chocolate eyes that she knew could melt when he was amused or feeling flirtatious, or turn to ice when he was so inclined.

They were ice now.

Catching her gaze, he lifted a cat carrier. A bright pink bedazzled carrier.

He had a cat.

Her entire being wanted to soften at this knowledge because that meant on some level at least he had to be a good guy, right?

Luckily her brain clicked on, remembering everything, every little detail of that long ago night. Like how she'd had to borrow a dress for the dance from a girl in her class who'd gleefully lorded it over her, how she'd had to beg her foster mother to let her go, how she'd stolen a Top Ramen from the locked pantry and eaten it dry in the bathroom so she wouldn't have to buy both her dinner and his, as was custom for the "backward" dance.

"We're closed," she said through the still locked glass door.

Not a word escaped his lips. He simply raised the cat carrier another inch, like he was God's gift.

And he had been. At least in high school.

Wishing she'd gotten some caffeine before dealing with this, she blew out a breath and stepped closer, annoyed at her eyes because they refused to leave his as she unlocked and then opened the door. Just another customer, she told herself. One that had ruined her life like it was nothing without so much as an apology . . .

"Morning," she said, determined to be polite.

Not a single flicker of recognition crossed his face and she found something even more annoying than this man being on her doorstep.

The fact that she'd been so forgettable he didn't even remember her.

"I'm closed until nine." She said this in her most pleasant voice although a little bit of eff-you *might've* been implied.

"I've got to be at work by nine," he said. "I want to board a cat for the day."

Keane had always been big and intimidating. It was what had made him such an effective jock. He'd ruled on the football field, the basketball court, *and* the baseball diamond. The perfect trifecta, the all-around package.

Every girl in the entire school—and also a good amount of the teachers—had spent an indecent amount of time eyeballing that package.

But just as Willa had given up men, she'd even longer ago given up thinking about that time, inarguably the worst years of her life. While Keane had been off breaking records and winning hearts, she'd been drowning under the pressures of school and work, not to mention basic survival.

She got that it wasn't his fault her memories of that time were horrific. Nor was it his fault that just looking at him brought them all back to her. But emotions weren't logical. "I'm sorry," she said, "but I'm all full up today."

"I'll pay double."

He had a voice like fine whiskey. Not that she ever drank fine whiskey. Even the cheap stuff was a treat. And maybe it was just her imagination, but she was having a hard time getting past the fact that he was both the same and yet had changed. He was still tall, of course, and built sexy as hell, damn him. Broad shoulders, lean hips, biceps straining his shirt as he held up the cat carrier.

He wore faded ripped jeans on his long legs and scuffed work boots. His only concession to the San Francisco winter was a long-sleeved T-shirt that enhanced all those ripped muscles and invited her to BITE ME in big block letters across his chest.

She wasn't going to lie to herself, she kind of wanted to. *Hard.*

He stood there exuding raw, sexual power and energy—not that she was noticing. Nor was she taking in his expression that said maybe he'd already had a bad day.

He could join her damn club.

And at that thought, she mentally smacked herself in the forehead. No! There would be *no* club joining. She'd set boundaries for herself. She was Switzerland. Neutral. No importing or exporting of anything including sexy smoldering glances, hot body parts, *nothing.*

Period.

Especially not with Keane Winters, thank you very much. And anyway, she didn't board animals for the general public. Yes, sometimes she boarded as special favors for clients, a service she called "fur-babysitting" because her capacity here was too small for official boarding. If and when she agreed to "babysit" overnight as a favor, it meant taking her boarders home with her, so she was extremely selective.

And handsome men who'd once been terribly mean boys who ditched painfully shy girls after she'd summoned up every ounce of her courage to ask him out to a dance did *not* fit her criteria. "I don't board—" she started, only to be interrupted by an unholy howl from inside the pink cat carrier.

It was automatic for her to reach for it, and Keane readily released it with what looked to be comical relief.

Turning her back on him, Willa carried the carrier to the counter, incredibly aware that Keane followed her through her shop, moving with an unusually easy grace for such a big guy.

The cat was continuously howling now so she quickly unzipped the carrier, expecting the animal inside to be dying giving the level of unhappiness it'd displayed.

The earsplitting caterwauling immediately stopped and a huge Siamese cat blinked vivid blue eyes owlishly up at her. It had a pale, creamy coat with a darker facial mask that matched its black ears, legs, and paws.

"Well aren't you beautiful," Willa said softly and slipped her hands into the box.

The cat immediately allowed herself to be lifted, pressing her face into Willa's throat for a cuddle.

"Aw," Willa said gently. "It's alright now, I've got you. You just hated that carrier, didn't you?"

"What the ever-loving hell," Keane said, hands on hips now as he glared at the cat. "Are you kidding me?"

"What?"

He scowled. "My great-aunt's sick and needs help. She dropped the cat off with me last night."

Well, damn. That was a pretty nice thing he'd done, taking the cat in for his sick aunt.

"The minute Sally left," Keane went on, "this thing went gonzo."

Willa looked down at the cat, who gazed back at her, quiet, serene, positively angelic. "What did she do?"

Keane snorted. "What *didn't* she do would be the better question. She hid under my bed and tore up my mattress. Then she helped herself to everything on my counters, knocking stuff to the floor, destroying my laptop and tablet and phone all in one fell swoop. And then she . . ." He trailed off and appeared to chomp on his back teeth.

"What?"

"Took a dump in my favorite running shoes."

Willa did her best not to laugh out loud and say "good girl." It took her a minute. "Maybe she's just upset to be away from home, and missing your aunt. Cats are creatures of habit. They don't like change." She spoke to Keane without taking her gaze off the cat, not wanting to look into the dark, mesmerizing eyes that didn't recognize her because if she did, she might be tempted to pick one of the tiaras displayed on her counter and hit him over the head with it.

"What's her name?" she asked.

"Petunia, but I'm going with Pita. Short for pain in the ass."

Willa stroked along the cat's back and Petunia pressed into her hand for more. A low and rumbly purr filled the room and Petunia's eyes slitted with pleasure.

Keane let out a breath as Willa continued to pet her. "Unbelievable," he said. "You're wearing catnip as perfume, right?"

Willa raised an eyebrow. "Is that the only reason you think she'd like me?"

"Yes."

Okay then. Willa opened her mouth to end this little game and tell him that she wasn't doing this, but then she looked into Petunia's deep-as-the-ocean blue eyes and felt her heart stir. *Crap.* "Fine," she heard herself say. "If you can provide proof of rabies and FVRCP vaccinations, I'll take her for today only."

"Thank you," he said with such genuine feeling, she glanced up at him.

A mistake.

His dark eyes had warmed to the color of melted dark chocolate. "One question."

"What?" she asked warily.

"Do you always wear X-rated headbands?"

Her hands flew to her head. She'd completely forgotten she was wearing the penis headband. "Are you referring to my reindeer antlers?"

"Reindeer antlers," he repeated.

"That's right."

"Whatever you say." He was smiling now, and of course the rat-fink bastard had a sexy-as-hell smile. And unbelievably her good parts stood up and took notice. Clearly her body hadn't gotten the memo on the no-man thing. Especially not *this* man.

"My name's Keane by the way," he said. "Keane Winters."

He paused, clearly expecting her to tell him her name in return, but she had a dilemma now. If she told him who she was and he suddenly recognized her, he'd also remember exactly how pathetic she'd once been. And if he *didn't* recognize her then that meant she was even more forgettable than she'd thought and she'd have to throw the penis headband at him after all.

"And you are . . . ?" he asked, rich voice filled with amusement at her pause.

Well, hell. Now or never, she supposed. "Willa Davis," she said and held her breath.

There was no change in his expression whatsoever. Forgettable then, and she ground her back teeth for a minute.

"I appreciate you doing this for me, Willa," he said.

She had to consciously unclench her teeth to speak. "I'm not doing it for you. I'm doing it for Petunia," she said, wanting to be crystal clear. "And you'll need to be back here to pick her up before closing."

"Deal."

"I've got a few questions for you," she said. "Like an emergency contact, your driver's license info, and"—God help her, she was going to hell if she asked this but she couldn't help herself, she wanted to jog his memory—"where you went to high school."

He arched a brow. "High school?"

"Yes, you never know what's going to be important."

He looked amused. "As long as I don't have to wear a headband of dicks, you can have whatever info you need."

Five extremely long minutes later he'd filled out the required form and provided the information needed after a quick call to his aunt—all apparently without getting his memory jogged. Then, with one last amused look at her reindeer antlers a.k.a. penis headband, he walked out the door.

Willa was still watching him go when Rory came to stand next to her, casually sipping her coffee as she handed over Willa's.

"Are we looking at his ass?" Rory wanted to know.

Yes, and to Willa's eternal annoyance, it was the best ass she'd ever seen. How unfair was that? The least he could've done was get some pudge. "Absolutely not."

"Well we're missing out, because *wow*."

Willa looked at her. "He's too old for you."

"He's thirty. What," she said at Willa's raised brow. "You've got the copy of his driver's license right here on the counter. I did the math, that's not a crime. And anyway, you're right, he's old. Really *old*."

"You do realize I'm only a few years behind him."

"You're old too," Rory said and nudged her shoulder to Willa's.

The equivalent of a big, fat, mushy hug.

"And for the record," the girl went on, "I was noticing his ass for *you*."

"Ha," Willa said. "The devil himself couldn't drag my old, dead corpse out on a date with him, even if he is hot as balls. I gave up men, remember? That's who I am right now, a woman who doesn't need a man."

"Who you are is a stubborn, obstinate woman who has a lot of love to give but is currently imitating a chicken. But hey, if you wanna let your past bad judgment calls rule your world and live like a nun, carry on just as you are."

"Gee," Willa said dryly. "Thanks."

"You're welcome. But I reserve the right to question your IQ. I hear you lose IQ points when you get old." She smiled sweetly. "Maybe you should start taking that Centrum Silver or something. Want me to run out and get some?"

Willa threw the penis headband at her, but Rory, being a youngster and all, successfully ducked in time.

Chapter 2

#OpenMouthInsertFoot

Two mornings later, Willa's alarm went off at zero dark thirty and she lay there for a minute drifting, dreaming . . . thinking. When Keane had returned for Petunia the other night, she'd been with a client so she hadn't had to deal with him.

But she'd made sure to look her fill.

And that bothered her. How could she like looking at him so much? Maybe it was because he was so inherently male and virile he could've walked right off the cover of *Alpha Male* magazine, if such a thing had existed.

The thing was, she wasn't supposed to care what he looked like, or how sexy his low-timbered voice was, or that he was taking care of his aunt's cat in spite of not liking said cat.

Because hello, ditched for the dance . . .

"Gah," she said to her bedroom and rolled over, sticking her head beneath her pillow.

She was too busy for a guy. Any guy. She had work and work was enough. She loved having the security of a bank account, when once upon a time she'd had nothing of her own and only herself to rely on.

She was proud of how far she'd come. Proud to be able to help kids who were in the same situation she'd once been in.

When her alarm went off, she jerked awake and groaned some more but rolled out of bed, blinking blearily at the clock.

Four in the morning.

She hated four in the morning as a general rule but today was an early day. She needed to hit the flower market and get some shopping done for an event she had going that night and also for her upcoming in-store Santa Extravaganza pet photo shoot, an annual event where customers would be able to get their pet's photo taken with Santa. It was a big moneymaker for her, and half of the profits went to the San Francisco animal shelters.

She dragged a grumpy Rory with her, where they bought supplies for the night's event, the photo booth, *and* additional foliage to boot.

"What's all that for?" Rory asked.

"More Christmas flavor."

Rory shook her head. "You've got a serious problem."

"Tell me something I don't know."

They got back to the shop by six thirty a.m. and

went to work. Sitting cross-legged on the counter of her shop with a sketch pad, Willa mapped out the evening's event, a wedding she'd been hired for as a wedding consultant, designer, and officiator.

For two giant poodles.

At seven on the dot, her friends Pru, Elle, and Haley showed up with breakfast, as they did several times a week since they all lived or worked in the building. Currently they were decimating a basket of Tina's muffins before scattering for their various jobs for the day. Haley wasn't yet in her lab coat for her optometrist internship upstairs, and had cute bright red spectacles perched on her nose. Pru wore her captain's attire for her job of captaining a tour boat off Pier 39. Elle was the building's office manager and looked the part in a cobalt blue suit dress with black and white gravity-defying open-toe pumps.

Willa looked her part too. Jeans and a camisole top despite the fact that it was winter. She kept her shop warm for the animals and her arms bare for when she was bathing and grooming.

The current discussion was men, and their pros and cons. Pru had a man. She was engaged to Finn, the guy who ran the Irish pub across the courtyard, and a really good guy along with being one of Willa's closest friends. So needless to say, Pru sat firmly on the pro side. "Look," she said in her defense of love. "Say you really need some orgasm RX, you know? If you're in love with someone, he'll go down on you and expect nothing back because he knows you'd do the same for him. Love is patient, love is kind." She smiled. "Love means oral sex without the pressure to reciprocate."

"Love is keeping batteries in your vibrator," Elle told her and the rest of them laughed, nodding. They all had a long list on the con side for men. Well, except for Haley, who dated women—when she was so inclined to date at all.

Although Willa had to admit, she did like the idea of orgasm RX . . .

"Yes, but what about spiders?" Pru ask. "A man will get the spiders."

There was a silence as the rest of them contemplated this unexpected benefit to having a man.

"I learned to capture and safely relocate," Haley finally said. "For Leeza."

Haley's last girlfriend had been a serious tree hugger. And a serial cheater, as it turned out.

"I just use the long hose on my vacuum cleaner," Elle said, looking smug. "No awkward morning-after conversation required."

"This is about Willa today so don't get me started on you," Pru told her. "You and Archer cause electric fires to break out when you so much as pass by each other. Remind me to circle back to that."

Elle shrugged it off. "You've heard of opposites attract?" she asked. "Well me and Archer, we're a classic case of opposites *distract*. As in we don't like each other."

They all laughed but choked it off when Elle gave them each a glacial look in turn.

Okay, so everyone knew she had a secret thing for Archer—except Elle herself apparently.

Well, and Archer . . .

Willa was just grateful to not be the center of attention anymore, although she wished they'd go back to the fascinating morning-after discussion because she hadn't had a lot of awkward morning afters. She tended to complicate her bad choices in men by sticking too long instead of running off. Maybe that was where she'd always gone wrong. Maybe next time she was stupid enough to give another guy a shot, it would be a strictly one-time thing. And then she'd run like hell.

"Tell me the truth," Pru said. "When it comes to me waxing poetic about mine and Finn's relationship, on a scale of one to that friend who just had a baby and wants to show you pics for hours, how annoying am I?"

Willa met Elle's and Haley's amused gazes and they each murmured a variation of "not that bad."

Pru sighed. "Shit. I'm totally that new mom with baby pics."

"Hey, knowing it is half the battle," Elle offered and being a master conversation manipulator, looked at Willa. "Tell us more about this guy with the cat."

"I can tell you he's hot," Rory said as she walked by carrying a case of hamster food. "Like *major* hot. And also Willa remembers him from high school. He stood her up for some dance, but he doesn't remember it or her."

"Well how rude," Haley said, instantly at Willa's back, which Willa appreciated.

"I don't think he was being rude," Rory said. "Willa had been bathing puppies and looked like a complete train wreck, honestly, all covered in soap suds and puppy drool and maybe some poop too. Even you guys wouldn't have recognized her."

"I looked how I always look," Willa said in her own defense. "And that part about high school was confidential."

"Oops, sorry," Rory said, not looking sorry at all. "I'll be in the back, grooming Thor."

Thor was Pru's dog, who had a penchant for rolling in stuff he shouldn't, the more disgusting the better. Pru blew Rory a grateful kiss and turned to Willa. "So back to hot-as-balls guy. More info please."

Willa sighed. "What is there to say? We went to school together and he never noticed me back then either so I should've known."

"How well did you know him?" Elle asked, eyes sharp. She was the logical one of the group, able to navigate through any and all bullshit with ease.

"Obviously not well," Willa said, hunching over her sketch pad.

"Hmm," Elle said.

"I don't have time to decipher that hmm," Willa warned her.

"You remember when Archer and Spence threatened to castrate your ex?"

Spence and Archer were the last members of their tight gang of friends. Spence was an IT genius. Archer an ex-cop. The two of them together had some serious skills. And yes, they'd stepped in when Willa had needed them to. "That was different," she said. Ethan had been an asshole, no doubt. "Keane's never going to be an ex, asshole or otherwise, because we're never going to be a thing. Now if we're done dissecting my life, I've got a lot to do before tonight's wedding."

She'd stayed up late working on the tuxes her client wanted the poodles to wear. Yes, tuxes. Just because she was in on the joke that South Bark Mutt Stop made more money on tiaras and weddings and gimmicks than actual grooming or supplies didn't mean she couldn't take the wishes of her clients seriously.

And hey, who knew, maybe if she ever got pets of her own other than the fosters she sometimes took in, and if she had more money than she knew what to do with, she might want a wedding for her dogs too. Although she sincerely doubted it. In her world, love had always been fleeting and temporary—sort of the opposite of what all the pomp and circumstance of a wedding conveyed.

Still, game to believe in lasting love as a possibility, at least for others, Willa dropped the giant poodle faux tux front over her own head and looked in the mirror. "What do we think?"

"Very cute," Pru said. "Now jump up and down and do whatever it is dogs do to make sure it holds up."

Willa jumped up and down like she was a dog in a show, holding her hands out in front of her, wrists bent as she hopped around to get the full effect of the tux. The girls were all still laughing when someone knocked on her front door.

Once again it was ten minutes before nine and in mid–dance step Willa stilled, experiencing a rush of déjà vu. The look on everyone's faces confirmed what she needed to know. Still, she slowly turned to the door hoping she was wrong.

Nope.

Not wrong.

Keane Winters stood at the door, watching her.

"Perfect," she said, her dignity in tatters. "How much do you think he saw?"

"Everything," Elle said.

"You should get the door," Pru said. "He looks every bit as hot as Rory said, but he also looks like he's in a rush."

"I'm not opening the door," Willa hissed, yanking off the tux front. "Not until you guys go. Go out the back and hurry!"

No one hurried. In fact, no one so much as budged.

Keane knocked for a second time and when Willa turned to face him again, he went brows up, the picture of gorgeous impatience.

"Well, honestly," Pru said. "Do men learn that look at birth or what?"

"Yes," Elle said thoughtfully. "They do. Willa, honey, don't you dare rush over there. You take your sweet-ass time and make sure to swipe that panic off your face and smile while you're at it. Won't do you any good to let him know he's getting to you."

"See," Willa said to Haley and Pru. "At least one of you isn't influenced by dark, knowing eyes and a darker smile and a pair of ohmigod-sexy guy jeans."

"Okay, I didn't say that," Elle said. "But I'm not so much influenced as curious as hell. Get the door, Wills. Let's see what he's made of."

"He just saw me dancing like a poodle," she said.

"Exactly, and you didn't scare him off. He's got to be made of stern stuff."

Willa sighed and headed to the door.

Again Keane held the pink bedazzled cat carrier, which should have made him look ridiculous. Instead it somehow upped his testosterone levels. His sharp eyes were on her but they turned warm in a way that melted her right through her center as she moved toward him. She stopped with the glass door between them, hands on hips, hoping she looked irritated even if that wasn't quite what she was feeling.

His gaze lowered from her face to run over her body, which gave her another unwelcome rush of heat. Dammit. Now she was irritated *and* aroused—not a good combo.

His mouth quirked at the saying on her apron that read *Dear Santa, I Can Explain*.

Drawing a deep breath, she opened the door. "You've got Petunia again. I hope that means your great-aunt Sally isn't still sick."

He looked surprised that she'd remembered his aunt's name, or that she'd care. "I don't know," he said a little gruffly. "She left me a message saying that I was in charge for the rest of the week but for two days now Pita's been happily destroying my jobsite. I'm throwing myself on your mercy here. Can you help?"

Wow. He must be really desperate since he was actually asking and not assuming. But since Petunia was a sweetheart, she knew she'd do it.

"I'll even tell you where I went to high school," he said, adding a smile that was shockingly charming.

Wow. He hadn't lost his touch when it came to turning it on. "Not necessary," she said, painfully aware of their audience.

Keane's attention was suddenly directed upward, just above her head. She followed his line of sight and found a sprig of mistletoe hanging from the overhead display of small, portable doggy pools. *Mistletoe? What the hell?* She glanced behind her and what do you know, suddenly Rory and Cara were a flurry of movement racing around looking very, *very* busy. "When did the mistletoe go up?" she asked them. "And why?"

"FOMO," Cara said from behind the counter.

"Fear of missing out," Rory translated. "She was hoping a hot guy would come in and the mistletoe would give her an excuse."

Willa narrowed her eyes and her two soon-to-be-dead employees scattered again.

"Interesting," Keane said, looking amused.

"I'm not kissing you."

His mouth curved. "If you take Pita for the day, *I'll* kiss *you*."

"Not necessary," she said, gratified no one could see her heart doing the two-step in her ears. "I'll take Petunia for the day. No kiss required or wanted."

Liar, liar . . .

Keane stepped inside. And because she didn't step back far enough, they very nearly touched. His hair was a little damp, she couldn't help but notice, like maybe he'd just showered. He smelled of sexy guy soap, a.k.a. amazing. He wore faded jeans with a rip along one thigh and another long-sleeved T-shirt with *SF Builders* on the pec, so her guess that he was in construction seemed correct.

He also was covered in cat hair.

From right behind him one of her regulars came in. Janie Sharp was in her thirties, had five kids under the age of ten, worked as a schoolteacher and was continuously late, harried, exhausted, and desperate.

Today, her three youngest were running around her in circles at full speed, screaming as they chased each other while Janie held a fishbowl high, trying to avoid spilling as she was continuously jostled. "I know," she yelled to Willa. "I'm early. But I'll have to kill myself if you don't help me out this morning."

This was a common refrain from Janie. "As long as you don't leave your kids," Willa said. Also a common refrain. At the odd sound from Keane, she glanced over at him. "She's only kidding about killing herself," she said. "But I'm not kidding about her kids."

Janie nodded. "They're devil spawn."

"Names?" Keane asked.

Janie blinked at him as if just seeing him for the first time. Her eyes glazed over a little bit and she might've drooled. "Dustin, Tanner, and Lizzie," she said faintly.

Keane snapped his fingers and the kids stopped running in circles around Janie. They stopped making noise. They stopped breathing.

Keane pointed at the first one. "Dustin or Tanner?"

"Tanner," the little boy said and shoved his thumb in his mouth.

Keane looked at the other two and they both started talking at once. He held up a finger and pointed at the little girl.

"I'm an angel," she said breathlessly. "My daddy says so."

"Did you know that angels look out for the people they care about?" Keane asked her. "They're in charge."

The little girl got a sly look on her face. "So I getta be in charge of Tan and Dust?"

"You *look out* for them." He turned his gaze on the two boys. "And in turn, you look out for her. Nothing should happen to her on your watch, ever. You get me?"

The two boys bobbed their heads up and down.

Janie stared down at her three quiet, respectful kids in utter shock. "It's a Christmas miracle come early," she whispered in awe and met Keane's gaze. "Do you babysit?"

Keane just smiled and for a moment, it stunned the entire room. He had a hell of a smile. One that brought to mind hot, long, deep, drugging kisses.

And more.

So much more . . . *"No,"* Willa said and took Janie's fishbowl. "You're not giving your kids to a perfect stranger."

"You got the perfect part right," Janie murmured and shook it off. "Okay, so we're going to Napa for an overnight. Can I leave you Fric and Frac?"

"Yes, and you know I'll take very good care of them," Willa promised and gave Janie a hug. "Get some rest."

When Janie was gone, Keane went brows up. "Fish? You board fish?"

"Babysit," she corrected, eyes narrowed. "Are you judging me?"

He shook his head. "I just brought you the cat from hell. I'm in no position to judge."

She gave a rough laugh and his gaze locked on her mouth, which gave her another quick zap of awareness.

"Thanks," he said. "For taking Pita today. It means a lot."

From behind the counter came a low "aw" and then a "shh!" that had her sending her friends a "shut it" look.

Keane swiveled to look too but as soon as he did, Elle, Pru, and Haley suddenly had their heads bowed over their phones.

Rory came through carrying another case of feed and took in Willa and Keane's close proximity. "Nice," she said. "I'm happy to see you came to your senses and gave up the no-men decree."

Willa narrowed her eyes.

"Oh, right," Rory said, slapping her own forehead. "Keep that to yourself, Rory. Almost forgot."

Keane slid Willa an amused look. "No-men decree?"

"Never you mind." She set the fishbowl on the counter and reached for Petunia. "You know the deal, right?"

"You mean where I pay double for being an ass and you pretend not to like me?" He flashed a lethal smile. "Yeah, same terms."

"I meant be here before closing." She sighed. "And I'm not going to bill you double."

His smile turned into a grin. "See? You *do* like me."

And then he was gone.

Willa turned to her friends and employees, all of whom were watching him go.

"That's a really great ass," Pru said.

"I agree," Haley said. "And I don't even like men."

Willa shrugged. "I didn't notice. I don't like him."

Everyone burst out laughing.

"We'd correct you," Elle said, still smiling, "but you're too stubborn and obstinate to see reason on the best of days and I don't think this is one of those . . ."

Yeah, yeah . . . She narrowed her eyes because they were still laughing, clearly believing she was totally fooling herself about not liking Keane.

And the worst part was, she knew it too.

Chapter 3

#BahHumbug

Keane Winters was used to crazy-busy and crazy-long days. Today in particular though, thanks to subcontractors not doing what they'd been contracted to do and the weather going to hell in the way of a crazy thunderstorm that intermittently knocked out electricity. And let's not forget the time-and-money-consuming detour to replace his phone and laptop thanks to his aunt's cat. At least she *looked* like a cat but Keane was pretty sure she was really the antichrist.

His phone buzzed and he dropped his tool belt to pull it from his pocket. One of his guys had sent him a link from the *San Francisco Chronicle*.

> Keane Winters, one of this year's San Francisco's People to Watch, is a self-made real estate developer on the rise . . .

He supposed the self-made part was true. Currently in the middle of flipping three properties in the North

Bay area, he'd been putting in so many hours that his core team was starting to lag. They all needed a break, but that wasn't happening anytime soon.

Winters specializes in buying up dilapidated projects in prime areas and turning them into heart-stopping, must-have properties. He doesn't find any use for sentimentality, ruthlessly selling each of them off as he completes them.

Also true. Financially, it didn't pay to hold on to the projects. There'd been a time not that long ago when he'd *had* to sell each off immediately upon completion or end up bankrupt. And yeah, maybe he'd lucked into that first deal, but there'd been no luck involved since. He was a risk taker and he knew how to make it pay off. As a result, he'd gotten good at burying sentimentality, not just with the properties he developed, but in his personal life too.

And as far as that personal life went, he'd been walking by South Bark after getting his coffee every morning for months and it'd never once occurred to him to check out the shop. He hadn't had a dog since Blue, who he'd lost the year before he'd left home, and he sure as hell wasn't in a hurry to feel devastated from loss like that again anytime soon.

Or ever.

But then his great-aunt Sally had dropped off Pita and he'd met the sexy owner of South Bark. Keane had no idea why Willa seemed irritated by the mere sight of him, but he felt anything *but* irritated by the sight of her. He thought maybe it was her eyes, the brightest green eyes he'd ever seen, not to mention her temperament, which appeared to match her strawberry blonde hair—way more strawberry than blonde.

He walked through the top floor of his favorite of his three current projects, Vallejo Street. The other two—North Beach and Mission Street—were purely strategic business decisions and would go right on the market the minute he finished them.

Buy low, renovate smart, sell high. That'd been his MO, always.

But the Vallejo Street house . . . He'd picked up the 1940 Victorian for way too much money five years ago on the one and only whim he could remember ever having. But he'd taken one look at the neglected old house and had seen potential in the three-story, five thousand square feet, regardless of the fact that it'd been practically falling off its axis.

Since then, he'd had to get into other projects fast and hard to recoup the lost seed money, and had worked on Vallejo Street only as time allowed.

Which was why it had taken so long to get it finished, or very nearly finished anyway. For the past year, the bottom floor had been serving as his office. He'd been living there as well. All that would have to change when he got it on the market, something he needed to do, as selling it would give him the capital for new projects.

He walked to one of the floor-to-ceiling windows and looked out. The day's light was almost gone. The city was coming to life with lights, backdropped by a view of the Golden Gate Bridge and the bay beyond that.

"Dude." This from Mason, his right-hand guy, who stood in the doorway. "We need to get the guys in here this week to help work on the loft since you and your little height phobia can't—Are you listening to me?"

"Sure," Keane said to the window. He could see the Pacific Pier Building and pictured Willa in her shop wearing one of her smartass aprons, running her world with matching smartass charm.

Someone snorted. Sass. His admin had come in too, and no one cut through bullshit faster than Sass.

"He's not listening to me," Mason complained.

"Not a single word," Sass agreed.

Keane's phone beeped his alarm. "Gotta go," he said. "I've got ten minutes to pick up Pita before South Bark closes."

"I could go get her for you," Sass offered. "What?" she asked when Mason's mouth fell open. "I offer to do nice stuff all the time."

"You offer to do nice stuff *never*," Mason said.

"All the time."

"Yeah? Name *one*," Mason challenged.

"Well, I wanted to smack you upside the back of your head all day," she said. "And I resisted. See? I think that was exceptionally nice."

Keane left while they were still arguing. It would take him less than five minutes to walk to South Bark but Pita wouldn't appreciate the chilly walk back, so he drove. Parking was the usual joke, so that by the time he got a spot twenty minutes had gone by.

He walked through the courtyard, taking a moment to admire the gorgeous architecture of the old place, the corbeled brick and exposed iron trusses, the large picture windows, the cobblestone beneath his feet, and the huge fountain centerpiece where idiots the city over came to toss a coin and wish for love.

All of it had been decorated for the holidays with garlands of evergreen entwined with twinkling white lights in every doorway and window frame, not to mention a huge-ass Christmas tree near the street entrance.

But that wasn't what stopped him. No, that honor went to the wedding prep going on. Or at least he assumed it was a wedding by the sheer volume of white flowers and lights, the ivory pillar candles set up in clusters paired with clove-dotted oranges and sprigs of holly running along the edge of half of a very crooked archway—

He stopped short as it fell over.

"Crap!"

The woman who yelled this had strawberry blonde hair, emphasis on strawberry.

Willa squatted low over the fallen pieces of the archway trying to . . . God knew what.

"Shit. Shit, shit, shit," she was muttering while shaking the hell out of the screw gun in her hand. "Why are you doing this to me?"

"It's not the screw gun," he said, coming up behind her. "It's operator error."

She jerked in response and, still squatting, lost her balance and fell to her butt. Craning her neck, she glared up at him. "What are you doing creeping up on me like that?"

He reached a hand down to her and pulled her to

her feet. And then grinned because she was wearing another smartass apron that read *OCD . . . Obsessive Christmas Disorder.*

With a low laugh for the utter truth of that statement, he took the screw gun from her.

"It's broken," she said.

He inspected it and shook his head. "No, you're just out of nails." He crouched, reaching for more from the box near her feet to reload the screw gun.

Since she was still just staring at him, he turned his attention to what she'd been doing. "You realize that this archway is only going to be three feet high, right?"

"That's perfect."

"In what universe is that perfect?" he asked.

"In the dog universe. It's a dog wedding."

That had him freezing for a beat before he felt a smile split his face.

She blinked. "Huh."

"What?" Did he have chocolate on his teeth from the candy bar he'd inhaled on the way over here, the only food he'd managed in the past four hours?

"You smiled," she said, almost an accusation.

"You've seen me smile."

"Not really, not since—" She cut herself off and took the gun from him. "Never mind. And thanks."

"There's really going to be a dog wedding? Here, in the courtyard?" he asked.

"In less than an hour unless I screw it all up. I'm the wedding planner." She paused as if waiting for something, some reaction from him, but he managed to keep his expression even.

"You're not going to laugh?" she asked. "Because you look like the kind of guy who would laugh at the idea of two dogs getting married."

"Listen," he said completely honestly. "I'm the guy who needed a fur-sitter because he was terrorized by a ten-pound cat, so I'm not throwing stones here. Speaking of which, where is the little holy terror?"

"She's in my shop safe and sound with plenty of food and water, napping in the warmest spot in the place—between Macaroni and Luna."

He must have looked blank because she said, "The two other pets I'm babysitting today. Well technically Cara, one of my employees, is doing the babysitting at the moment."

"I hope you aren't attached to those other pets," he said. "Because Pita will tear them up one side and down the other."

Willa merely laughed and pulled her phone from one of her apron pockets, a few dog treats cascading out as well, hitting the cobblestone beneath their feet.

With an exclamation, she squatted down to scoop them up at the same time that Keane did, cracking the bottom of his chin on top of her head.

This time they both fell to their butts.

"Ow!" she said, holding her head. "And I'm so sorry, are you okay?"

He blinked past the stars in his vision. "Lived through worse," he assured her, and reached out to gently rub the top of her head. Her hair was soft and silky and smelled amazing. "You?"

"Oh, my noggin's hard as stone, just ask anyone who knows me," she quipped.

Their gazes met and held and he realized that their legs were entangled and was struck by the close proximity and the unbidden and primal urge he had to pull her into his lap.

Clearly not on the same page, she picked up her phone and went back to thumbing through her pics. *"Ha,"* she exclaimed triumphantly. *"Here."* She leaned in to show him her phone's screen, her arm bumping into his. When he bent closer, her hair brushed against his jaw, a strand of it sticking stubbornly to his stubble.

"See?" she asked.

He blinked away the daze she'd put him in and realized she was showing him a pic of the front room in her store. And just as she'd said, there in front of a holly-strewn fake mantel lay a huge pit bull and a teeny-tiny teacup . . . piglet. Entwined.

Between them was a familiar-looking white ball of fluff with the black face of his nightmares. And that nightmare's face was pressed trustingly to the pit bull's. For a long beat Keane just stared at it. "Photoshop, right?" he finally asked. "Just to fuck with me?"

She laughed, and he found himself smiling at just the sound. But soon as he did, her amusement faded, almost as if she'd just reminded herself that she didn't like him. Standing, she turned away. "Well, finally."

"What?"

"Archer and Spence are here."

"The dogs?"

"No, two of my best friends."

"I met your best friends," he said. "They were the ones who watched our conversation this morning like we were a Netflix marathon, right?"

"I have a whole gang of BFFs," she said. "Archer and Spence are on wedding security detail tonight." The cell phone on her hip rang. She looked at the screen and swore.

"The antichrist committed murder, didn't she," he guessed.

"No, of course not! I've got a cake emergency."

"Well I can't compete with that. Go ahead," he said. "I'll build the dog archway."

She hesitated. "It has to be perfect."

Keane had built houses from the ground up and she was questioning his ability to put together an archway. For dogs. "Cake emergency," he reminded her.

"Shit. Okay . . ." She looked at him very seriously. "Do you need any help?"

He stuck his tongue in his cheek. "I'm pretty sure I can handle it."

Looking torn, she blew out a sigh. "Okay, if you're sure. And . . . thanks."

He merely waved Ms. Doubtful One off, though he wasn't above watching her rush away. Yeah, his gaze locked on her sweet ass in those snug skinny jeans tucked into some seriously kickass boots. He was still watching, neck craned to catch the last of her as he turned back to his work and . . . nearly plowed into two guys standing there shoulder to shoulder staring at him. The two who Willa had pointed out as Archer and Spence.

Neither spoke.

"So . . . you guys here for the bride or the groom?" Keane asked.

No one blinked.

"It's a joke," Keane said. "Because the groom and the bride are dogs. See, it's funny."

Neither smiled.

"Tough crowd," he muttered.

"We're here for Willa," one of them said. The bigger, more 'tude-ridden one, who looked like he'd seen the darker side of the world and maybe still lived there. The other guy was leaner but just as fit, his eyes assessing Keane with careful interest.

"Hey." This was Willa herself, yelling from the other side of the courtyard's fountain. "Play nice!" She pointed at her two friends. "Especially you two."

Spence and Archer busted out sweet-looking smiles for her and added cheerful waves. Then the minute she turned away, they went back to deadpan staring at Keane.

"Okay, great talk," he said. "I'm going to build this dog gazebo now. You can either stand there or give me a hand."

The bigger guy spoke. "The last guy she went out with played games with her head." His tone was quiet, his gaze direct and steady.

The other guy, clearly the more easygoing of the two, nodded. "They never did find the body, did they?"

The other guy slowly shook his head.

Okay then. "Good to know," Keane said lightly but suddenly he was feeling anything but light. He didn't like the thought of anyone screwing with Willa. Still fixated on that, he turned his back on her bodyguards and got to work. When he straightened to hoist the arch, suddenly there were four extra hands—both guys lending their strength to the cause.

Still not talking.

After that they were apparently a threesome and recruited as such to be the official setting-up-chairs committee. One hundred and fifty chairs to be exact.

For a dog wedding.

The three of them were hot and sweaty in no time even with the cold December air brushing over them.

"At least it's easier than that time she made us help her do that South Beach wedding, remember, Arch?" the leaner guy asked, giving Keane his first clue on which was Archer and which was Spence.

Archer just grunted as he lined up the last row, his gaze drifting to the edge of the courtyard where Elle stood in a siren red dress working both a cell phone and an iPad.

Spence followed his friend's gaze. "How is it she never gets dirty or sweaty?"

Archer shook his head. "Dirt and sweat don't stick to Elle; she isn't human."

Spence laughed. "So she's still mad at you then."

"She's always mad at me."

"You ever figure out why?"

Archer didn't answer.

Willa came up with three bottles of water. "Chilly night," she said.

Keane, who'd been still getting the occasional frosty looks from Spence and Archer, snorted.

Willa took this in and then looked at them each in turn. "What's going on?"

No one said a word.

She reached up and grabbed Spence by the ear. He manfully winced instead of yelped. "What the hell, Wills."

"What's the weird vibe? What's going on?"

Spence carefully pried her fingers from his ear. "Why didn't you twist off Archer's ear?"

"Because Archer's probably wearing two guns and a knife," she said.

Keane glanced over at the guy. Archer's body language hadn't changed. He was deceptively casual, his gaze hard and alert. Military or law enforcement, he figured.

Willa went hands on hips.

Archer didn't cave, but Spence did. "We were just making sure this one passed muster after Ethan—" He broke off at the look on Willa's face.

Keane had two older sisters. They'd mostly ignored him unless he'd put himself in the line of fire. During those times, their gazes had shot out promised retribution that might or might not include maiming and torturing. Death was a given.

Willa had the look down.

"This one?" Willa repeated. "Oh my God."

Spence opened his mouth but Willa shook her head and pointed at him.

"No," she said. "You know what? This is really all my own fault."

"No, it's not," Archer said firmly. "Ethan was an asshole serial creeper—"

"I meant it's my fault that I'm friends with you two!" And then without so much as glancing over, she jabbed a finger in Keane's face, nearly taking out an eye. "He isn't a date," she said. "He isn't a future date. And he sure as hell isn't a *past* one."

Keane opened his mouth but then shut it again. This was the second time now she'd referred to a past between them. He was so busy mentally rewinding the conversation that he nearly missed Spence and Archer taking off. He didn't, however, miss Spence's sympathetic glance as he left.

"Listen," Willa said when it was just the two of them. "I'm grateful for your help, very grateful actually, but—"

"How do you know I'm not a future date?" Well, hell, he hadn't realized that had bugged him so much.

Willa looked just as flabbergasted. "I just know," she finally said. "I—" She broke off when a little boy not more than four years old tugged on her apron. She immediately smiled, a warm, sweet smile that dazzled Keane more than it should as she hunkered low to be eye-to-eye with the kid.

"Hey, Keller." She straightened his mini tux jacket. "You look handsome tonight."

"My daddies say they're ready."

"Perfect, because so are we."

Keller tipped his head way back to look up at Keane. "You're wearing funny shoes for a wedding."

"They're work boots," Keane told him. "And speaking of footwear, yours are on the wrong feet."

Keller looked down at his shoes and scratched his head before tipping his head up again. "But I don't have any other feet," he finally said.

Fair enough, Keane thought but Willa helped the kid sit down and fix his shoes. Then she went back to being an adorable but utter tyrant, bossing everyone into doing her bidding. No one complained. In fact, everyone seemed happy to jump to her every command.

He could use her on his jobsites.

Ten minutes later the wedding was taking place, complete with marriage certificates that each dog put a paw print on, and a video recording by Rory. There'd apparently been a registry as well because a stack of wrapped gifts from South Bark sat on a table.

"I've just run out of those bedazzled leashes," Willa was saying to someone, consulting an iPad after the ceremony. "But I'll be happy to take an order."

Yeah, Keane was starting to see a whole other side to Willa and her entrepreneurial skills. And he had to admit, he liked this side of her. She was smart as hell, but surrounded by all the fluff as she was, she'd nearly fooled him.

After, when the crowd thinned and then dissipated altogether, he stuck around and helped her with the takedown.

"This isn't necessary," she said.

"Because I'm not a present or future?"

She gave him a long look and then turned to struggle with the archway.

Moving in close to help, he reached around her to add his strength to separate the two pieces of the arch.

Her back to his front, she stilled, and so did he because a zap of what felt like two hundred volts of electricity went straight through him.

"What was that?" she whispered, not moving a single inch.

He'd given this some thought so he had a ready answer. "Animal magnetism."

She unfroze at that, slipped out from beneath his arms to face him. "Oh no. No, no, no. That's one thing we absolutely do *not* have."

He laughed a little because apparently she'd given it no thought at all. Not super great on the ego. "You really going to tell me you don't feel it?"

She chewed on that for a moment. "I'm telling you I don't *want* to feel it," she finally said.

Welcome to my club, he thought.

Chapter 4

#FactsJustGetInTheWay

The days that followed the wedding blurred together for Willa, swamped as she was with the early holiday rush. Not that she minded since the shop, like always, filled all the holes inside her, the ones her rough early years had left.

Yep, she was completely fulfilled.

But then she'd seen Keane Winters and something had happened, something weird and unsettling. He made her realize that she hadn't plugged all her holes at all, that there was at least one still open and gaping inside her.

With a groan, she got up to face her day. Her apartment was also in the Pacific Pier Building, four flights up from her shop. The place was small but cozy. The living room and kitchen were really all one room, divided by a small bar top. On the wall between her living room and short hallway that led to her bedroom was a small door that opened to a dumbwaiter, a throwback to the days when this building was one very large ranching family's central compound. That was back in the late eighteen hundreds, when there'd still been actual cows in the Cow Hollow district of San Francisco.

The dumbwaiter door was locked now but sometimes mysterious gifts ended up in there for her, like cookies or muffins. And then there was the time Archer had a training exercise for his men in the guise of a scavenger hunt, and one of the items required to obtain had been Finn, who'd ended up stuck in the dumbwaiter while making a run for it.

Archer's idea of funny.

In any case, there was nothing in there now no matter how much she wished for some muffins, so she showered and dressed. Today's work uniform consisted of her favorite pair of jeans, which only had one hole in a knee, and another lightweight camisole. She topped that with an easy-to-remove sweater for grooming clients.

She wasn't surprised when she got to work and the knock came on her shop's door at ten minutes before opening. Nor was she surprised at the traitorous leap her pulse gave. It'd been two weeks since Keane had shown up that first morning. Since then, there'd been no rhythm or reason to the days he came in. Sometimes he'd show up for a few days in a row and then nothing for another few days. Whenever she asked about his aunt, he got a solemn look on his face but shook his head. *"Not better yet,"* he always said.

Willa hated to admit she had an ear cocked every

morning, wondering if she'd see him. Hated even more that she always put on mascara and a lip stain just in case. As his knock echoed in the shop, she forced herself to remain still.

"You're going to want a look at this," Elle said from Willa's right. She was leaning against the front counter sipping her hot tea. The kind she ordered in from England because she was a complete tea snob.

"Nope, I don't," Willa said. She didn't have to look because she knew what she'd see—some version of Hot Builder Guy with those T-shirts that stretched taut over his broad shoulders, emphasizing a whole lot of muscles apparently gained the old-fashioned way—by sheer manual labor. His hair would be carelessly tousled, like he hadn't given his looks a second thought. And why should he? When you looked like that, you didn't even need a damn mirror.

"He looks good in clothes," Elle said appreciatively. "I'll give him that. Let him in, Willa."

"I just poured my milk," she complained.

"Yes, and I'm totally judging you based on your choice of plain Cheerios, you unfrosted weirdo." Elle's gaze hadn't left the front door. "But holy cow hotness, Batman, really, you want to see this."

"Why?"

"He's in a suit, that's why. My eyes don't know what to do with themselves."

Willa whipped around so fast she gave herself whiplash.

Keane's sharp eyes were scanning the store. When they settled on her, she felt it all the way from her roots to her toes and some very special spots in between. Every. Time. "Damn."

"Told you," Elle said. "I thought you said he was a carpenter of some sort."

"He listed himself as self-employed on my forms when he left Petunia that first day," she murmured, unable to tear her gaze off him standing there looking like God's gift.

If God's gift came carrying a pink bedazzled carrier . . .

"I can't decide which is the hotter look for him," Elle said. "Hot and suited up, or hot and in Levi's."

"It might be a draw," Willa admitted.

"So you *do* like him," Elle said triumphantly.

"No, but I'm not dead. I mean look at him."

"Believe me," Elle said. "I'm looking. So are you really going to stand there and tell me you're still not moved by him at all?"

"Hello, did you miss the part where he not only stood me up, he also doesn't remember doing it?" Willa asked.

"And are you missing the part where that happened a long time ago?" Elle asked. "Because he totally stepped in and helped you at that wedding. Is it possible you're overdramatizing?"

"I'm not overdramatizing, I *never* overdramatize!" Willa stopped talking as she realized she was waving her arms, spoon in the air and everything. "Fine. It's my red hair. You can't fight genetics."

"Uh-huh." Elle's expression softened. "Honey, I know your past wasn't exactly easy, but I think you've got him all tangled up in that emotional landmine. And before you tell me it's none of my business, you should know that I'm only saying so because I get it, I really do."

Willa sighed because she knew Elle did. She'd had an even rougher time than Willa, and she hated that for the both of them. "Getting stood up like that by him during that particular time in my life was . . . memorably traumatic," she said. "So yeah, there's no doubt I'm projecting. But you remember the torture of high school, right? Or maybe you don't, maybe you were popular like Keane was. I, on the other hand . . ." She shook her head. "I was invisible," she admitted. "And it really messed with my self-esteem."

Elle's smile faded. "Okay. So we stay mad at him then."

Willa's heart squeezed. "Thank you," she said and moved toward the door.

Keane's morning had started at dawn and had already been long, involving a near brawl with an engineer, kissing up to a client who couldn't make up her mind to save her own life, and a way-too-long meeting with the interior decorator for North Beach, who loved to hear himself talk. Now as he stood at South Bark's locked door, he had twenty minutes to get back for another meeting.

Willa took her sweet-ass time opening up, and when she did, she stared at him like she'd never seen him before.

"Keane?" she asked, whispered really, as if she wasn't quite sure.

"Yeah." *Who the hell else?*

"Just checking." Her gaze ran over him slowly. "I thought maybe you had a twin or something."

"Yeah, and the cat hates both of us."

She laughed. It was unexpected, to say the least, and he stared at her. Her bright green eyes were lit up, her smile more than a little contagious. He didn't have time for chitchat but when it came to this woman, he couldn't seem to help himself. "I'm not kidding," he said.

"I know," she said. "That's why it's so funny." Her jeans were worn and faded and fit her petite curvy body like a beloved old friend. He loved her little top, which read *Naughty AND Nice* across her breasts and had teeny-tiny straps and was thin enough to reveal she was both wet and chilly.

Her strawberry blonde hair was in wild layers, some of them in her eyes, and she knew exactly why he was there but she went brows up, wanting him to ask. This should've annoyed the hell out of him but instead he was amused. "Tell me you have time for Pita today," he said, doing their usual dance, willing to beg if he had to. Yesterday Pita had used a very expensive set of blueprints as her personal claw sharpener an hour before a meeting in which he'd needed those plans.

"You changed your work uniform," she said instead of answering. "You're in a suit."

"A necessary evil today."

"You look . . . different."

Torn between satisfaction that she was noticing his looks at all and unexpected annoyance that she'd judged him by his clothes, he didn't answer right away.

Being judged wasn't exactly a new thing for him. He'd been judged by his parents as a kid for not being solely academic. He'd been judged in school for not being just a jock or an academic, but somewhere in the middle, and as a result, he worked hard to fit in anywhere and was proud of his ability to do so. "You judging me by my clothes?"

"Not even a little bit," she said in a tone that he'd heard before, the same tone that again suggested he should know what the hell she was talking about.

"Okay," he said. "I cave. I want to buy a vowel."

She glanced over her shoulder at Elle, who lifted a shoulder. "Give him hell, honey," she said and hopped off the counter, leaving out the courtyard-side door.

Keane didn't have time for this. "What am I missing?" he asked, determined to figure out why she'd twice now referred to a past. And suddenly an odd and uncomfortable thought came to him. "Do we know each other or something?"

"Why?" she asked, eyes suddenly sharp. "Do you remember me from somewhere?"

"No."

Willa stared at him for a long beat and then shook her head. "No, we don't know each other. At all. And to be clear," she added, those brilliant eyes narrowed now, "I liked you better as a carpenter." With that, she took Pita from him and walked away.

At two minutes past six that evening, Keane flung his truck into park and jogged in the pouring rain across the street to South Bark.

The front door was locked, lights off—except for the strings and strings *and strings* of Christmas lights wound through the inside of the shop, making it look like the North Pole at Christmastime.

On steroids.

And crack.

The sign read CLOSED but there was a piece of paper attached to it that said:

Unless you're an extremely rude person who's late in picking up their precious bundle of love, use the back door.

Gee, he thought dryly, who could she possibly be referring to . . . ? He strode through the courtyard and entered the back door to South Bark to find Willa up to her elbows in suds, bathing a huge Doberman.

"Who's a good boy," Willa was saying to the dog in a light, silly voice that had the dog panting happily into her face. "That's right," she cooed, "you are, aren't you? Aren't you a good boy?"

"Well I don't like to brag," Keane said, leaning against the doorjamb. "But I do have my moments."

She jerked and whirled around to face him. "I didn't hear you come in." She looked him over. "You changed."

He looked down at his jeans and long-sleeved T-shirt. "I ended up working on some electrical for a good part of the day until the storm hit," he said. "I didn't want to accidentally electrocute myself in a suit and make things easy for the undertaker."

She didn't smile. "You were working on electricity in these conditions?"

"The job doesn't always wait for good weather. And no worries, I haven't accidentally electrocuted myself in years."

She didn't respond to this but drained the tub and wrapped Carl in a huge towel. She attached his lead to a stand. "Give me a second," she said to Keane and vanished into the hallway.

She didn't go far because he heard her say, "Need a favor, can you finish up with Carl for me?"

"Depends." Rory's voice. "Is his owner here?"

"Max?" Willa asked. "No, he's with Archer on a job but he'll be here soon to pick up Carl, who just needs to be dried and combed through. Why? Is there a problem with Max?"

"No," Rory said quickly. Too quickly. "Fine," she said on a sigh. "I can't stop thinking about him."

"And I can't stop thinking about grilled cheese," Willa said.

Rory laughed. "That would be a lot easier." She paused. "He asked me out again."

"I see," Willa said, her voice softer now. "Honey, he's one of the good guys. Archer wouldn't have him on his team otherwise."

"My radar's still broken."

"Well, I get that," Willa said commiseratively and then the two of them walked back into the room.

Rory rolled up her sleeves. "I've got this." She smiled at Carl. "And you're a far better date than the marathon of *American Horror Story* I was planning anyway." She kissed the dog right between the huge, pointy ears.

Carl licked her face from chin to forehead, making the girl laugh.

Willa gestured for Keane to follow her down that hallway to what looked to be her office.

Pita was sprawled on her back across a wood desk, all four legs sticking straight up in the air like she'd been dead and stiff for days.

Keane stopped short in shock.

Not Willa. She laughed and moved to the desk to tickle Pita's belly.

The cat yawned wide and stretched, rubbing her face up against Willa's wrist, and a ridiculous sense of relief came to Keane.

He didn't have to call Sally and tell her that Pita was dead. At least not tonight.

"Daddy's come to pick you up," Willa said, nuzzling the cat.

"Funny," Keane said and noticed the empty fishbowl next to Pita. "Were you fish sitting again?"

"Was," she said and let out a slow, sad breath. "I've been letting Petunia have the run of the place because she's so sweet and the customers love her, but I turned my head for a few minutes to assist Rory with some grooming and . . ." She swallowed hard. "I think Petunia was hungry."

His heart stopped. "Jesus. Are you kidding me?"

"Yes."

He blinked at her. "What?"

"Yes, I'm kidding you."

He just stared at her. "That was mean."

"Don't be late again," she said, but damn if her smug smile wasn't lighting up his rough day like nothing else had. How she managed to do that while irritating the shit out of him at the same time was anyone's guess. "I'm sorry I was late, I'll pay late fees."

Willa shook her head. "It was only a few minutes and you were working on electricity. I wouldn't have wanted you to rush and get zapped."

"Aw," he said. "More proof that you do care about me."

"I care about the paycheck."

He laughed. "Duly noted." He knew he should get Pita and leave. He was starving, he still had paperwork to tackle, and certainly she had things to do too, but he didn't make a move to go.

They were still staring at each other when a woman stuck her head in the office. Keane recognized her as Kylie, one of the woodworkers who ran Reclaimed Woods, a shop across the courtyard that created gorgeous homemade furnishings. He'd bought several things from her in the past year. He smiled in greeting as he realized she had a very tiny dog's head peeking out the breast pocket of her denim jacket.

"Hey, Keane," she said and Willa looked surprised that they knew each other. "He's a customer," Kylie told her. "A good one. Listen," she went on in a rush, her hand cupping the puppy's head protectively. "I'm watching this little guy for a friend."

"Adorable," Willa said, moving closer to touch. "Breed?"

"Hard to say, he's only three weeks old. He's still bottle-fed too, but I'm thinking Chihuahua."

Not what Keane was thinking, not with those paws that were nearly bigger than his ears.

"It's too cold for him, I think," Kylie said. "He shakes all the time. I'm worried he's going to rattle the teeth right out of his head. All two of them."

"I've got just the thing." Willa pulled what looked like a stack of tiny doll sweaters from a bin by her desk.

"You're a lifesaver," Kylie said, taking four, one of which was a Santa costume. "Bill me." She turned to Keane. "When you get a chance, stop in. I just finished that reclaimed wood furniture set you saw me working on, what, six months ago now?"

"I will."

She flashed a smile, blew a kiss to Willa for the sweaters, and then was gone.

Willa slid him a look as she opened her laptop and hit some keys. "I saw the look on your face when you saw the dog sweaters. I make more money on dog sweaters, bedazzled collars, tiaras, and dog weddings than I do from anything else."

"You make money however you make money, Willa. It's a good thing."

She paused and looked at him for a long beat, like she was testing his genuineness.

"When I saw you in action at that wedding," he said, "I was impressed. People and animals are important to you and you run a really smart business from that."

"Animals ground me," Willa said quietly. "But yeah, I did my homework before I opened this place to make sure I could make a living at it. It's turned out better than my wildest dreams."

"You should be proud of yourself and what you've built here."

She paused, looking a little startled, like maybe no one had ever said such a thing to her before. And then she abruptly changed the subject, like she'd just realized she was being nice. "Any news on your aunt?"

He shook his head. "I'm not sure." It was a hell of a thing to have to admit because he was a guy who prided himself on always having the answers, or at least being able to get them. But the truth was, as it pertained to his family, he'd never known much.

He also hadn't given it a lot of thought until Sally had shown up on his doorstep just over two weeks ago now, leaning on a cane with one hand, her other clutching Pita's pink carrier. He'd taken the cat because she'd seemed so frail and worried, and he'd wanted to alleviate some of her stress.

He'd never expected to *still* have the cat.

Willa scooped Pita up from the desk and the damn cat nuzzled right into her neck. And for the first time in his life, Keane found himself jealous of a cat. "Seriously, what's your secret with her? You wear tuna as perfume?"

Willa laughed, a soft musical sound, and nuzzled the cat right back. "Let's just say I speak her language."

"Yeah? What language is that?"

"Something a man like you wouldn't understand." She kissed Pita's face and gently coaxed her into the carrier. "The language of loneliness."

Keane felt something shift in his chest and go tight. "You might be surprised."

She stared at him for a beat and then suddenly got very busy, zipping up the carrier, looking anywhere but at him, and he realized she was embarrassed. He slid his hand over hers, stilling her movements. "Have dinner with me."

She blinked in surprise.

Yeah, he was just as surprised.

"I'm sorry," she said haltingly. "I shouldn't have— Honestly, I wasn't angling for a date—"

"I know," he said. "But I'm standing here because I want to keep talking to you, only my stomach is growling and demanding sustenance. Come on, Willa. We're both off work and neither of us are wearing wedding rings. Let's go eat."

She stared at him. "Just like that?"

"Just like that."

"It doesn't seem like a smart idea," she said.

"Why not?"

She hesitated and he wanted to ask her about what Archer and Spence had alluded to that night, about her ex being a complete asshole, but that was none of his business. It didn't mean that he didn't want to hunt up the guy and teach him a lesson.

Or two.

"Lots of reasons," she finally said.

"Name one."

She opened her mouth and then closed it. "I can't really seem to come up with a single reason."

"Because there isn't one," he said. "Look, if I was Elle, would you go out to dinner with me then?"

"Of course. She's my friend."

"And Spence? Or Archer? If I was one of them, would you eat with me?"

"Again," she said, eyes narrowing. "Yes."

"But not me."

"No."

He took the cat carrier from her hands and set it on her desk. Then he stepped in so that they were toe to toe and dipped down a little to look right into her eyes.

She sucked in a breath. And that wasn't her only reaction either. Her pupils dilated and her nipples went hard against the thin material of that cute little shirt with the cute little straps.

She'd been very busy distracting him with her sharp tongue and quick wit, so he'd almost missed it. But this insane attraction he had for her? *She felt it too.* "Tell me what to do here," he said quietly. "I know you're hungry. I can hear your stomach growling louder than mine."

She slapped her hands over her lower belly, her fingers first bumping into his abs, which jumped at her touch.

"Dammit," she said, her eyes wide on his, the pulse at the base of her throat going batshit crazy. "It's a noisy beast."

"So let me feed it," he said.

"Maybe I don't like you."

"Maybe?"

"Haven't yet decided," she admitted.

Never one to back away from a challenge, he smiled. "So you'll let me know. You ready?"

When she still hesitated, he gently rasped the pad of his thumb over the pulse point on her throat. "Do I make you nervous, Willa?"

She lifted her chin. "Of course not," she said, her mouth so close to his that he couldn't help but stare at it, gripped by a driving need to cover it with his.

"Especially," she added softly with a light of mischief in those green depths, "since I could knee you in the family jewels right now if I needed to."

"I appreciate your restraint," he said. "Can we go get food now?"

"I guess."

He laughed. "Don't overwhelm me with enthusiasm."

"Just don't . . . read anything into this," she said.

He looked into her eyes and yeah, saw definite attraction for him. Reluctant attraction.

He'd take it.

He scooped the carrier in one hand and grabbed hers in his other.

"Afraid I'll change my mind?" she asked, looking amused.

"More afraid you'll carry out that threat to my family jewels."

Her startled laugh warmed him to his toes. *Game on,* he thought. Even if he had no idea what that game was.

Chapter 5

#TheFirstCutIsTheDeepest

Willa had no idea what the hell she thought she was doing agreeing to go out with Keane for dinner, but apparently her feet knew because they took her back into the grooming room to tell Rory.

The girl was crossed-legged on the floor in front of Carl, brushing him. Sitting facing her, Carl's head was higher than Rory's but he sat still happily, smiling.

Carl loved attention, all of it.

"I'm heading out," Willa said.

"Thanks for the newsflash."

"I'm going with Keane."

Rory froze. Only her eyes swiveled to Willa. "Has hell frozen over?"

Willa sighed. Given that all her current feelings for Keane were mixed up with her past feelings for him, she could hardly explain it to someone else much less herself. "It's just dinner."

"Uh-huh," Rory murmured, stroking an ecstatic Carl. "Remember you're the one who said the devil himself couldn't drag your cold, dead corpse out on a date with Keane even if he was hot as balls."

"Shh!" Willa took a quick look behind her but thankfully Keane hadn't followed. "It's all very . . . complicated."

"Complicated," Rory repeated, amused. "Maybe we should have the birds-and-bees talk, like you always try to have with me when I'm attracted to the wrong-for-me guys."

"Funny," Willa said. The fact was, both of them were attracted to the wrong men, *still*.

But Rory was on a roll, ticking off points on her fingers. "No sleeping with him on the first date, no matter how amazing he kisses—"

"Oh my God, keep your voice down!" Willa looked behind her again. "I'm not going to sleep with him on the first date." Even if the low, sexy tone of his voice did very interesting, *very* distracting things to her body. Nope, she wasn't going down that road because that road led to her downfall every time. This was just dinner, that was it. It was the only way she could ensure her emotional security. No more falling for a guy too quickly. Nope. Not gonna happen.

Rory wasn't done reciting the notes. "A public setting, don't take your eyes off your drink, and don't have more than one."

Any humor in this reversal of roles faded fast at that as the conversation took a turn she hadn't expected but should have. Neither of them would ever forget the night Rory had become a part of Willa's life.

Rory had been in the foster system for ten years when she turned eighteen and had been set loose into the big, bad world all on her own.

And oh how well Willa knew the feeling. It'd felt like she was being thrown away.

Rory had met a guy at a bar who'd seemed fun, gregarious, and charismatic. She'd somehow missed his stalker, predator characteristics.

Willa had been on a walk through the Marina Green one night when she'd found Rory in the park, sick as a dog from the drug that had been dumped into her drink. Willa had taken her to the hospital, helped her recover from the events she couldn't even remember, given her a job, and basically bullied her back to life.

Willa knew that Rory felt like she owed her for all that but she didn't. She also knew that Rory would do absolutely anything for her, which she took very seriously. She had to. Because once upon a time she'd been that lost little girl too.

Rory was watching her, her eyes giving away her worry.

"I'll be fine," Willa said. "Really."

Just then came a single knock on the back door. Max stood there in cargoes, work shirt, and full utility gear, looking pretty badass, clearly coming in off a job for Archer. "Hey," he said, eyes tracking straight to Rory. "How's it going?"

Since Rory had apparently swallowed her tongue,

Willa smiled at him. "Great. Rory's just finishing up Carl." She looked at Rory. "Lock up for me?"

Still silent—hugely unlike her—Rory nodded.

Willa thought maybe she was missing a piece of the puzzle here but she couldn't very well ask Rory with Max standing tall and handsome right there, his eyes also holding secrets. Willa gave Carl a kiss on the head and then the same to Rory, making the girl laugh.

"Just go already," Rory said, looking embarrassed.

"Be safe," Willa said to her.

"I'll make sure of it," Max said and Willa met his serious gaze.

Yep. Definitely missing a piece of the puzzle. "Thanks."

He nodded and five minutes later she and Keane walked out to his truck. He set the cat carrier carefully in the backseat like maybe it was a ticking bomb but made her smile when he hesitated and then locked a seatbelt around it.

When he caught her watching, he shrugged. "She's just ornery enough to knock herself off the seat and die and then come back to haunt me, so I'm taking all necessary precautions." He opened the passenger door for her but caught her before she could slide in. "You're cold."

Actually, she was freezing. "I forgot my jacket this morning—No, don't give me yours," she said when he made to take his off.

So instead he spread it open and wrapped as much of it around her as possible. Chest to chest, thighs to thighs . . . and everything in between mashed up against each other all cozy like.

Except it didn't feel cozy.

It felt . . . sexy as hell.

It would've taken more control than she had to keep her hands to herself. She wrapped herself around him, letting her fingers trail up the sculpted muscles of his back.

At her touch, his gaze met hers, dark and heated. Oh boy. She was in trouble here, and she forced herself to back away and get into her seat.

A minute later, he'd rounded the front of the truck and slid in behind the wheel. He craned around to eyeball Pita like she was a pissed-off rattlesnake.

Willa laughed and Keane turned all that concentrated hotness on her. "What?"

"I'm picturing Petunia coming back from the dead to haunt you."

With a small smile, he leaned in close and slid his fingers along her jaw. "You think that's funny?"

"I'd do the same thing."

His mouth quirked. "Revengeful, huh?"

"Absolutely."

His fingers still on her jaw, he let his thumb slide lightly over her lower lip, making it hunger for a touch.

His touch.

No, make that his mouth. She wanted his mouth on hers and wasn't that just annoying as hell. "This isn't happening," she said out loud, because surely that would make it true.

"What isn't?" he asked. "Dinner with me despite you saying that the devil himself couldn't drag your cold, dead corpse out on a date with me, even if I was . . . how did you put it? Hot as balls?"

"I didn't say that!" She felt her face flush. She was doing her best to desperately hold on to her resentment over their past, but even she could admit she was quickly losing the battle here, to curiosity.

And lust.

"If you're going to eavesdrop," she said with as much dignity as she could, which wasn't much, "at least get your facts straight."

He just laughed, a sexy sound that woke up all her happy spots, damn him. And he knew it too. She sunk in her seat a little, crossed her arms over her chest and looked out the window. "Be amused all you want, I'm holding firm."

He didn't look worried.

Which in turn worried her.

They made a stop on Vallejo Street, at the top of the hill lined with beautiful old Victorians. Here the houses were big and gorgeous and expensive. The one in front of them had some scaffolding wrapped around it, which didn't take away from the absolutely gorgeousness of the place.

"Wait here," Keane said and reached behind him to grab the cat carrier. "I'm just going to run the antichrist inside before we go so she doesn't have to sit in the truck during dinner."

"You live here?"

"It's one of my renovation projects. It's also my office and where I temporarily park my head at night."

"It's beautiful," she breathed, unable to take her eyes

off of it. "One of the most beautiful homes I've ever seen."

He smiled. "Thanks but you should've seen it when I first got ahold of it several years ago. You wouldn't have given it a second look." He started to get out of the truck but then hesitated. "You'll still be here when I get back, right?"

She wanted to see inside that amazing house. "You could take me with you to guarantee it."

"I trust you," he said.

She didn't buy that for a second. What she did buy was that he didn't want her to go inside. "You leave dishes in the sink?" she asked. "Clothes all over the floor? Or maybe you've got someone in there waiting on you . . ." She was just joking but she didn't like thinking it could be true.

"You mean a woman?"

Well when he said it like that, it did sound dumb. "Never mind," she said. "Do what you have to do."

He stilled a beat and then set the carrier down again and leaned in close to her. With one hand on the headrest at the back of her head and the other on the seat at her opposite hip, he caged her in, his face an inch from hers.

Smiling.

The ass. He was temptation personified and he knew it. And also, he smelled good. She had no idea how he'd managed to work all day long doing what he did and still smell amazing, but he did. She closed her eyes, making herself sit still instead of doing as she wanted—which would've been smushing her face into the crook of his neck and inhaling him like she was a third grader with a bottle of glue.

"You want to come upstairs, Willa?" he asked, voice pure sex.

What she wanted was to put her hands back on his chest now that she knew it was as hard as it looked. Instead she gripped either side of her seat with white knuckles. "Of course not."

"I think you do. I think you want something else too."

"What I want," she said as coolly as she could, "is dinner as promised."

"Liar," he chided softly.

"Well that's just rude, calling your date a liar."

"So it *is* a date." His tone was very male and very smug. It should've pissed her off but instead it did something hot and erotic to her insides.

Clearly knowing it, he smiled at her and then dragged his teeth over his lower lip as he contemplated her.

Gah. She wanted to do that. And she wanted to do more too. She wanted him shockingly badly and suddenly she couldn't remember why she shouldn't. She tried to access her thought processes on the subject but her brain hiccupped and froze. Which surely was the only reason she let go of the death grip on her seat, slid her fingers into his hair, and . . . brushed her mouth over his.

He didn't move, not a single muscle, but when she pulled back, his eyes had gone dark as night, piercing her with their intensity.

"Don't read that the wrong way," she whispered.

"Is there a wrong way to take it when a beautiful woman kisses you?"

"Um . . ."

He laughed low in his throat, like maybe she delighted him, and then he mirrored what she'd done. He slid his hands up her throat and into her hair, intensifying the pleasure already wreaking havoc inside her body so that desire laced its way from her chest to her stomach, and then much lower.

"Um . . ."

His lips curved. "You said that already."

She laughed nervously, feeling sixteen and stupid all over again, but seriously, if his voice got any lower she was going to embarrass herself here. It was so deep and husky that she could *feel* his words. "I . . ."

He waited for her to speak but honestly, she had nothing. Not a single thought in her head.

He smiled, a wicked, naughty smile, and the hand in her hair slowly pulled her head back. And then he lowered his perfect mouth to hers in a devastatingly slow and unhurried kiss, sealing his lips to hers as one powerful arm curled around her hip to keep her in place.

Pulsing waves of heat unfurled inside of her and she gave a helpless moan, prompting him to tighten his grip on her and deepen the connection with a better angle and a lot more tongue.

She'd started this, she'd been in charge, but she was no longer even remotely in control. For a beat she let her fingers wander, eliciting a rumbly groan from deep in his throat, the sound incredibly erotic. Then she pulled back and stared up at him.

"I have no idea what I did to deserve that," he murmured quietly, stroking a finger along her temple. "But I'm going to drop Pita off now before this goes too far."

Their gazes held and she could see the humor shining in his, crinkling at the edges. Right, she thought. Good. One of them could still think.

"Okay?" he asked, which was when she realized she had two fistfuls of his shirt, holding him to her.

"Sure." She made herself loosen her grip, smoothing out the wrinkles she'd left, and again she could feel his tight abs through the cotton. Very tight.

She wanted to lick him like a lollipop.

But he didn't want this to go too far. Not with her. She needed to remember that. Maybe she should write it down so she didn't forget. She was nodding to herself like a bobblehead when he said her name and then waited until she looked at him.

"Not that I don't want it to go too far," he said, his gaze revealing heat and the raw power she was getting used to seeing in those dark depths when he looked at her. "But not in my truck, Willa. Not with you." He got out of the car and waited while she did the same. Then he picked up the carrier with Petunia in it and with his other hand, grabbed hers.

"It's okay," she said quickly. "I can wait here."

"Don't chicken out now," he said, looking amused. "You can satiate your curiosity and check to make sure I'm not double booked tonight all at the same time."

She tried to pull free of his grip, but he had her, and she laughed a little to herself—*the sexy jackass*—as he nudged her inside ahead of him.

She immediately forgot why she was mad. The main level was rich with Victorian architectural details: beautiful trim, a crafted stairway with ornate wood railings and stairs. Gorgeously charming light fixtures hung in the entry and living room, paying homage to the period style of the home.

"Wow," she murmured, taking in the surprisingly wide-open space that was still liberally protected from the renovation with tarp runners across the hardwood floors. She could see into the open kitchen and den as well as the still unfinished loft above and to the left. The dining room and living area were clearly being used as office space.

What she didn't see was a single Christmas decoration. "You said you live here?" she asked.

"Temporarily."

"There's no holiday decorations."

"No." He couched low to set down the carrier and unzipped it. Rising to his full height, he stared down at the thing, hands on hips as if braced for warfare. "I have three projects going right now. This is one of them."

She looked around in marvel. "How did you get started doing this?"

"The short of it is that I begged, borrowed, and stole the money for the first fallen property and then kicked some serious ass to not lose my shorts over the deal."

"Fallen?" she asked.

"In that first case, a foreclosure. I slapped some lipstick on it and quickly turned it around for a small profit, emphasis on *small*." He gave a quick smile. "I got better as time went on."

"Someone had to walk away from their home?" she asked. "And you gained from that?"

"They chose to walk," he said pragmatically. "The bank wanted their money back. I ate mac and cheese for an entire year to make it work."

Okay, she got that. Because as he'd told her, you make money however you make money. She took in the gorgeous, incredible details of his work and marveled at his talent. "It's amazing."

"You wouldn't have said so if you'd seen it before," he said. "It was just about a complete teardown. I've had this place the longest. It's taken the most work of any other project. I really need to get it on the market, should've already done it by now."

She was boggled. "How could you get rid of this place? You put such heart and soul into it."

"It's worth a lot of money," he said, not giving a lot away although there was something to his body language, the set of his wide shoulders maybe, that told her she wasn't getting the whole story.

"The profit will go into my next project," he said.

And yet he hadn't sold it. Possibly it meant too much to him, and she could certainly see why. "Maybe you're attached to it," she said.

He shook his head in surprise. "I don't get attached."

She looked at him. "Ever?"

"There's no place for it in my world."

"Huh," she said, thinking of all of *her* attachments. Her friends, who were also her family. Rory, Cara, and all the others she hired and took on. "I get attached to everything and everyone," she admitted.

"No kidding."

This took her aback. "What does that mean?"

He glanced at her and laughed softly. "I've seen you in action, Willa. It seems that once you make a friend, you keep them until the end of time. Same thing with animals. I'm pretty sure you've never met a two-legged or four-legged creature you don't fall for. You collect hearts and souls like most women collect shoes."

"Hey. I collect plenty of shoes." And anyway, he was only partially right. Maybe she did collect hearts and souls, but she didn't keep them. Being a foster kid had taught her that all too well. You only borrowed the people—and animals—you loved. You didn't get to keep them.

Even when you wanted to.

"I really do love this place," she murmured, turning in a slow circle. "It's so warm and welcoming. If this house was mine, I'd never leave it."

"That's the thing, it's not my home, not really."

"Where is your home then?" she asked.

He paused. "I've not really settled on one yet." He looked around as if seeing it for the first time. "If I was ready, I'd want it to be a place like this but for now it's just where I sleep and work. I've got some small finish work to get to yet before I can put it on the market."

She watched him as he spoke. He'd turned to watch the carrier but that wasn't what grabbed her attention and held.

No, it was that he wasn't buying what he was trying to sell her. Whether he really was done with the property or not, she had no idea, but she had the feeling he wasn't *ready* to be done.

Maybe . . . maybe he could get attached to things after all. Things like this house. And . . . her.

This wayward, out-of-nowhere thought set off all her inner alarms. She had to work at keeping her face blank through her panic. This wasn't going to happen. She wouldn't allow it. Not here, not with him, because she knew from experience that once the pit bull that was her heart snapped its jaws onto something, it took a miracle to let go.

Chapter 6

#HitMeWithYourBestShot

While Willa stood there reeling a little bit about her unwanted feelings for Keane, the world kept spinning on its rotation, completely oblivious to her unhappy epiphany.

It was her greatest wish that Keane would remain oblivious as well, which meant that she had to be careful because he wasn't the sort of guy to miss much.

Or anything.

Luckily, Petunia chose that moment to stroll out of her carrier, nose in the air, tail swishing prissily back and forth, her entire demeanor projecting Queen Bee.

Until she saw Willa. Then she immediately let out a happy chirp and trotted over, her tubby belly swinging to and fro as she wound herself around Willa's legs, purring.

"Ingrate," Keane said mildly.

Willa relaxed a little. Okay, they were moving

on. This was good. This was *great,* and she let out a long breath that caught in her throat at Keane's next words.

"What's the matter?"

"Nothing."

His expression was doubtful. "It's something. Something's different. Is it the house somehow, or the kiss?"

Oh for God's sake. Most men were oblivious. Why had she had to kiss the one who wasn't?

No, they most definitely did not need to talk about it.

Petunia, clearly tired of humans, stalked off and Willa watched her go, wistful. Why wasn't she a cat? *Why hadn't she stayed in the truck?*

"Willa."

"Um . . . hold on a sec, my phone's going off." She pulled it from her pocket like she'd just received an important text. She brought up a new message and quickly typed.

Her:
Alskjfa;oiw;af;o3ij;asjfe

She got an immediate response.

HeadOfAllTheThings:
Are you just texting me gibberish so you look busy in front of someone you don't want to talk to again? Who is it this time, that UPS guy with gingivitis?

Willa started to thumb in a response, but Keane came up behind her, *right* behind her, and even though he wasn't actually touching her, she could feel his heat, the tempered strength in his big body, and she got a rush so strong her knees wobbled.

Her phone pinged another incoming text and assuming it was Elle teasing her, she ignored it. But behind her Keane wrapped his fingers around her wrist and brought the screen up so that they could see the readout. It wasn't Elle.

> **AssholeExDONOTAnswer:**
> **Miss you.**

"I especially like your contact name for him," Keane said. "The infamous Ethan?"

Willa nodded dully because really she was just stunned to hear from the guy at all after so much had happened. Ethan had started off so normal but he'd slowly morphed into a possessive, jealous, angry guy. It'd happened gradually enough that at first she thought she was overreacting. She'd reminded herself he'd been good to her, and as a people pleaser she'd doubled her efforts to make him see he had nothing to worry about.

Classic mistake.

When he'd blown up at her at the pub one night for dancing with Finn and tried to physically haul her out of the place, she'd taken a stand. Actually, she'd tossed a drink in his face and he'd screamed like a baby.

That's when he'd been ejected from the pub by Archer.

And then Willa had ejected him from her life.

The next day she'd found her cash drawer in the shop

emptied of three hundred bucks and a stack of her gift cards verified and missing.

For a long time she'd blamed herself and then she'd found her mad and had ached for an apology. But that ache had faded, replaced with some hard-won maturity. She no longer was that same woman who'd give a perfect stranger the shirt off her back. Nope, she'd care for a perfect stranger's cat though, and at that thought, she snorted.

"It's funny?" Keane asked.

"Not funny ha-ha. More like"—she mimed a gun with her first finger and thumb, bringing it up to her temple—"blow my brains out funny."

Keane didn't look amused. "This is the serial creeper, right?"

Since he seemed more than a little tense all of a sudden, she smiled to show him she wasn't bothered by this blast from her past. Hell, she was getting used to it. "Give me a sec?"

He nodded but didn't go away. Okaaay. So she composed her answering text with an audience:

> The person you're trying to reach has forwarded this text to the police, who are still trying to locate you. Please text your current addy and place of employment to make it easy for them but know it's not necessary as this was a felony case and they'll be tracking you down by triangulation of your cell-phone pings.

She felt Keane, a big, strong presence at her back. "Exactly what did this guy do to you?"

Nothing she wanted to get into right now. Or ever. "Nothing but live up to the contact name I gave him."

"I especially like the cell-phone-ping thing," Keane said.

She laughed a little. "I don't actually know if that's a thing. I saw it on *Criminal Minds* once and it stuck with me."

"Nice." His voice was warm and approving. "Now forward the text to the cops like you said."

She grimaced. "I was actually just fibbing about that part. But I did promise Archer I'd let him take care of it personally if Ethan contacted me again. Archer used to be a cop and he hasn't lost any of his skills." She craned her neck and met Keane's gaze. "I think he's been really looking forward to this."

"Good. Forward the text."

"Now?"

"Now."

Okay then. She forwarded the text to Archer. "Feel better?" she asked as her phone buzzed with Archer's immediate response:

On it. Don't worry.

"Yeah," Keane said. "I feel better."

They left the house, with Willa giving it a final look back as they walked out to his truck. It felt a little silly to fall for a house but that's what she'd done.

Keane drove to the Embarcadero. It had a view that eclipsed any other place in the city, at least in Willa's opinion. They walked along the water and stopped to take in the heart-stopping view of the bay.

"Thought we'd eat here," Keane said of the Waterfront Restaurant behind them.

She hesitated. "When you said 'let's get some food,' I thought we'd get a burger or a taco," she said. "I don't think I'm dressed for this."

He let his gaze run over her, taking in her sweater and skinny jeans. She'd need to lose ten pounds before she could get anywhere even close to skinny.

"I like what you're wearing," he said. "You're beautiful."

This actually left her speechless.

"And anyway, I'm hungry for more than just a quickie."

She stared at him. "Is that a double entendre?"

"Actually, it might have been a triple entendre."

She laughed and looked at the restaurant front. She'd walked by the place enough times, always drooling over the great view and menu, but she'd never actually been inside.

Turned out, the food was fantastic.

And so was the company, dammit.

As they ate, they watched the moon hang above the water. A salty breeze brushed through the outside patio, mingling with the warm air coming out of the standing heaters beside every dining table.

It was unexpectedly . . . romantic. So much so that she had to keep reminding her hormones to take a chill pill, not that they listened. She was far too attracted to Keane for her own good. He was smart, funny, sexy . . . At some point she came up with the brilliant idea to concentrate on what she *didn't* like. "Why aren't there any holiday decorations up at your place?" she asked.

"Because you bought out all the decorations in the entire city."

Okay, so she had to laugh at that. "Elle thinks my shop looks like Christmas and New Year had a baby who threw up on everything."

He smiled and she thought *bingo,* something else she didn't like about him—he didn't appreciate her admittedly obsessive need to celebrate the holidays, supersize style.

"It could've been worse," he said. "I didn't see Santa himself represented anywhere in your shop."

"He's coming soon," she admitted. "I'm doing a Santa Extravaganza. Customers bring their pets in to be primped and then can get into a photo booth with Santa."

"Nice. Love your entrepreneurial spirit." He smiled. "So do you go nuts for all the holidays or just Christmas?"

Because the question was genuine and there didn't seem to be any sense of mocking in his dark gaze, she answered with more honesty than she'd intended. "Yes, all the holidays. It's a holdover from when I was a kid and didn't always get to celebrate them."

His smile faded as he looked at her and she suddenly developed a fascination with her last sip of wine.

"Parents not into the holidays?" he asked.

She shrugged. "My dad got himself killed while hunting with his buddies when I was two. My mom was young when she had me, too young. She's . . . not really cut out for parenting."

An understatement. She'd gotten better over the years, enough to call and check in once in a while.

And ask for money.

Keane slid his hand to hers on the table and gently squeezed her fingers. "I'm glad you treat yourself to the holidays then. So does Father Time come on New Year's?"

"No," she said on a laugh and then admitted the rest. "But Cupid comes on Valentine's Day."

He stared at her and then burst out laughing, a sound she was all too quickly becoming addicted to. Damn. She quickly wracked her brain to come up with more things she didn't like about him. Such as he seemed unwilling—not incapable, which would've been different, but *unwilling*—to get attached to Petunia. Also, he clearly didn't fully appreciate her holiday decorating skills. And then there was the fact that he kissed like sex on a stick—No, wait. That was a pro not a con.

"How about you?" she asked. "What's your take on holidays?"

"I don't have a reason as good as you do for going one way or the other," he said. "I was a late-in-life unhappy surprise to a couple of college professors who'd already raised two daughters. They were really into their work. Holidays got in the way of that work."

Well that sounded lonely. And sad. "So you didn't get to celebrate much either?" she asked, suddenly feeling . . . small. Back in school she'd judged him for being a jock, when maybe sports had been all he'd had.

And if that thought didn't open up a whole big can of worms . . .

"No, not much celebration at the Winters's house," he said. "And you didn't want *my* pity, Willa, so don't you dare give me any. I didn't know any different. It didn't bother me."

"But . . ." She swallowed the rest of that sentence because he was right. He'd treated her pride with respect and she needed to do the same. "Do you all keep in touch?"

"Not as much as we should." Regret slashed through his features. "I hardly even knew I had a great-aunt Sally until she showed up on my doorstep just over two weeks ago now."

Willa had spent a few years searching for long-lost family to no avail. She was riveted by this peek into Keane's life. "Really?"

"Yeah. She's my grandma's sister," he said, "and apparently there was some big feud fifty years ago involving the two of them falling for the same man."

"Wow. Who ended up with the guy?"

"My grandma," he said. "And then I guess she caught her sister flirting with him and accused Sally of trying to steal him out from right beneath her nose. It divided the family."

"That's awful."

"I'm pretty sure even without the scandal, we'd have all drifted apart," he said. "We're not much for emotion, us Winterses. We like to keep it all closed off and we're good at it."

She shook her head because though she knew he believed that, she'd seen him display emotion, plenty of it. Frustration and exhaustion when he'd first brought her Petunia. Anger, though he'd done his best to hide it from her, when she'd gotten the text from Ethan.

And then there'd been the sheer blast of passion and heat when he'd kissed her.

Yeah, he felt plenty. He just didn't like it.

And that she could understand. She didn't like it when emotions got the better of her either. The difference between him and her was that he could zip them up and walk away.

She wasn't made like that.

After dinner, they walked some more, ending up inside the colorful and packed Marketplace in the Ferry Building. She bought a loaf of fresh bread and Keane picked up what looked like an expensive whiskey. When she started to panic that the evening was feeling way too much like a real date, she pretended to be shocked at the time and suggested she had to get home.

Keane gave no indication of being annoyed or disappointed, just took her hand and walked her back to his truck. When he drove around the block of her building, making her realize he was looking for a parking spot, the facts sunk in.

One, his five o'clock shadow had a shadow and made her physically ache with yearning to feel it brush over her skin.

Two, he had a bottle of alcohol.

Three, he was clearly planning to walk her up to her apartment.

It all added up to an uncomfortable truth—if he so much as looked at her mouth in that innately masculine, watchful way of his, she'd probably jump his sexy bones.

"Don't worry about finding a spot," she said quickly, reaching for the door handle as he slowed down, his gaze on a car up ahead that was getting ready to pull out. "I can get out right here." She smiled at him brightly and hoped the whites of her eyes weren't showing, revealing her panic. "Thankssomuchfordinner," she managed and hopped out.

"Willa. Wait—"

But nope, she couldn't. She needed to get the heck out of Dodge before she did something incredibly stupid. So she ran into the courtyard of her building without looking back.

It was second nature to slow at the fountain and search her pockets. Dog treats. Her keys. And *yes,* a nickel, which she tossed into the water to make her usual wish.

Old Man Eddie, the homeless guy who lived in the alley, poked his head out. He was sitting on his box between two Dumpsters—his favorite spot because from his perch he could see both the courtyard and the street. He was always chipper and smiling, but tonight his smile was devoid of its usual wattage.

"Any of your wishes come true yet?" he asked.

"Not yet. Are you okay?"

He lifted a shoulder. "Waiting for my holiday cheer to kick in."

A lot of people in the building took turns making sure Eddie had everything he needed, but mostly it was Spence, herself, and Elle in charge. They'd tried getting him into a shelter several times but he preferred his alley. She peered over and could see why he hadn't found his holiday cheer yet: it was dark and dank. "Brought you dinner," she said and handed him her doggie bag. "Lobster linguine. Bad for our diet, but totally amazing."

"Thanks, dudette. What's the hurry? Bad date?"

"Worse," she said. "*Great* date."

Clutching the leftovers, he nodded like he got it all too well. "Thanks for dinner. Think I'll walk to the Presidio first though. All the Victorians are decorated with wreaths and lights, and some of them have baskets of candy out."

"Be safe," she said and watched him go, her own problems dissolving as her mind raced to find a way to help Eddie find his cheer.

And then it came to her.

Changing directions, she ran to her shop. Quickly letting herself in, she pulled down a string of lights that she'd put up along her checkout counter. She grabbed an extension cord and her staple gun too. Less than three minutes later she was in Eddie's alley, stapling the string of lights above his spot—between the two Dumpsters.

Stepping back, she eyed her work. The lights lit the alley up in brilliant colors, warming the area and giving some cheer to it as well. Nodding in satisfaction, she left.

When she exited the elevator on the fourth floor five minutes later she was shaking with cold and so deep into her own thoughts that the tall, built shadow of a man standing there scared her nearly out of her own skin.

"Dammit, Keane," she gasped, hand to her heart. "You startled me."

"Did you really just decorate the alley for the homeless guy that lives there?" he asked.

"Maybe. And his name is Eddie."

Keane's eyes were warm and went a long way toward heating her up. So did his smile.

"Are you laughing at me?" she asked.

"I'd never laugh at a woman who decorates dark alleys and carries a mean stapler gun at crotch level."

She looked down at the tool in her hand and rolled her eyes. "The alley looked lonely."

"You mean Eddie looked lonely and you wanted to do something for him."

That too.

He tipped her face up and she found his eyes more serious now. "You're pretty amazing," he said. "You know that?"

She squirmed a little bit at the unexpected praise but he didn't give her any room. "If I ask you a serious question, Willa, will you give me an honest answer?"

She hesitated. "Maybe." And maybe not . . .

"Why don't you want to like me?"

She blinked. "What?"

"You heard me. I'm missing something, something big I think. No more playing, Willa; tell me. You gave up the right to keep it a secret after you kissed me."

"You kissed me back," she whispered.

"Yes, and I'm going to kiss you again soon as you finish talking."

"No, actually, you're not." She drew in a shaky deep

breath, held it for a minute, and then let it go in one long shudder. "Fine, I'll tell you the truth," she said, tired of holding it in anyway. "But just remember, you asked."

He nodded.

"We went to high school together for a year." Once that escaped, the rest came out really fast, as if that could help ease the reliving of the humiliating experience. "You were the popular jock and I was . . . a nobody. You stood me up for my first—and last—dance." Just saying it out loud made her mad all over again. "And then to add insult to injury, you don't even remember."

He just stared at her. "Run that by me one more time. Slower. And in English."

"No," she said, turning to her front door. "I'm not going to say it again. It was hard enough to live with and even harder to say it the one time."

He caught her and with gentle steel pulled her back around and pressed her up against the hallway wall. Hands still on her arms, he leaned in, holding her there. "Why don't I remember you?"

"Because you're an ass?" she asked sweetly, pushing ineffectively at his chest. "Back up."

"In a minute." He wasn't going to be distracted. "You weren't in any of my classes."

"No. I was a freshman when you were a senior. There was a Sadie Hawkins dance and you were the only guy in the whole school I wanted to go with. I was new there so I didn't have friends to talk any sense into me. I caught you coming out of one of your football practices and I thought . . . Well, never mind what I thought. You were in a hurry, which I didn't realize until I stopped you." She squeezed her eyes shut as remembered humiliation washed over her. "I spoke too fast then too. Way too fast. You had to ask me to repeat the question. Twice."

He let out a breath, closed his eyes, and dropped his forehead to hers. "Tell me I was nice about it. Tell me I wasn't a complete eighteen-year-old dick."

"You don't get to ask that of me," she said and gave him another push. "Because I was so forgettable that you don't even remember me."

"Yeah, so I was a complete eighteen-year-old dick," he muttered. *"Shit."* He tightened his grip on her when she tried to break free. "Listen to me, Willa, because I want to make something perfectly clear here." He opened his eyes and held hers prisoner. "You're the most unforgettable person I've ever met."

She let out a soft sigh of unintentional need because pathetic as it was, the words felt like a balm on her raw soul. "Don't—"

"Tell me what I said to you that day."

"You said 'sounds cool.'" She dropped her forehead to his chest. "And I practically floated home. I didn't have a dress. Or shoes. Or money to get into the dance. I had to beg, borrow, and steal, but I managed to do it, to get myself together enough that I'd be worthy of a date with Keane Winters."

A rough sound of regret escaped him. "I had a real problem with girls back then," he said. "I didn't know how to say no."

"Cue the violins."

He grimaced. "I know. But there were these sports groupies and—"

"Oh my God." She covered her ears. "Stop talking! I don't want to know any of this."

"I'm just saying that they used to hang around outside of practice and then jump us when we left the locker room. If you were there, I probably thought you were one of them."

Willing to concede that this might actually be true, she lifted a shoulder but managed to hold on to most of her mad. "You should have known by taking one look at me that I wasn't a damn groupie."

"You'd think. But eighteen-year-old guys are assholes." He looked genuinely regretful. "Tell me the rest."

"Nothing more to tell. You didn't show. And you never so much as looked at me again."

"Willa—"

"End of story," she said. "Both back then and now." She ducked beneath his arms and fumbled for her keys, practically falling into her apartment. She shut the door harder than was strictly necessary and didn't know if she was disappointed or relieved when he didn't even attempt to follow her.

Chapter 7

#FallenAndCantGetUp

Keane woke up to a heavy pressure on his chest that felt like a heart attack—no doubt the result of wracking his brain all night long, trying to remember Willa from high school.

To his chagrin, he still couldn't.

He'd been telling her the utter truth when he'd said that a lot of girls had waited on the players after practices. He'd ignored most of them and when they'd refused to be ignored, he'd flashed a smile and done his best to flirt his way to the parking lot rather than hurt anyone's feelings.

So it killed him that he'd hurt Willa.

But the truth was, he hadn't given a lot of thought to how any of those girls had taken his ridiculous and stupid comments designed to help him escape. It hadn't been until he'd gotten to college that he'd lost some of his shyness around women.

Okay, all of it.

He'd met his first real girlfriend—Julie Carmen—his freshman year and they'd gotten serious fast, fueled by the sheer, mind-numbing hunger of eighteen-year-old lust.

By the end of that first year, he was no longer thinking with his head, at least not the one on top of his shoulders. For the first time in his life he had someone so into him that she wanted to spend every waking moment with him, and he'd gotten off on that. He'd wanted to marry her, ridiculous as that sounded now. He'd told himself to play it cool, to hold back, but he had no real experience with that and ended up blurting it out at a football game over hot dogs and beer.

Real smooth.

Julie had been cool about it and he'd been . . . happy, truly happy for the first time in his life. That had lasted two weeks until she'd dumped him, saying she'd only been in it for a good time and because he had a hot body, and she was sorry but he wanted way more from her than she could give.

He hadn't reverted to his shyness around women. Instead he'd accepted that he wasn't good with or made for long term, a fact made easy to back up since he had no desire to give his heart away again.

But one-night stands . . . he'd gone on to excel there, for quite a few tumble-filled years. Until now, in fact. Willa was unlike any woman he'd ever met. She was passionate, smart, sexy . . . and she made him laugh.

And her smile could light up his entire day.

He wasn't actually sure what to do with that, but he knew he wanted to do something.

The weight on his chest got heavier. Yep, probably a heart attack. Well, hey, he'd nearly made it to thirty and it'd been a pretty good run too.

No regrets.

Well maybe one—that he wouldn't get to kiss Willa again or see that soft and dazed look on her face after he did, the one that said she wanted him every bit as much as he wanted her.

The pressure on his chest shifted, getting even heavier now. He opened his eyes and nearly had a stroke instead of a heart attack.

Pita was sitting on his ribcage, her head bent to his, nose to nose, staring at him.

"Meow," she said in a tone suggesting not only that she was starving, but that he was in danger of having his face eaten off if he didn't get up and feed her.

Remembering Willa's admonishment that he hadn't tried to connect with the damn thing, he lifted a hand and patted her on the head.

Pita's eyes narrowed.

"Right, you're a cat not a dog." He stroked a hand down her back instead and she lifted into his touch, her eyes half closed in what he hoped was pleasure.

"You like that?" he murmured, thinking *middle ground!* So he did it again, stroked her along her spindly spine for a second time.

A rumble came from Pita's throat, rough and

uneven, like a motor starting up for the first time in a decade.

"Wow," he said. "Is that an actual purr? Better be careful, you might start to almost like me."

On his third stroke down her back, she bit him. Hard. Not enough to break the skin but she sank her teeth in a bit and held there, her eyes narrowed to slits.

"Still not friends," he gritted out. "Noted. Now let go." When she didn't, he sat up and dislodged her, and with an irritated chirp, she leapt to the end of the bed, turning her back on him and lifting her hind leg, going to work cleaning her lady town.

He looked down at his hand. No blood, good sign. He slid out of bed and . . .

Stepped in something disgustingly runny and still warm. Cat yak. He hopped around and swore the air blue for a while and then managed to clean up without yakking himself.

Barely.

He found the little antichrist sitting up high on the unfinished loft floor, peeking over the edge down at where he stood in the kitchen.

"Are you kidding me?" he asked.

"Mew."

Shit, she was stuck. There was a ladder against the wall because Mason had been working up there this week. Keane, hating heights, had avoided going up there at all and had absolutely no idea how she'd managed to climb the construction ladder in the first place.

Blowing out a sigh, he climbed up halfway and held out his arms. "Come on then."

Pita lifted a paw and began to wash her face.

He dropped his head and laughed. What else could he do? Clearly the cat didn't give a shit that he had a height phobia. And yeah, it was a ridiculous phobia for a builder to have but that didn't change a damn thing.

He glanced down—oh shit, he hated that—and assured himself it was only eight feet. Then he kept going. "Cat," he said at the top and reached for her.

She jumped, but not for him. Instead she hit the ladder over his shoulder, lithely running past him like she was Tinker Bell complete with wings.

From the top, Keane looked down and felt himself start to sweat. Grinding his back teeth, he climbed down and found Pita staring disdainfully at her food bowl, which was still full from last night.

This got his attention. "You didn't eat? Since when don't you eat?"

She swished her tail and gave a "mew" that he figured translated to *that shit is for cats and I'm a Queen Bee, remember?*

He took a closer look and realized she seemed a little thin, at least for her, which concerned him in a way her attitude hadn't. He'd called Sally three times this week alone but hadn't gotten a return call. What if Pita wasted away and died before Sally came for her? How would he explain that?

Worried, he went hunting through his admittedly not well-stocked cabinets and found a can of tuna. *Score.* "Cats love tuna," he told Pita. "Willa says so."

Pita just stared at him censurably with those deep blue eyes.

Finding a can opener took a while, making him realize something a little startling. He'd lived here for
going on six months now and though it was by far his
favorite property he'd ever owned . . . he'd not ever
really moved in. Yes, he had all his stuff here but that
wasn't much. He'd moved around frequently over the
years, from one property to the next as he fixed them
up and sold them, so he'd gotten good at traveling light.

Maybe too good.

Once he got his hands on a can opener, he waved
it triumphantly at Pita, who looked distinctly unimpressed. He opened the can and dumped it into another
bowl and set it in front of her.

She froze and then sniffed it with the caution of a
royal food-taster.

"It's albacore," he said. "The good stuff."

She gave it another brief sniff and then turned and
walked away.

He stared after her. "Seriously? You lick your own
ass but turn your nose up at fucking tuna?"

He was still staring after her in disbelief when his
cell phone rang. "Keane Winters," he snapped, not
reading the display. "Cat for sale."

There was a long pause.

"Hello?" he said.

"Are you selling *my* cat?" came a soft and slightly
shaken older woman's voice.

Shit. His great-aunt Sally. "Sorry, bad joke," he
said and grimaced, shoving his free hand through his
hair. "And am I ever glad to hear from you. I've been
calling—"

"I know." Her voice sounded a little faint. "I'm out front, may I come in?"

"Yes, of course." Was she kidding? She was here to pick up Pita and for that he'd roll out the red carpet. "You didn't have to call first—"

"I didn't want to interrupt any . . . meetings you might have had. With women."

He choked back a laugh as he moved through the house toward the front. What was it with people thinking he had a lineup of chicks every night? "I'll make sure to keep all the women locked up in the bedroom while you're here," he said.

She gasped in his ear.

"I'm kidding, Aunt Sally. It's just me." Not that he wouldn't mind having Willa sprawled out in his bed right about now . . .

He opened the door. Sally was bundled up in a thick coat, hat, scarf, gloves, and boots, and since she was under five feet tall, she looked a bit like a hobbit. Hat quivering, she walked ahead of him into the foyer and then stopped abruptly, her back to him as she studied his place.

"It's beautiful," she said softly. "You do beautiful work. I never understood your parents' contempt for what you do with your bare hands."

Leaving him stunned, she called for the cat. "Petunia, darling, come to Mommy."

Pita came running, eyes bright, a happy chirp escaping her, the same sound she used with Willa too.

Old woman and cat had a long hug and then his aunt finally straightened slowly, her back still to him.

There was an awkward silence that he had no idea how to broach. It was safe to say he didn't know his own parents all that well. Yes, they'd raised him. Somewhat. But the truth was he'd been a latchkey kid who'd spent most of his time at sporting events, with friends, or in front of a gaming system. When he'd turned eighteen and moved out, there'd been a blast of overwhelming relief from his parents. They'd been virtual strangers to each other and in the years since they hadn't gotten to know each other any better.

He knew his aunt even less. "How are you feeling?" he asked.

She was silent for a long moment. "Do you ever have regrets about our family?" she asked instead of answering. "How little we all bother with each other?"

One thing the Winterses didn't do was discuss feelings. Ever. In fact, they buried them deep and pretended they didn't exist. So he stared at her stiff spine, an uncomfortable feeling swirling in his gut.

She sighed. "Right. Listen, I'm sorry about this, Keane."

Oh shit. "Tell me what's wrong."

She stayed where she was but he realized her shoulders were a little slumped as she pulled open her large handbag. From it, she pulled out a plastic Ziploc baggie filled with what were unmistakably cat toys. "For Petunia," she said.

"But—"

"And I've got her special blankie too. She'll need it for nap times."

"Aunt Sally." Gently he turned her to face him. "What's going on?"

"I can't take her back yet." Her rheumy blue eyes went suspiciously watery. "I need you to keep her a little bit longer. Do you think you can do that without selling her?"

"I was kidding about that." Mostly. As for the question of could he handle Pita . . . He'd handled a lot of shit in his life so theoretically he could handle one little cat.

And then there was the built-in bonus—he'd have a reason for Willa to let him back into her shop, and yeah, he was pretty sure he needed to give her a reason. "Talk to me."

"It's nothing for you to worry about." She reached up to pat his head like he was a child, but being a whole lot shorter than him she had to settle for an awkward pat to his forearm. "I'm having some cat food delivered," she said. "Petunia needs routine."

"And what do you need?"

She inhaled a shaky breath. "I need to make this transition as easy as possible for her."

Keane took her small, frail hand in his much bigger one. "Done. But now you, Aunt Sally. What can I do for you?"

There was another long pause and then a suspicious sniff, and in the way of men everywhere the world over, his heart froze in utter terror.

"I didn't know you as a child," she said quietly. "And that was my own doing. Nor did I bother with you when you got older, not until I needed you anyway. And that's also my shame." She squeezed his fingers. "You're a good man, Keane Winters, and you deserved better from me. From all of us. I've got no right to ask this of you, but please. *Please* take care of my baby."

And then she was gone.

He turned and stared down at the cat, who stared right back. "I think we're stuck with each other now."

Her eyes said she was unimpressed. And then she turned and, with her tail high in the air, stalked off.

"No more yakking in my bedroom, you hear me?" he called after her.

And shit, now he was talking to a cat. Shaking his head at himself, he shoved his feet into his running shoes—his *new* running shoes since Pita had taken a dump in his beloved, perfectly broken-in ones two weeks before—and hit the concrete.

He didn't have a set route. Running was for clearing his brain, and he let his feet take him where they wanted to go. Sometimes that was along the Embarcadero, or through Fort Mason. Or the Presidio, or the Lyon Street steps.

Today it was Cow Hollow.

He wanted to talk to Archer, wanted to make sure he was doing something about Ethan contacting Willa. All Keane knew of Archer was that the guy clearly took care of his own, and he did consider Willa one of his own. He'd seen that firsthand at the dog wedding.

Keane didn't expect Archer to be at work this early. He assumed he'd have to leave a message. But when he got to the Pacific Pier Building and took the stairs to Archer's second-floor offices, Archer was standing in the front room with Elle, the both of them staring down at an iPad screen together. There were two other men, one younger with a Doberman at his side, the other dressed like he'd just come back from a takedown, complete with more than one gun. He was talking when Keane entered, pointing at the iPad as if explaining something.

Archer lifted his head, eyes intense and hard. Whatever he'd been looking at had pissed him off. It clearly wasn't a good time but Keane didn't care. "About that text Willa got last night from her asshole ex," he said.

Archer exchanged a long look with the other men. "Taken care of," he finally said.

"Take care of how?" he wanted to know. "She shouldn't have to deal with him. I want to make sure she doesn't have to."

"She won't," Archer said grimly. "He won't contact her again."

Keane waited for a better explanation, but apparently Archer didn't feel the need to explain himself.

Elle shook her head at Archer and turned to Keane. "Good morning, by the way. And this is Joe," she said of the guy all weaponed up. "He's Archer's second in command. And Max," she said of the younger guy. "And this handsome four-legged guy"—she patted the huge dog on the head—"is Carl. And what Archer meant to say is that he and Max got Ethan. And because he had a warrant out for his arrest for being rough with other women and also stealing from them as well, they put his pansy ass in jail."

Keane's jaw was so tight he could barely speak. "When?"

"About an hour after she sent me the text last night," Archer said.

Elle smiled a little tightly but her eyes were warm. "As you know, Willa is incredibly special, to all of us. We've got her back." She paused. "And it's nice to know that you do as well. Isn't it, Archer?"

Archer slid her a look. She gave him one back, prompting him to blow out a sigh. "Yeah," he said and then his eyes hardened again. "Don't fuck it up. Don't fuck her up."

"Okay then," Elle said cheerfully. "Moving on. Welcome to the gang, Keane. You're one of us now, right, Archer?"

"As long as he doesn't fuck it up," Archer repeated.

Keane held the guy's gaze and gave a short nod. He wouldn't fuck it up. He couldn't.

Because he already had.

Back outside on the sidewalk, he stood in the early-morning dawn, a thick layer of fog casting everything in blues and grays. The lights were on inside Willa's shop, though the sign on the door said CLOSED.

He could see in the windows, see movement past the bright string of holiday lights and boughs of holly. Willa was there.

In another man's arms.

Chapter 8

#TisTheSeason

Willa had slept like crap. She wanted to blame it on the sheer amount of food she'd inhaled at dinner last night with Keane but even she, a woman who knew the value of putting her head in the sand once in a while, couldn't fool herself.

It hadn't been dinner. It was Keane: his smile, his eyes.

His kiss . . .

It was also the sombering certainty that he couldn't—or wouldn't—get any more attached to her than he had anything else in his life. Not his family, his work, Petunia . . .

And certainly not her.

She rolled out of bed and showered and since she'd run out of coffee, skipped makeup. No need to risk poking out an eye with a mascara wand when she had only major catastrophic medical insurance.

She ran down the four flights of stairs and called it exercise, entering her shop with three minutes to spare before a longtime client showed up. Carrie had standing reservations for one-day-a-week babysitting services for Luna, her new teacup piglet, and Macaroni, her "baby," a.k.a. sixty-five-pound, sweet-as-pie pit bull.

Thirteen-year-old Macaroni had arthritis, no teeth, questionable bowel control, and hip dysplasia, but he was pure heart. So much so that Carrie hadn't been able to put him down as her family had been gently suggesting.

Macaroni loved Willa and the feeling was mutual. He was a lot of work but he was absolutely the highlight of her week.

Except Carrie didn't show up. Figuring she was just running late, Willa began working on setting up the Santa Extravaganza Photo Booth for the upcoming weekend. She lost track of time until Spence appeared with two coffees in hand looking unaccustomedly solemn.

Spence was the brain of their gang. Quiet but not even remotely shy, he'd been recruited for a government think tank right from college—which he'd finished with a mechanical engineering degree at age eighteen. He'd never said much about that job but he'd hated it. A few years later he and some of his coworkers had gone to work for themselves. Last year they'd sold their start-up and struck gold. Willa had no idea if he'd gotten a penny or a million bucks; he never talked about it.

Since then he hadn't found his next thing. They all

knew he was unhappy and hated that for him, but if Spence didn't want to talk, Spence didn't talk. He'd been keeping busy with a variety of things and one of them was that he showed up at her shop several times a week to handle her pet-walking duties for her, which she loved. Nothing like a sexy geek to help increase business.

In fact, he was closer to Carrie and her pets than Willa since Carrie was dating one of Spence's ex-partners. "Come in," Willa called out to him. "Macaroni isn't here yet."

"I know." Spence came closer, set down the two coffees, and reached for her hand. "Honey, Macaroni passed away this morning."

Willa felt her heart stop, just stop. "Oh no," she breathed and pressed a hand to her chest, not that it alleviated any pain. "How?"

"In his sleep. No pain," he said softly and pulled her in just as she burst into tears.

A few minutes later, thankful she hadn't bothered with mascara after all, she shuddered out a sigh, still within the warm safety of Spence's arms. Damn, crying was exhausting. She needed to get it together and call Carrie to see how she could help. She needed to get to work. She needed to do a lot of things. That's when her gaze fell to the window and the man standing on the corner outside, his eyes locked on her.

Keane.

In the next beat, the shop door opened and there he was, bigger than life, looking a little tense, a frown on his lips, his eyes on Spence's arms still around her.

"What's wrong?" he asked.

"A client's dog passed away this morning," Spence told him. "Willa and Macaroni were really tight."

Was it her imagination or did he relax slightly?

"Aw, hell," he said, voice warm and genuine now. "That sucks."

"Yeah." Spence ruffled Willa's hair. "It does."

Willa took some tissues from the box on her counter and mopped herself up, aware of Keane watching her. He'd been thrown by finding her in Spence's arms but he'd recovered quick, which was a point in his favor, she could admit. He'd also been running. He was in black basketball shorts, with compression shorts peeking out beneath, and a long-sleeve dry-fit shirt that clung to his broad shoulders and chest, revealing every line of sinew on him.

And there were many.

His black baseball cap sat backward on his head and reflective aviator sunglasses covered his eyes. He shoved the glasses to the top of his head over his baseball cap, revealing his dark eyes filled with concern.

She felt a little dizzy just looking at him, a fact she attributed to the lack of breakfast and the weight of grief.

"I'm sorry," he said quietly and she thought maybe he wasn't just talking about Macaroni. "What can I do?"

She was unprepared for the warmth that spread inside her at that. Unprepared and ill-equipped to handle. For weeks, inner alarms had been going off every time she got too close to him, blaring warnings at her, pummeling her with the memory of being stood up by him, and the even worse blow of him not remembering her.

But now that she'd told him about it and heard his reaction and explanation, something had happened to her mad. It was as if someone had reached out and turned the volume down. *Way* down.

Off, actually.

Or maybe it'd been the kiss. It was incredibly hard to hold on to resentment for someone when you'd had your tongue down their throat. Plus, he kissed like magic.

Spence pointed to the coffee on the counter. "Make sure she caffeinates before you attempt conversation," he warned Keane and then kissed Willa on the cheek. "I'm leaving you in good hands," he said to her.

She stared up into his warm eyes. "How do you know?" She really hoped he had some wisdom to depart here. She needed it, bad.

Spence's smile was crooked and just a little sad. "Because you know as well as I do, people change."

He was referring to himself. He'd changed a lot—he'd had to in order to survive. Or maybe he'd meant the rest of them. Elle and Haley and Finn, even the far more closed-off Archer, they'd all had big changes in their lives, things that irrevocably affected them.

But actually, she thought maybe he'd meant her, because they both knew how much she'd grown since she'd opened South Bark. Through her work and the love of her friends, she'd found a direction. That had given her confidence and anchored her in a way she'd never been before.

Spence held her gaze for a minute, silently reminding her that she was no longer that meek wallflower she'd been in high school, that she knew more than anyone else things weren't always what they seemed, that people weren't always what they seemed, and also . . . some deserved a second chance.

Aware that Keane was soaking up this conversation, both spoken and unspoken, she blew out a breath and nodded.

"You know where to find me if you need me," Spence said. He nodded at Keane and then was gone.

Willa realized she was staring blindly after him when the to-go cup of coffee got waved back and forth beneath her nose. She latched on to it like it was the last air in the room.

"Jesus, your fingers are frozen," Keane said and wrapped his much warmer hands around hers on the cup, sandwiching her in his heat.

She could feel the roughness of the calluses on his hands and she liked that. He was real, very real. She took a sip of the coffee, and then another, and then finally just gulped it down, feeling the caffeine sink into her system with a soft, relieved sigh.

"Better?" Keane asked, dipping down a little to look into her eyes. "Yeah," he said, a slice of amusement in his gaze as he answered his own question. "There you are. You don't open for another hour, right?"

She glanced at her clock. "No, but—"

He pulled off her apron. "Love this one, by the way," he said, smiling at the printed words *I Don't Have to Be Good—I'm CUTE!* "And it's true," he said, grabbing her jacket from the hook by the door and wrapping her up in it. He went so far as to zip it up for her and pull her hood up over her head, tucking loose strands of her hair back out of her face.

The feel of his fingers on her temple and jaw, as rough and callused as his palms had been, should've felt intrusive.

Which was just about the opposite of how they felt. "Keane—"

"Shh," he said and took her hand. "I know I've given you absolutely zero reason to trust me but I'm going to ask you to anyway."

Yeah, she wasn't really all that good with trust.

He must have seen that in her gaze because he laughed softly, not at all insulted. "Reading you loud and clear but let's try this," he said. "How about you forget the asshole punk I was in high school for a minute, the one who'd say or do anything to get out of practice without having to talk to anyone, okay? Go off the guy I am today, standing here in front of you. Can you trust that guy?"

This time she hesitated on the other side of the fence, and apparently not above taking advantage of that, Keane said, "Close enough," and tugged her out the door.

Chapter 9

#NoSoupForYou

Willa couldn't believe she was doing this but apparently her feet had seceded from the States of Willa.

"Lock up," Keane told her and waited while she did just that. Then he took her hand again like maybe she was a flight risk.

And she was. "I don't want to talk about it," she said.

He laughed roughly. "Which *it?*"

"Any of the its. *All* of the its." Feeling like a shrew, she sighed and turned to face him. "But as for the one it in particular, the one where you stood me up—"

He opened his mouth to say something and she put her fingers over his mouth. "I'm moving on from that," she said softly. "I'm not a grudge holder—never have been, never will be—so it's silly for me to hang on to my mad over something that you honestly don't even remember—"

Wrapping his fingers around her wrist, he kissed her

fingertips before pulling them from his mouth. "Or intended," he said. "Because, Willa, I can promise you, I *never* intended to hurt you."

Staring into his eyes, she slowly nodded. "I know."

He held her gaze and nodded back, and then he walked her through the courtyard of her building, where he tugged her into Tina's Coffee Bar.

The six-foot-tall mahogany-skinned barista was serving and she winked at Willa. "Been a while since you were in here with a man, honey. Didn't like your last one, but I sure do like this one." She gave Keane a big white smile. "And good morning to you too, sugar. Haven't seen you much this week. How's the Vallejo Street renovation coming?"

"Almost done," Keane said.

Tina gave a big, deep laugh. "You've been saying that for months. Maybe you've grown too attached."

Keane just smiled. "How are the muffins this morning?"

"Out of this world, don't you doubt that for a single second."

Keane grinned at her. "I'll take half a dozen of your finest."

Two minutes later, Willa and Keane were outside. The morning was still gray but their way was lit by the strings of twinkling white lights, casting the cobblestones in black and white bold relief.

She watched Keane take in the two newest Christmas trees, one in front of O'Riley's Pub, the other in front of Reclaimed Woods, both decorated in simple red and gold balls. The only sound around them was the soft trickle of the water flowing from the fountain and some lovelorn crickets mourning the dawn's lack of warmth.

"Legend states that if you make a wish with a true heart, true love will find you," she said.

He met her gaze. "Legend also states that if you put your tooth under your pillow the Tooth Fairy will leave you cash."

She slowed, as always the fountain calling to her to make a wish. Keane slowed too, looking at her with a question.

She searched her pockets for change, but could only come up with a dog treat. "Damn." It was the swear jar's fault, all her spare change always ended up in there.

"What?"

"I wanted to make a wish," she said.

A small smile crossed his face. "You want to make a wish? You've lived here for how long and you've never made one?"

"Oh, I have." She paused. "I like to."

This garnered her a raised brow. "How many times have you wished?"

She bit her lower lip.

"More than once?"

Well, crap. How had they gotten on this subject? "Um . . ."

"More than . . . five?"

"Gee, would you look at the time?" she asked and tried to go but he caught her and brought her back around, his smile now a broad grin.

"Fine," she said. "If you must know, I toss a coin in every time I walk by."

He lost the battle with his laughter and she stared at him. Seriously, he had the best laugh. "It worked for Pru, I'll have you know," she told him. "She wished for true love to find Finn, and then he fell in love with her."

And Willa had been wishing ever since, even knowing how ridiculous and silly it was.

"So . . . you've been wishing for true love for who exactly?" he asked.

She stared at him in dismay. How had she not thought this through? "Me," she admitted, slapping her pockets because surely she had even a penny. "But I intend to fix that right now. I'll just wish for love for someone else."

"Who?" he asked warily.

She narrowed her eyes at his fear. "You. Got any change?"

He laughed. "Absolutely not." Then he pulled a dime from his pocket and held it up. "But how about this. *I'll* wish for you." And on that, he tossed the coin into the water.

Plop.

"There," he said. "Done. Hope it works out for you." He sounded fairly certain that it would and equally certain that it wouldn't be with him.

Which was good to know. Except it was also a little bit not good at all. "So you've never made a wish on true love before?" she asked.

He laughed. "No. That was a first."

"Because . . . you don't believe in true love?"

To his credit, he didn't brush off the question or try to tease his way out of answering. Seeming to understand how much it meant to her, he shrugged. "For some people, yes."

She nodded even as she felt a small slash of disappointment go through her. How silly was that? It wasn't as if love had worked out for her either. But she knew what the real problem was. It was that Keane had been clear about not wanting or needing anything serious in his life and yet here she was, finally feeling ready for just that in hers.

"And you?" he asked.

She stared at the water because it was far easier to talk to the fountain than hold Keane's too-honest gaze. "I've seen bits and pieces of it here and there. I know love's out there."

His eyes were solemn, intense, as he turned her to face him. "But?" he asked quietly. "I'm sensing a pretty big *but* here."

"But sometimes I'm not quite sure it's out there for *me*."

His gaze searched hers. "That seems pretty jaded for someone who wants everyone to believe in the magic of the holidays."

"Christmas has a happy connotation that brings joy and warmth. It comes every year, rain or shine. You can count on it."

"But not on love," he finished for her. His hand came up and he brushed a strand of hair from her temple, his fingers lingering. "I don't think it's always like that,

Willa. For some people, love's real and long-lasting. Forever."

"For some people," she repeated. "But not you? If you believe in love, why don't you believe in it for yourself?"

He shook his head. "I don't feel things deeply. I never have."

She stared at him, dismayed. "You don't really believe that."

"I do."

"But . . . I've seen you with Petunia."

He laughed. "Exactly. You've seen me dump her on you. I'm willing to pay a cat-sitter rather than deal with her."

"When you're at work, yes," she said. "But you've never once asked me to board her overnight when you were home."

"You board overnight?" he asked hopefully.

She laughed and smacked him lightly on the chest. "You know what I mean. You're frustrated by her and yet you still spend the money and time to make sure she gets good care when you're busy."

"Because she's my aunt's cat," he pointed out.

"Which is yet more proof. You're not close to your aunt but you took on her cat for her, without question or qualm."

"Oh, there was qualm," he said. "Buckets and buckets of qualm."

"You bought me muffins," she said softly, undeterred. "You wanted to cheer me up because I was upset."

"No, that was a sheer male knee-jerk attempt to make sure you didn't cry again. As a whole, we'll pretty much do anything to get a woman to stop crying."

"So what are we doing here, if you don't, or can't, feel things, if you don't ever want to find The One. What do you want from me?"

He flashed a wicked grin that made her body quiver hopefully but she snorted. "Right," she said. "'Animal magnetism.'"

"Just because I don't plan on finding The One doesn't mean I'm not interested in The One For Now."

She rolled her eyes. "Whatever. But I still think you're not giving yourself enough credit and you can't change my mind about that."

"What a shock," he murmured beneath his breath but his eyes were amused. Then that amusement faded. "From the outside looking in, I had a very traditional upbringing compared to you. Two parents, two older sisters, all college professors of science, their lives tightly run, everything entered into a planner, put in a neat little compartmentalized box." His smile was short. "But then along came me. I didn't fit in the box. I was wild, noisy, and destructive as hell. I was rough on the entire family and usually got left behind with a caretaker. My own doing," he said with a head shake. "It's not so much that I don't get attached, as I'm not easy to get attached *to*."

Willa's heart gave a hard squeeze. He'd learned too young that even the people who were supposed to un- conditionally love you didn't always—something she knew all too well. Only she'd compensated by going in the opposite direction and loving everything and everyone. "You didn't get a lot of affection," she said softly. "You weren't shown much emotion. That's why you think you don't know how to feel or give it."

"I don't think it," he said. "I know it."

Back in high school, she'd not been aware of any of this. She'd simply set her sights on inviting him to the dance, knowing only that he'd been a solid athlete and also an equally solid student, and that kids and teachers alike had flocked to him.

He'd had an easy smile and a natural confidence that had made him seem impenetrable at the time. Now, looking back on it, she could see that he'd used his charisma as a personal shield and she'd not looked past it.

Which made her just as guilty as everyone else in his life.

He nodded for her to sit on the stone bench she'd personally lined with boughs of holly and little jingle bells weeks ago now. It was early enough that few people came through the courtyard. There was the occasional runner or dog walker, but mostly they had the place to themselves. With the low-lying fog, it felt like they were all alone.

It was incredibly intimate.

They ate muffins in companionable silence for as long as she could stand it, but silence had never been her strong suit. Eventually her curiosity got the best of her. "When Tina said maybe you've grown attached to your place, why did you say not likely?"

"I told you." He shrugged. "I always sell them when I'm finished."

"Because you don't get attached."

"Right."

"But we decided that isn't exactly strictly true," she pointed out.

"No, *you* decided."

She blew out an annoyed sigh.

He didn't ask her to translate the sigh. Clearly it wasn't necessary. Instead, he turned his head and met her gaze. "You say more with silence than any woman I've ever met. Spit it out, Willa, before you choke on it."

Where did she start with alphas . . . "It's your home."

"It won't be a home until someone's living in it."

"You're living in it!"

He smiled at her exasperated tone and ran a finger down her nose. "I annoy you."

"In so, so, *so* many ways," she said on a laugh. "Seriously, you have no idea."

"I have some."

"Is that right?" she asked. "Because I'd think that annoyance is one of those messy emotions you don't bother with."

His eyes darkened. "I bother with some emotions."

"Yeah? Which ones?"

He calmly took the half-eaten muffin out of her hand and dropped it back into the bag.

"I wanted that," she said.

"And I want this." He moved faster than she imagined anyone as big as he was could move. Before she could so much as draw another breath of air, he pulled her hard against him, his hands fisting in her hair, his mouth seeking hers.

The kiss started out gentle, but quickly got serious and not so gentle. His lips parted hers, their tongues touched, and she heard herself moan. His hot mouth left hers and made its way along her jaw, her throat, where he planted openmouthed kisses that made her shiver for more. If she hadn't been sitting, her knees wouldn't have held her up, because he kissed away her annoyance, her good sense, any ability to think, *everything*.

Except her ability to feel.

And oh God, what she felt. She could barely even hold on, she was so dizzy with the hunger ripping through her, but then he pulled back and stared at her, his hair crazy from her fingers, those chocolate eyes fierce and hot, his breathing no more steady than hers.

She pressed her palms to his chest to try and ground herself but she still felt like she was floating on air. "Wha . . . ?" It was all she could manage. Clearly, their chemistry had exploded her brain cells. She shook her head to clear it. "Okay, I stand corrected. There are some emotions you do exceptionally well. Like lust." She paused. He'd been upfront with her, and brutally honest to boot. They weren't going to be each other's The One, but they could have this. He was game.

And in spite of herself, so was she. "Why did you stop?"

He looked at her for a long moment, at first in surprise and then with a slow smile. He knew he'd coaxed her over to the dark side. "We're in the middle of the courtyard," he said.

"We don't have to be." She couldn't believe she said

it but, well, she meant it. She was still plastered up against his big, hard body, emphasis on *hard,* and all she could think about was what he'd feel like without the barriers of their clothing.

But Keane wasn't making a move to take her back to his place.

Or hers.

Instead, he had his hands on her shoulders, holding her away from him. Embarrassed, she started to get up but he held on. "No," she said, "I get it. You're . . . feeling things and you don't like to. Not for your house, not for Petunia, and certainly not for me—"

She broke off with a gasp as he hauled her back into him, right onto his lap this time. One of his big hands palmed her ass to hold her still against an unmistakable bulge of a rock-hard erection.

"See, you're feeling *something*," she said breathlessly. "So *why* aren't we running for one of our places?"

"Because by the time I got you there, you'll have changed your mind," he said. "You've had a rough morning. I don't want this to be a spur-of-the-moment decision I push you into because of the crazy heat between us. And then there's the work factor. We're both on the clock in a few minutes and, Willa"—he held her gaze—"when we go there, we're going to need more than a few minutes."

At that low, gruff tone, she went damp.

"So," he said firmly. "We're going to sit here enjoying the morning and each other's company."

"But . . ." She lowered her voice to a mere whisper. "We could be doing that naked."

He groaned and dropped his head to her shoulder as part of his anatomy seemed to swell beneath her. "It's not nice to tease."

Who was teasing?

Reading her mind, he laughed soft in his throat and it was sexy as hell. "Talk," he said. "We're going to talk until we both have to go to work."

She blew out a sigh and her gaze snagged on the nearest Christmas tree. "Did you have Christmas trees growing up?"

"Yeah. My parents always hosted the holiday party for their entire department and the decorations had to be perfect. Which meant I could look but not touch."

She turned her head and met his gaze. "Why am I getting the feeling you didn't always do as you were told?"

He laughed again and she felt like she'd won the lottery. "I never did what I was told," he said. "One year I sneaked downstairs in the middle of the night and tried to climb the tree."

"What happened?"

"It fell over on me. Broke all the ornaments and I cut open my chin." He rubbed his jaw, smiling ruefully. "I was a total miscreant. My parents told me I was going to get coal for Christmas that year."

"Did you?"

"No, I got a one-way ticket to my dad's brother's ranch in Texas for the entire winter break, where I shoveled horseshit for three long weeks."

She searched his expression, which was calm and easy. In direct opposition to the erection nudging her butt. "You don't look particularly scarred by that experience," she said.

"My uncle loved to build things. He had all these amazing tools and machinery." He leaned back, one arm along the back of the bench, his fingers playing with the ends of her hair. She wasn't even sure he was aware of doing it.

"It was the first time I'd seen anything like it," he said. "The first time I got to watch someone work with their hands. He had an entire barn filled with antique tools." He smiled. "He gave me one, a vintage level. I still have it. Someday I'll collect others to go with it. I definitely got bitten by the builder bug that winter. Looking back, it's actually one of my best childhood memories." He nudged her shoulder with his. "Now you. Tell me something from one of your past Christmases."

She searched her brain for a happy memory to match his. "My mom gave me a necklace when I was little once," she said. "It had a charm with the letter *W* engraved in gold, with all these little rhinestones outlining the *W*. I loved it." She smiled. "I wore it to school and some mean girl named Britney said it was fake and from a bubble-gum machine. She grabbed it and it broke."

"I hope you punched her in the nose," Keane said.

She bit her lower lip. "I stomped on her foot and made her cry, even though she was right. The necklace was fake. It turned my neck green."

He grinned and she felt the breath catch in her throat as she watched the early-morning light magnify his beautiful smile. "Atta girl," he said.

She laughed a little, finding humor in the bittersweet memory for the first time.

When their coffee and muffins were gone, he stood and pulled her up with him. Her phone was going off and so was his.

"Real life's calling," he said reluctantly.

Right. She had a business to open and he had God knew what to build today, and they both had people depending on them to do their jobs. "Thanks for the muffins," she said and started to walk off.

He caught her.

"We still have unfinished business," he said in that sexy voice with the smile that made her stupid.

"That's nothing new."

He tightened his grip on her hand when she would have pulled free. "I didn't thank you for trusting me enough to tell me about high school."

"I wouldn't take it quite as far as trusting you," she said. "I haven't signed on the dotted line for the trust-you program yet."

"A wise woman." He gave her fingers a meaning-ful squeeze as he reeled her in and planted a soft but scorching-hot kiss on her mouth. "But I might surprise you."

She watched him walk away and then sank back to the bough-lined bench so hard that the little bells tacked to either side jangled as loudly as her nerves.

"That was interesting."

Willa looked up at Elle. She was wearing form-fitting black trousers, FMP's, and a power-red fitted blazer over a white lace tee, all of which emphasized her curves and general badassery.

"You look amazing," Willa said. "How do you walk in those shoes without killing yourself?"

"No changing the subject. I went to grab a coffee and saw you two pressed up against each other like there'd been some sort of superglue incident."

Well, crap. "Are you sure?" Willa asked. "Because it's pretty foggy this morning and—"

Elle pointed at her. "You know who might buy that? No one. Because that was one smoking-hot kiss. I mean I get it, the man is sex on stilts. But you keep trying to tell us you don't like him like that so imagine my surprise to find you two out here attempting to exchange tonsils."

Oh God. It *had* been smoking hot, incredibly so. In fact, she could still feel the hard, rippling muscles beneath his shirt, the slow and reassuringly steady beat of his heart under the palm of her hand. The way it'd sped up when his mouth had covered hers.

"Not that anyone believes you about not liking him, by the way," Elle said. "When he showed up in Archer's office this morning looking all hot and edgy, needing to kick some serious Ethan ass, I—"

"Wait, what?" Willa asked, sitting up straight. "Keane went to Archer's office?"

Elle went brows up. "He didn't tell you."

"Do I look like he did?"

"No," Elle murmured thoughtfully, tapping a perfectly manicured fingernail to her chin. "Which actually makes him even hotter now."

"For keeping secrets?"

"For caring so much about your safety. That, or he already knows how stubborn and obstinate you are."

Willa shook her head. She couldn't go there right now. "Did anyone else see the kiss?"

Just then, Rory stuck her head out the back door of South Bark. "Okay, not that I'm judging or anything," she called out, "but are you going to stand around all day kissing hot guys who you pretend not to like, or are we going to get some work done?"

"I think it's safe to say someone else saw," Elle said dryly.

Chapter 10

#AllThatAndABagOfChips

Keane went back to Vallejo Street for what should've been a hot shower but he decided cold would be best under the circumstances. He was pretty certain a guy couldn't die from a bad case of needing to be buried balls deep inside a certain strawberry blonde, green-eyed pixie, but he figured the icy shower might ensure it.

It didn't help.

After, he didn't go to either North Beach or the Mission District project, both of which needed his attention. Nor did he hit his desk to unbury himself from paperwork. Instead he got busy on the finish work at the Vallejo Street house—the trim, the floorboards, the hardware for the windows and doors . . . the last of what had to be done before the place could be put on the market.

At first, Pita watched him suspiciously from the open doorway. Then she slowly and deliberately worked her way into the room to bat at a few wood shavings. When she got too close to his planer, he stopped. "Back up, cat. Nothing to see here."

Instead, she sat and stared at him, her tail twitching.

"Suit yourself." When he looked up an hour later, she'd curled up on the wood floor in the sole sunspot and had fallen asleep. He heard the sound of Sass's heels coming down the hallway and looked up as she appeared.

"Bad news," she said.

"We didn't get the permits for the Mission project?"

"Worse," she said.

"There's not really a Santa Claus?"

She didn't laugh. Didn't snort. Didn't ream him out for being an insensitive dumbass. Shit. "What is it?" he asked. "Just tell me."

"It's your great-aunt Sally," she said quietly. "Her doctor's admin called here because you're listed as her next of kin."

This was news to him. "What's wrong?"

"Apparently she needs to go into an assisted-living facility."

"Why, what's wrong with her?" Answers to this question bombarded him. Heart failure. Cancer . . .

"Rheumatoid arthritis," Sass said. "It's acting up and she can't get around like she used to, taking care of an apartment or herself without help. They've got a facility lined up—it's the one she wants, but there's a problem."

"Killing me, Sass," he said, pressing a thumb and a finger into his eye sockets.

"She doesn't have the money, Keane. She needs five grand up front for the first month."

"Tell them they'll have it today," he said.

"You know how many zeroes that is, right? And her insurance won't kick in until month three, so—"

"Tell them they'll have whatever they need, Sass."

"Okay." Her voice was softer now, more gentle. "I realize you're all alpha and manly and won't want to hear this, but I have to say it anyway—this is incredibly generous of you—"

"Is there anything else?"

"Actually, yes," she said, "and for you this is going to be the worst part, so girdle your loins, pull up your big-girl panties, and anything else you have to do to face the music."

"I swear to God, Sass, just tell me all of it or—"

"She can't have a pet at this place," she said quickly. "Not even a goldfish."

Keane turned around and stared at Pita, still sleeping calmly, even sweetly, in that sunspot. He might've been warmed by the sight if it hadn't been for the wrecked box of finishing nails that she'd pulled apart, which lay all around her like the fallen dead.

"Keane?"

Shit. He blew out a breath, dropped his tool belt, and headed to the door. "Text me the address for the place."

"Only if you promise me you're not going over there guns blazing to dump that sweet little cat on them. You'll get Sally kicked out before she's even in there."

Not that he would love nothing more than to dump the antichrist on someone, *anyone,* but even he wasn't that much of a bastard. "Just get me the damn info, including their phone number."

"Why don't you let me handle the transfer," she started, sounding worried. "I'll get someone to help her pack and—"

"I want to see the place and check up on it, okay? She doesn't have any other family who'll give a shit."

She stared at him, eyes suspiciously shiny, and Keane stilled. "What are you doing?"

She tilted her head up and stared at the ceiling, blinking rapidly. "Nothing." But she sniffed and waved a hand back and forth in front of her face.

Oh, Jesus. "You're . . . crying?"

"Well, it's all your fault!" she burst out with. "You're being sweet and it's my time of the month!"

He wasn't equipped for this. "First of all, I'm not even close to sweet. And second, I bought you stuff for that, it's in the hall bathroom."

"See?" she sobbed and tossed up her hands. *"Sweet."*

He tried calling his aunt's cell but she didn't answer. He drove to the facility and checked it out. It was a nice, clean, surprisingly cheerful place. After, he went to his aunt's and found her stressing over the arrangements, so he helped her pack and took her to the facility himself.

He felt like shit leaving her there but she seemed relieved to have it done and clearly wanted him out of her hair, so he went back to work.

At the end of the day his body was demanding food, so he found himself at O'Riley's Pub seeking their famous wings.

And maybe also a Willa sighting.

The pub was one half bar, one half seated dining. The walls were dark wood that gave an old-world feel to the place. Brass lanterns hung from the rafters, and old fence baseboards finished the look, which said antique charm and friendly warmth. And much like the rest of the building, there was holiday décor everywhere. Boughs of holly, strings of twinkling lights, tinsel, and a huge Christmas tree sitting right in the middle of the place.

He wondered if Finn had let Willa loose in here. Seemed likely. Music drifted out of invisible speakers. One wall was all windows that opened to the courtyard. The street view came via a rack of accordion wood-and-glass doors revealing a nice glimpse of Fort Mason Park and the Marina Green down the hill, and the Golden Gate Bridge behind that.

But he paid no attention to any of it. Instead, his gaze went straight to the end of the bar where the O'Riley brothers and their close-knit gang could usually be found.

Willa was in the middle of a huddle with Elle, Pru, Haley, Finn, Archer, and Spence. As he moved closer, he could hear them arguing over several tree toppers sitting on the bar in front of them.

"It's my turn to decide and I think that one's the best," Haley said, her attention on what looked like an intricately woven angel. "Last year was Spence's turn, and I go after Spence."

"No, last year was *Finn's* turn," Spence said, pointing to a ceramic star. "And I go after Finn."

"But it's got to be the dog," Willa said, stroking a stuffed Saint Bernard with holly around his neck. "He's a rescue dog." She caught sight of Keane and gave a quick, genuine smile. "Hey," she said. "What are you doing here?"

Apparently looking for you, he thought, his day suddenly not seeming so shitty.

"We'll have a dart-off," Archer said, back to the topic at hand. "Three teams of two. Haley, Spence, and Willa will each pick one of the rest of us to be on their team. Best team wins choice of tree topper for their captain. Get your asses to the back."

When Archer gave people an order, they obeyed. Everyone got up and headed to the back room where the darts were played.

Elle was right on Archer's heels until he put up a hand to stop her.

Elle went hands on hips. "What have we said about using your words?" she asked him.

"You're not playing," Archer said.

Elle looked around her like she couldn't believe he'd said such a thing. "And since when are you the boss of me?"

Archer pointed to her impossibly high heels. They were black and strappy and revealed her sky blue toenail polish and a silver toe ring. "No one plays darts in sandals," he said.

"Sandals?" She laughed. "Honey, these are *Gucci.*"

"I don't care if they're flip-flops, it's safety before beauty. You need to lose them to play, because I'm not risking your toes, even if you're willing to do so."

"Let me be crystal clear," she said. "*Not* losing the heels."

"Then you're not playing."

"Fine." Elle stuck a finger in his face. "I hope your team gets its ass kicked."

Archer looked unaffected. "Never going to happen."

"You're down a player now," Elle said.

Archer turned to Keane. "You play?"

Yeah, he played. He'd been a champion in his bar crawl days, but he gave a slight shrug. "A little."

Willa stopped in front of Keane, eyes narrowed. "A little or a lot?" she demanded. "Do I want you or Finn?"

"Hey," Finn said. "Standing right here."

Keane never took his gaze off Willa. "You want me," he said with quiet steel.

She flushed to her roots, and he grinned at her.

"I beat all of you just last week," Finn grumbled. "Even Archer."

There were pool tables and two dartboards in the back room. Everyone lined up at the dartboards. Archer and Haley, Spence and Finn, and . . . him and Willa.

Haley was good, and no surprise, Archer was great. Spence and Finn were both off the charts.

"See?" Finn said to the room.

Willa . . . sucked. There was no other word for it.

"Dammit," she griped when her dart fell off the board.

"I've got you," Keane said and hit a bull's-eye.

Willa pumped a triumphant fist in the air. "Yes!" She threw herself at Keane and when he caught her, she gave him a smacking kiss right on the lips. Grinning, she stepped back. "The Saint Bernard topper it is!"

"There's going to be no living with her now," Finn said. "You all know that, right?"

Archer looked at Keane. "You can aim, you're tough under pressure, and even better yet, you can lie. Tell me you can shoot and you're hired—*Shit,*" he muttered, his attention going to the dance floor. Elle was out there, her heels still firmly in place on her feet, dancing with some guy Keane had never seen before. Dirty dancing.

Archer moved toward them and cut in. Elle looked pissed but allowed it. Sparks flew between them and Keane turned to Willa. "Is that something new?"

"Those two?" Willa laughed. "They fight like that whenever they're together."

"Yeah, that's not what I mean."

She looked confused and he grinned. "Never mind," he said. "I'll explain when you're older."

She eyed Archer and Elle again. "They both insist there's nothing going on."

He didn't buy it but it wasn't his business.

Willa inhaled a deep breath. "It's getting late. I should go."

"Dance with me first."

She laughed.

"I'm serious."

Her eyes widened and she sent a startled look to the dance floor. "If you think I suck at darts, you should see me on the dance floor. I'm a really bad dancer."

"So am I."

She rolled her eyes. "Like I'm supposed to believe you're bad at anything."

He flashed a smile. "How will you know unless you give me a shot?"

"That's one thing I really shouldn't do."

"Chicken?" he asked softly.

She narrowed her eyes. "Never." And then she stomped off to the dance floor.

He caught up with her just as the music changed, slowed. Slipping an arm around her waist, he pulled her in, tucking that wayward lock of hair behind her ear.

She shivered.

"Cold?" he asked, running his free hand along her arm, urging it up to slip around his neck.

"No." Her warm breath brushed his jaw as she stepped into him. "I'm starting to think you're a little like that chocolate bar I keep in my fridge for emergencies."

"Irresistible?"

"Bad for me."

He laughed and let the music drift over them, enjoying the feel of her warm, soft body against his, the way she gripped him tight, one hand at the back of his neck, the other at the small of his back, fisted in his shirt. He could feel her heart pounding against his but it wasn't until she trembled that he tipped her head up.

She shook her head at his unasked question. "Okay, maybe you're also a *little* irresistible," she murmured. "It's just that you're always so . . ."

"What?"

"Everything."

He turned his palm up and entwined their fingers together, bringing their joined hands to his mouth as they swayed in sync to the music, her steps unsure and too fast. He matched her steps to his, slowing her down, looking into her eyes.

"You're scared," he realized, not talking about dancing anymore.

"Terrified," she confessed. She wasn't talking about dancing either. "Join me, won't you?"

"There's nothing to fear here, Willa."

"Because we're just two consenting adults who are hugely attracted to one another, and we both know the score. No falling. Just some good, old-fashioned fun." Her huge eyes blinked up at his. "Right?"

"Right," he murmured against her lips. "But you forgot something."

"What's that?"

"You do make me laugh, and I dig that. So yes to the fun, but, Willa, nothing I feel about you is old-fashioned." He ran the tips of his fingers lightly down her back until they came to a stop at the low waistband of her jeans, stroking the bare skin between the hem of her sweater and the denim. Another shudder wracked her and he pulled her even closer to him, their bodies forming an unbroken line from chest to toe.

Closing her eyes, she sighed softly and tipped her face up to his. As he lowered his mouth to hers, she parted her lips for his eagerly. He swallowed her soft moan, rocking her in tune to the music as they kissed. "You do so know how to dance," she accused softly.

His hands traveled up her slim spine. "I know other things too. Like how much I want to touch you."

She laughed nervously. "Keane—"

"Shh," he whispered into her hair. "Later."

Both the street and courtyard doors of the pub were closed to the winter air, but every time someone came in or out, a breeze whisked through, brushing over their heated skin.

When the song ended, Keane tipped Willa's face up to meet his, rasping his thumb over her lower lip. "Thanks for showing me how to dance."

She sank her teeth into the pad of his thumb just hard enough to sting, making him laugh.

She was as dangerous as Pita.

The air around them crackled, much the way it had around Archer and Elle earlier, the heat between them pulsing and ebbing in the crowded pub. But unlike Archer and Elle, Keane knew exactly what it was.

"I really do have to go," Willa said.

"I'll walk you up."

"That's . . ." Her gaze fell to his mouth. "Probably a bad idea."

He had to smile. "There's no doubt." If she wanted him to push her on this issue, she was going to be disappointed. It wasn't his style to push. When they slept together—and God, he really hoped that was going to happen—it would be because she wanted him and she was ready, and not because he talked her into it. So he took her hand and they walked out into the courtyard.

There really was a *whole* lot of Christmas going on out here. The fountain misted softly in the evening chill, lit red and green from the lights.

Old Man Eddie was out here, manning the fire pit. He pulled a sprig of mistletoe from his pocket and tossed it to Willa.

In return, she handed him her leftovers. "Wings," she said. "Extra sauce."

"Thanks, darlin'. I love my lights. Meant a lot that you'd do that for me."

"Anything," Willa said.

And Keane knew she meant it. It was part of what made her special, and different from just about anyone he'd ever known. She really would give a stranger the shirt off her back.

In the stairwell, Keane met her gaze. "You have plans for that mistletoe?"

She smiled but waited until she was at the top of the stairs, turning to walk backward toward her apartment as she flashed him a grin. "Some things a man should find out for himself."

He caught her at her door and pushed her up against it. He had no idea if they were going to push their limits or what, but he wanted her to think of him after he walked away. To that end, he wrapped his fingers around her wrist, the one still holding the sprig of mistletoe, and raised it slowly up the wall until it was above her head, held to the wall by both of them.

Then he lowered his head and brushed her mouth with his. And then—to torture them both—again.

Moaning, she dropped the mistletoe and tugged her hand free to grip the front of his shirt with two fists. She was still holding tight when he lifted his head.

"It's the damn mistletoe," she whispered.

He let out a low laugh. "Babe, it's not the mistletoe."

Chapter 11

#SillyRabbit

Willa dropped her head to Keane's chest and *thunked* it a few times, hoping it would clear her thoughts. Instead, since his chest was hard as concrete, she gave herself a mini concussion. "What am I going to do with you?" she asked.

"I've got a few suggestions."

She lifted her head and took in the heated amusement in his dark gaze. And something else too, something that stole her breath and made it all but impossible to look away. "Keane," she whispered and shifted in closer.

His hands went to her hips and he lowered his head slowly. A sigh shuddered out of her and she closed her eyes as his lips fell on hers. Dropping the mistletoe, she wrapped her arms around his neck, the silky strands of his hair slipping through her fingers.

With a rough sound that came from deep in his chest

he pulled her closer, his hands threading through her hair to change the angle of the kiss, taking it deeper. With one tug he bared her throat and dragged his mouth from hers only to scrape his teeth along her skin.

She gasped in pleasure and need and probably would have slid to the floor in a boneless heap if his muscled thigh hadn't been thrust between hers, both holding her up and creating a heat at her core that made her forget why she wasn't ready for him.

Her body couldn't be *more* ready.

But then he gentled his touch and nuzzled his face in the crook of her neck. Sweet. Tender. And with what sounded like a low chuckle, he pulled back.

She struggled to open her eyes. "Wow," she whispered.

With a soft laugh that turned her on even more, he brushed one last kiss to her temple. "Lock up, Willa. Dream of me."

And she knew she would.

Keane woke up on Sunday to a clanking, clattering that sounded like a flock of birds had gotten into his bedroom and were beating their wings against the window trying to get out.

Sitting straight up in bed, he whipped his head to the window, expecting to see a blood bath.

Instead he saw his shades all out of whack with a suspicious cat-size bulge behind them. Then a black face and searing blue eyes peeked from between two slats. And then four paws.

"Mew."

"So you're stuck," he said.

"Mew."

Shaking his head, he got up and attempted to separate her from the shades. She wasn't having it. In fact, she lost her collective shit.

"This would be a lot easier if you stopped hissing and spitting at me," he said.

Her ears went back and she tried to bite him.

"Do that again and I'll leave you here," he warned.

She switched to a low, continuous growl. When he finally got her loose, she stalked off, head high, tail switching back and forth, pissy to her very core.

Shaking his head, he turned to the shades.

Destroyed.

He searched out his cell phone and called Sass. She didn't pick up so he left a message. "I know it's Sunday, but if you're around, I could use some help. Call me back."

He disconnected and met Pita's still pissy gaze. She'd come back in, probably to remind him that she was an inch from starving to death. "She's not going to call me back," he said.

He tried Mason next. Also went to voice mail. Shit. He fed the heathen and hit the shower. He was halfway through when he felt like he was being watched. He opened his eyes after rinsing off his shampoo and found Pita sitting on the tile just outside the shower, staring him down.

It wasn't often he felt vulnerable, but he had the urge to cup himself. "Problem?" he asked her.

She gave one slow-as-an-owl blink. "Mew."

She didn't sound angry. In fact, she sounded . . . lonely. Seeming to prove that point, she actually took a step into the walk-in shower.

"Watch out," he warned her. "You're not going to like it."

And indeed, when the water hit her square in the face, she slitted her eyes and glared at him as she retreated back to the safety zone. Lifting a paw she began to meticulously wash her face free of the evil water that had dared land on her.

"I told you so," he said and stilled.

I told you so.

It'd been a common refrain of his parents whenever he'd done something they'd considered stupid. And admittedly, he'd done a lot of stupid. Such as when he'd broken his leg in his sophomore year of college and lost his football scholarship.

"Smarts never fail you," his father had said. *"Science never fails you. Being a professor is a job that won't fail you. I told you that you needed a backup plan."*

"Holy shit," Keane muttered, shaking my head. "I just opened my mouth and my father came out."

Pita sneezed but it sounded like a derisive snort.

A little traumatized, Keane got dressed and then stood there in his foyer, staring down at Pita, who'd followed him to the door. "I have to go to the North Beach job to check on yesterday's progress," he said. "Wait here and don't destroy anything."

She gave him one blink, slow as an owl.

"Shit." She was totally going to destroy something.

Maybe several somethings. "Listen . . ." He crouched low to look her in the eyes. "I can't take you to kitty day care today; it's closed. And Sass and Mason are ignoring me because it's Sunday."

She just kept staring at him. Didn't even blink.

"Shit," he said again and pointed to the carrier. "Your only other option is to come with me but that's a bad idea—"

Before he'd finished the sentence, Pita had walked right into her carrier without fuss or a single hiss.

Shocked, he zipped up the bright pink bedazzled case and met the blue eyes through the mesh. "Look, I know you're unhappy about all of this, but we're stuck with each other for now."

She did more of that no-blinking thing.

"How about this," he said. "I promise to do the best I can, and in return you promise to stop taking a dump in my shoes."

Pita turned her back on him.

"Okay then. Good talk." He carried her out the door and to the truck, driving her to North Beach. When he parked on the street in front of a café two doors down from his building, a group of women stood on the sidewalk talking to each other at ninety miles an hour.

". . . Just wait until you bite into their warm cinnamon buns . . ."

". . . Couldn't have found a better place to have your thirtieth-birthday girls' bash . . ."

". . . Ohmigod don't turn around, but there's a hot guy at your six and he's carrying his cat in a pink bedazzled carrier—I said *don't turn around!*"

But they'd all turned around. Six of them, smiling at him.

Nodding at them set off an avalanche of waves and more smiles as he walked to his place.

"Now those are buns I could sink my teeth into," one of them murmured.

Keane resisted running up the stairs. Entering the house, he came to a shocked stop as Mason and Sass jumped apart, looking tousled and guilty.

They all stared at each other for an awkward beat and then Mason got very busy with his nail gun while Sass began thumbing through her work iPad as if it were on fire.

"What the fuck," Keane said.

Mason accidentally discharged a nail into the floor.

Sass went hands on hips and took the Defensive Highway. "Hey, what we do behind your back is *our* business."

"True," Keane said.

"And we never let it affect work," she said. "Never."

"Okay," he said.

"I wouldn't," Sass added, softer now. "I love this job."

"Sass," Keane said on a low laugh. "I don't care what the two of you do on your off hours, as long as I don't have to see it. What I meant by what the fuck is . . . what the fuck are you two doing here working but not picking up your phones?"

"You said last week all hands on deck until we finish," Mason said, apparently finding his voice. "Whelp, all hands are on deck."

"Yes, but I called you," Keane said with what he thought was remarkable patience. "Both of you. No one answered."

"Because you wanted a cat-sitter," Sass said. "And much as I do love this job, evil-cat sitting is not in my job description."

"Or mine," Mason said.

Keane stared at them. "You didn't know that's what I wanted."

Sass shifted her gaze pointedly at the cat carrier he was still carrying. "You don't hire stupid people."

He blew out a breath and set the cat carrier down.

"What are you doing?" Mason asked, eyes wide with horror. "Don't let it out."

"It's a she."

"*It* will attack me," Mason said.

Sass rolled her eyes. "Mas here thinks the cat is Evil Incarnate."

"*It is,*" Mason said.

"She rubs against his legs," Sass said. "He's convinced that the cat is trying to establish that she's the dominant in their relationship."

"She left me *half* a field mouse," Mason said.

"She's noticed your lack of hunting skills and inability to feed yourself," Sass told him. "She's trying to show you how to hunt. It's a compliment."

"*Half* a field mouse," Mason repeated.

Keane shook his head and unzipped the carrier. "No one leave any doors open," he directed. Then he got Pita a bowl of water and food, and finally did his walk-through.

Then he left Mason a list of things he wanted done and he and Pita headed back to Vallejo Street, where he strapped on his tool belt. The favorite part of any of the jobs he took on was always the woodwork. Carpentry had been his first love and it was still the thing that fulfilled him the most. On this job, he'd really gone old-school in the traditional Victorian sense, bringing back the original oak plank flooring and ornate wood trim, which was what he was working on today. Sanding and varnishing. The trim would go next.

An hour into it, he paused to pull out his vibrating phone. It was Sally finally calling him back with a FaceTime call. He answered and was treated to . . . a huge mouth. The skin around the mouth was puckered with age. The lips had been painted in red lipstick.

"Hello?" the mouth said. "Keane? Goddamn new-fangled phone," she muttered. "Can't hear a damn thing."

"Aunt Sally, I'm here," he told her. "You settled in okay?"

"What?"

"You don't have to hold the phone up to your mouth like that. You can just talk normal—"

"Huh? What's that? *Speak up, boy.*"

Keane sighed. "I said you can just talk normal."

"I am talking normal," she yelled, still holding the phone so close to her face that only her mouth showed. "I'm calling to talk to Petunia. Put her on the line."

"You want to talk to the cat."

"Do you have hearing problems? That's what I said. Now put her on for me."

"Sure." Keane moved into the kitchen, because that's where Pita hung out most, near her food bowl. The food bowl was empty.

No sign of Pita.

"Hang on," he said into the phone and then pressed it against his thigh to block video and sound. "Pita," he called. "Pita, come." He felt ridiculous. Cats didn't "come." Neither did the antichrist. "Cat," he said. "Petunia?"

Still nothing. He strode through the house and stilled in the dining room. Oh fuck, he thought, staring down at the hole in the floor. The air duct, without its grate, because it was on a sawhorse with some trim drying after being lacquered.

He dropped to his knees and peered down the open vent, but couldn't see a thing. "Pita?"

There was a loaded silence, then a rustling, followed by a miserable-sounding "mew."

His heart stopped. "Okay, not funny. Get your fuzzy, furry ass back up here," he demanded, still holding the phone tight to his thigh.

This time the "mew" sounded fainter, like she'd moved further into the vent. He brought the phone back up. "Hey, Aunt Sally, I've got another call I have to take. I'll call you right back, okay?"

"Is there something wrong?" the red, wrinkled lips asked.

"No worries," Keane assured her and hung up. He retrieved Pita's food bowl, refilled it, and then jangled the bowl above the open vent. "Hear that?" he called down the hole. "That's your food. Come and get it."

Nothing. Not even a rustle this time.

"Christ." Keane got to his feet and strode into the next room, where he knew the venting system led to. He tore off that grate, flicked on the flashlight app from his phone and peered into the hole. "Pita?"

More nothing.

"Dammit, cat." He turned off the flashlight and rubbed his temples. At a complete loss, he did the first thing that came to mind. He called the only person he knew that the cat actually liked.

"Hello?" Willa answered, sounding soft and sleepy.

"I woke you. I'm sorry."

"Keane?"

"Yeah," he said. "I've got a problem."

"Still?" She yawned. "Aren't you supposed to call a doctor if that conditions persists for more than four hours?"

He froze for a beat and then laughed. Pinching the bridge of his nose, he shook his head. "Not that kind of problem." He paused. "And I'm pretty sure there's no guy on earth who'd actually go to a doctor for that."

"Yet another reason why men die younger than women. What's the problem, Keane?"

"Pita."

"You have her today too?"

"Yeah. My aunt had to go into a rehab facility with assisted living. While I was working, Pita went down a vent and either joined a rat compound or she's just enjoying fucking with me like every other female I know, but I can no longer see or hear her."

Silence.

"Willa?"

"Your aunt had to go into a home?"

Hadn't he just said so? "Yes, and—"

"And you're holding on to Pita for her? Indefinitely?"

"Well I *was*," he said. "Now I'm pretty sure I've accidentally killed her."

"I'll be right there."

Chapter 12

#WheresTheBeef

After Keane's call, Willa slipped out of bed for the second time that morning. The first had been an hour ago at the desperate knock at her door.

That had been Kylie. "Remember Vinnie?" her friend had asked, pulling the tiny puppy from her pocket. "My so-called pal never came back for him, can you believe it?" She kissed the top of the puppy's head, which was bigger than his body. "I think she abandoned him, *and* me . . ."

Oh boy. Willa looked into Vinnie's warm puppy eyes and felt herself melt. "So what's your plan?"

"I'm keeping him," Kylie said firmly. "He'll be a Christmas present to myself. My problem is that I have to go to work. Is there any way you can help me today?"

Which was how Willa had ended up back in bed cuddling a three-week-old puppy until Keane had called.

Now she scooped Vinnie up, cuddling the tiny handful close. "We've got a search-and-rescue situation, buddy. You up for it?"

Vinnie yawned bigger than his entire body, which wasn't all that hard. Juggling the little guy, Willa ran around handling her morning routine as quickly as possible. She had to set Vinnie down to brush her teeth, which turned out to be a mistake because when she turned back around, she found him sitting proudly next to what looked like a pile of fresh Play-Doh. Except it wasn't so much fresh as incredibly stinky.

He was looking at her as if to say, *It wasn't me, nor was it me who just chewed the shoelace off your shoes. I have no idea who'd do something like that, especially given the poo situation; that'd just be mean.*

With a sigh, she cleaned up the mess and then pulled sweats on over her pj's. She grabbed the baby bottle Kylie had left with her for Vinnie, who got very excited at the sight of it and began panting happily, short little legs bicycling in the air as if he could fly to the bottle.

"In a sec," she promised. She grabbed her bag and a jacket and ran out the door, ordering an Uber on her cell as she waited for the elevator.

The car ride was a luxury she couldn't quite afford but it was pouring rain and she had Vinnie, and Keane had sounded . . .

Vulnerable.

She'd have gone for that alone because . . . well, curiosity had killed the cat and all. But it wasn't just nosiness that had her hurrying.

She cared about Petunia, and more than that, she cared about him.

"Not good," she told the puppy as he finished his bottle, tucking him into her sweatshirt beneath her jacket to keep him warm. "Not good at all."

Sticking his head out the collar of her sweatshirt, Vinnie licked her chin. His eyes, bigger than his head, were warm and happy as he stared up at her in adoration.

"Okay, so here's how we're going to play this," she said. "When we get there, we're not, repeat *not*, going to get attached to the hot, sexy guy that lives there, okay? It's no use getting attached to someone who isn't going to get attached back."

"Then why go to his house this early if you're not going to get attached?" the Uber driver asked. "Didn't your mother teach you better than that?"

"Hey, no eavesdropping," she said. "Or judging."

"How much you like this guy?" he asked, his gaze scanning her clothes from his rearview mirror. "Because maybe you want to dress nicer."

Said the guy in a grungy gray T-shirt and hair so wild and crazy it touched the roof of his car. "These are my favorite sweats," she said.

"But they're not getting-laid sweats. They're more like . . . birth control sweats."

She looked down at herself as they stopped in front of Keane's building. Good thing she wasn't worried about getting laid.

Wait . . . was she? Well, too late to worry about it now.

"Leave me a good review?" the driver asked as she got out.

Willa sighed. "Sure."

Keane had barely refrained from tearing down the wall—the *new* wall—between the living room and the dining room to get to Pita when he heard Willa's knock.

She stood there in the pouring rain, hood on her parka up.

"Hey," she said, clearly just out of bed and looking sexy adorable. "S&R at your service."

He knew how hard she worked, and that today was probably a rare day off for her, and yet she'd come when he'd called. Okay, so she was there for the cat and not him, but still, he felt pretty wowed by that.

By her.

It didn't happen often in his world, help freely given like this with nothing expected in return, nothing to be held over his head later. And that meant a lot.

He pulled her inside, getting her out of the rain, which was dripping off her.

"You're in a tool belt," she said, staring at it.

"Yeah." Was he mistaken or had her eyes dilated. "Why?"

She wet her lips and stared at the tool belt some more. "No reason."

He laughed softly. "You like the tool belt?"

She flushed. "Well, it's a cliché for a damn reason. They're sort of . . . sexy."

"Good to know," he said, biting back his smile. "And thanks for coming."

Willa pushed her hood back and met his gaze, her eyes heavy-lidded from what he assumed was sleep. Her silky hair was more than a little wild, flopping into her eyes, clinging to her jaw. He slid the jacket off of her in the hopes of keeping her dry. This left her in sweat bottoms that said *SWAT* up one thigh, rain boots, and a snug long-sleeved hoodie that clung to her curves and told him she wasn't wearing a bra.

His mouth went dry.

From the hoodie pocket a little puppy head poked out. *"Ruff!"* he squeaked out so hard that his huge ears quivered.

"Vinnie's back," she said of the palm-sized dog. "I'm babysitting." She looked around. "Wow. This place is seriously just . . . *wow.*" She turned in a slow circle. "I meant to ask you, the molding—is that original woodwork?"

"Original and restored."

"Gorgeous," she said, walking through, her voice low and reverent. "Seriously, if this was my home, I'd never leave it."

Uncomfortable with the praise and yet feeling his chest swell with pride, he didn't say anything. But it was his fantasy home too.

"And you're really going to flip it?" she asked, meeting his gaze.

He shrugged. "That's the plan. I sell everything I renovate. It's my income."

"Right." She nodded. "You don't get attached to things, I get it. So where can I put Vinnie while we search for Petunia?"

He drew a deep breath and walked her into the kitchen, the leather of his tool belt creaking as he moved, although he was pretty sure she wasn't finding that so sexy at the moment.

She set Vinnie up in the deep laundry sink, layering it with a soft blanket and then setting his special dog bed in there—a tissue box—with his water and a few toys. "Stay here and be a good boy," she said. "And I'll give you a treat."

"Does that apply to all the males in the room?" Keane asked.

She sent him a long look.

Okay, so no. Shaking his head at himself for even wishing for things that weren't for him, he turned and walked into the dining room. "Here," he said, crouching low at the vent. "She went in here."

Willa eyed the air duct. "Where does it lead?"

"The den. I pulled the vent cover from that one too but she wouldn't come out." He wasn't a guy who panicked. Ever. But he felt a knot in the center of his chest and was pretty sure he was pretty close to panic now.

"Chances are that she can't back out," Willa said. "She's a little . . . *husky*." She whispered this last word, as if Pita could not only hear them but also understand English. "Which direction does the vent go?"

He pointed to the left. "The next room over."

Willa moved to the wall between them and put her ear to it. "Petunia!" she called out and stilled, listening.

There came a very faint "mew."

"Shit," Keane said. "That's it." He rose to his feet and left the room, grabbing his hatchet from his large job tool box. He moved back to where he'd left Willa. "Stand back."

She turned and looked at him, her eyes going wide. "What the hell are you going to do with that?"

Wasn't it obvious? "Tear the wall down."

"Wow," she said, and this time she *definitely* wasn't impressed. "Hold off a second there, Paul Bunyan." She went back to the second vent. Down on her hands and knees, she once again called out to Pita. "Petunia? I know you can't turn around and go back, and that you're in the dark and probably very unhappy about all of that, but you have to push forward, okay? You've got to come to me or the Big Bad Wolf here is going to huff and puff and chop this whole place down. And you should know, he's going to rip into some beautiful molding and break my heart."

"Mew."

"That's it," she cooed, still on her hands and knees, her pert ass up in the air, her sweats stretched tight across her cheeks. "Come to me, baby."

He groaned. "Killing me."

Still in position, in fact one of his very favorite positions, she craned her neck and looked at him. "I'm trying to save your wall here."

"Carry on," he said, his voice an octave lower than before.

She stared at his mouth for a beat, swallowed hard, and then turned back to her task. "Petunia?"

Nothing.

Keane shifted closer and Willa pointed at him. "Don't you even think about touching that wall."

His sexy tyrant.

"I mean it," she said.

He had to laugh. "I hate to break this to you, Willa, but you've finally met someone as stubborn and obstinate as you. Pita's not coming out of there, not even for your sweet nothings because—"

Because nothing. There was a rustling and then the saddest looking lump of filthy fur stuck her head out of the duct, and Keane nearly dropped to his knees in relief. "I can't believe she came out of there at just the sound of your voice."

"I'm good but not that good," Willa said as Pita snatched something from her palm and ate it like she'd been gone for five days without food instead of an hour. "It's a pupperoni treat. Works every time. Aw," she said to the dirty cat. "You poor baby. That must have been so traumatic for you."

"Hugely," Keane said, swiping his brow. "You should hold me."

She laughed and he found himself smiling at her like an idiot. "You always carry pupperoni treats in your pocket?"

"Always," she said and sat on the floor with Pita, not looking at all bothered by the fact that she was now filthy too. From another pocket she pulled out a comb and proceeded to use it to get most of the dirt and dust off the cat.

"I'm not even going to ask what else you carry on you at all times," he said, moving close, crouching at her side to stare into the cat's half-closed-in-ecstasy eyes. "You've put her in a trance."

"Most cats get a little hypnotized with pleasure when you comb them," she said and smiled. "Actually most females."

"Huh. Now that's one thing about your kind that I didn't know."

"You think that's the only thing?" she asked with just enough irony in her voice to have him taking a longer look at her.

"You have something you want me to know?" he asked.

"Absolutely not." But she blushed a gorgeous color of red and he had to admit to being more than a little curious.

Apparently having had enough of the pampering, Pita climbed out of Willa's lap.

"Hold up," he said to the cat. He called Sally back and pointed the FaceTime call toward Pita.

Sally talked baby talk and the cat stopped and stared unblinking into the camera, listening intently.

After, Sally thanked Keane and disconnected. Pita stalked off, tail and head high.

"That was sweet of you," Willa said.

"That's me, a real sweetheart. And you're welcome, princess," he called to Pita's retreating figure. Grabbing Willa's hand, he pulled her upright.

Her hands went to his chest, but instead of using him to straighten herself, she held on, sliding her hands up and around his neck, rocking against him in the process.

"That thing is happening again," she whispered.

Yeah. It most definitely was. "That 'thing' likes you," he said. "A lot."

She snorted. "I didn't mean that. Although"—she pressed into him some more, wriggling her hips not so subtly against his erection—"I definitely noticed."

"Hard not to."

She snorted again at that but curious as hell, he had to ask. "So what *did* you mean?"

She bit her lower lip and got very busy staring at his shirt. He slid a hand up her back and into her hair, tugging until she looked up at him.

Her gaze locked on his mouth.

"I meant that thing where I want to do things to you," she said.

He smiled. "Not seeing the problem here, babe."

She shook her head and went to pull away. "I can't stay. Big day. It's the Santa Extravaganza at the shop."

"I thought you weren't working today."

"I'm not. My employees handle this event for me; they always do. I'm just setting up and making sure everything looks good."

He caught her and when she tensed, he very gently pulled her back in, giving her plenty of room to escape if she really wanted. "So I do scare you."

"No." She shook her head. "The only things I'm scared of are creepy crawlies and Santa Claus. Which is why I have my girls handle Santa Extravaganza for me."

He paused. "Okay, we're going to circle back to that," he said, "but first, if you're not scared of me, why are we . . . 'not ready' again?"

She gave a small smile that held more than a few secrets. "Maybe I'm just . . . cautious."

Smart woman, he had to admit. "And the Santa Claus fear?"

"How are we supposed to trust a full-grown man who wants little kids to sit on his lap and whisper their deepest secrets?" she quipped.

"But you love Christmas."

"Christmas, yes. Santa, not so much."

"So why do the Santa Extravaganza then?" he asked.

She shrugged as if uncomfortable with this subject. "It's a huge moneymaker and I give half the profits to the SPCA. They need the dough." She headed to the door, scooping up Vinnie on her way out. She gave the tiniest dog on the planet a kiss on his face that made Keane feel envious as hell, and walked out the door.

Chapter 13

#KeepCalmAndBeMerry

At the end of the day, Keane found Pita napping . . . on his pillow. He started to remove her but she flattened herself, becoming five-hundred-plus pounds, and he blew out a breath because they both knew arguing with her was a waste of time. And in any case, she'd had a rough day and he understood rough days. "I'm going out for a little bit," he told her. "And while I'm gone you're not going to destroy a damn thing, right?"

She yawned, stood, plumped up his pillow with her two front paws like she was making biscuits, and then plopped back down and closed her eyes.

"Behave," he said firmly.

She met his gaze, her own serene, and he was pretty sure he'd just made a deal with the devil.

Thinking *fuck it,* he headed toward O'Riley's. Sure, there were fifty places to get dinner between his place and the pub, maybe even more than fifty, but there was never any question of where he'd end up after work.

He wanted to see Willa.

From the beginning he'd known he was fascinated by her, but he hadn't realized it would become so much more than a physical attraction.

He still had absolutely zero idea how to process that.

It was no longer raining, but the air was frigid. Shoving his hands in his jacket pockets, he lowered his head against the wind. Entering the building through the courtyard, he stopped by the fountain when Old Man Eddie stepped out of the alley.

Eddie was at least eighty, and that was being kind— something time hadn't been to him. He had Wild Man of Borneo shock white hair and in spite of the cold air, wore board shorts and a Grateful Dead sweatshirt that looked as if he'd been wearing it since the seventies.

"So you're Willa's now," the guy said. "Right?"

Keane gave him a closer look. "Not sure how that's any of your business."

The guy beamed. "Good answer, man. And I like that you didn't deny it. Our Willa, she's had a rough go of things. But she's picked herself up by the bootstraps and made something of herself, so she deserves only the best. Are you the best?"

"Rough *how?*"

Eddie simply smiled and patted him on the arm. "Yeah. You'll do." And then he turned and walked away.

"Rough how?" Keane asked again.

But Eddie had vanished.

Keane let out a long, slow breath. As he knew all too well, the past was the past, but it still killed him to think about Willa as a young kid, on her own.

At the fountain, a woman was searching her pockets for something. She was early twenties and looked distressed as she whirled around, eyes narrowed.

He realized it was Haley, Willa's optometrist friend.

"Lose something?" he asked.

"No. Well, yes," she corrected. "I wanted to make a stupid wish on the stupid legend but I can't find any stupid coins . . ." She sat on the stone ledge and pulled off her shoe, shaking it. When nothing came out, she sighed. "Damn. I always have a least a penny in there."

He pulled a quarter from his pocket. "Here."

"Oh, no, I couldn't—"

"Take it," he said, dropping it in her hand. "For your 'stupid' wish on the 'stupid' legend."

She laughed. "You're making fun but it really is stupid. And yet here I am . . ." She tossed up her hands. "It's just that it worked for Pru and it appears to have worked for Willa." She gave him a long look making him realize she meant him.

He shook his head. "We're not—"

"Oh no." She pointed at him. "Don't ruin my hope! I mean it's Willa. She pours herself into taking care of everyone, the kids she employs, the animals, her friends." She smiled a little. "Well I don't have to tell you; you know firsthand."

He absolutely did. Willa had taken on Pita for him when she had less than zero reason to like him. She'd taken him on as a friend when he wasn't sure he deserved it.

"She deserves love," Haley said. "She gives one hundred percent to everyone and everything but herself so we all knew it was going to be something big when she fell. Someone who really knocked her off her feet." She smiled. "You've got the big down anyway."

"I'm not sure it's what you think," he said quietly.

"Yeah, well, nothing ever is." She turned back to the water. "If you'll excuse me."

"Sure," he said and left her to her privacy.

The pub was packed. Lights twinkled above all the laughter and voices and "Santa Looked a Lot Like Daddy" was busting out of hidden speakers.

And speaking of Santa, he was sitting at the bar calm as you please, tossing back a shot of something.

Keane made his way to the far right end of the bar, where Willa sat with Elle, Spence, and Archer. There was a row of empty glasses and a pitcher of eggnog in front of them. Elle and Spence were deep in discussion about Spence's workout routine.

"You have to eat healthy more than once to get in shape," he said to Elle.

"Cruel and unfair," she answered and jabbed a finger at Archer, who was shoving some chili fries into his mouth. "Then explain *him*."

Archer swiveled his gaze Elle's way and swallowed a huge bite. "What?"

Elle made a noise of disgust. "You eat like you're afraid it's going out of style and yet you never gain a single ounce of fat."

Archer gave a slow smile. "Genetics, babe. I was born this way."

Elle rolled her eyes so hard that Keane was surprised they didn't fall right out of her head. Shifting past all of them, he headed toward Willa. No longer in sweats, she wore a black skirt, tights, boots, and the brightest red Christmas sweater he'd ever seen. Her gaze was glued to Santa in the middle of the bar and Keane would've sworn she was twitching. He purposely maneuvered to block her view of the guy. "Hey."

"Hey." Her smile didn't quite meet her eyes. "Be right back," she said and, slipping off her stool, headed into the back.

Keane looked at Elle, who was also watching Willa go, her eyes solemn and concerned. "I know she's not a Santa fan," he said. "But what am I missing?"

"A lot," Elle said but didn't further enlighten him.

And he knew she wouldn't. Elle could keep state secrets safe. He looked at Spence, who seemed sympathetic but he shook his head. Archer might as well have been a brick wall, so Keane turned to Haley, who'd just come in, apparently having made her wish.

She grimaced.

"Tell me," he said.

"Her mom dated a drunk Santa who chased her around the house wanting her to sit on his lap. Back then they called it funny for a grown-ass man to terrorize a little girl."

"And now they call it a fucking felony," Keane said grimly.

Elle and Archer both turned to look at him with a new appraisal—and approval—in their gazes. But they still weren't talking.

And he got that. Good friends stood at each other's backs unfailingly. He was grateful Willa had that. After how her childhood had gone, she needed that.

But he wanted in her inner circle and he wanted that shockingly badly. He made his way down the bar. "Hey," he said, tapping Santa on the shoulder.

Santa turned to face him with the slow care of the very inebriated. "Whadda want?"

"There's free drinks down on Second Street for Santas," Keane said.

The guy's eyes brightened. "Yeah?" He got to his feet, weaving a little. "Thanks, man."

When Santa headed for the door, Keane followed the path Willa had taken. The hallway ended at the kitchen. There were a couple of other doors as well. Offices, he assumed. The bathroom door was shut so he waited there, holding up the wall and contemplating the utter silence on the other side of the door. After another few minutes went by, he pushed off the wall and knocked. "Willa."

Nothing.

It wasn't the first time today that one of the females in his life has refused to speak to him but something didn't feel right. "I'm coming in," he warned and opened the door.

The bathroom had two stalls, a sink, and was pleasantly clean.

And empty.

The window was wide open to the night, the cold air rushing in.

She'd gone out the window.

He strode across the room and stuck his head and shoulders out, taking in the corner of the courtyard and the fire escape only a few feet away. Craning his neck, he looked up and saw a quick glimpse of a slim foot as it vanished over the edge of the roof.

Five stories up.

"Shit," he said, his vision wavering. "Why is it always something high up?" Muttering some more, he pushed himself through the window, bashing his shoulders against the casing as he squeezed through. *Squeeze* being the operative word.

Also he hadn't thought ahead to the landing problem coming out headfirst, so there was an awkward moment when he nearly took a dive out face-first before he managed to right himself.

He stared at the damn fire escape and then rattled it. It held and he blew out a breath. "You've fucking lost it," he told himself as he began to climb.

He passed the second floor and began to sweat. He was outright shaking as he counted each story off to himself to keep his sanity. "Three." He held his breath and kept going. "Four."

Finally, level with the roof, he made the mistake of looking down. "Fuck. Five. *Fuck.*" He had to force himself up and over the ledge, and flopped gracelessly to the rooftop.

Chapter 14

#HoHoHo

Willa turned her head at the sound of a body hitting the rooftop, wide-eyed at the sight of Keane flat on his back like the bones in his legs had just dissolved.

"Keane?" she asked in disbelief.

He didn't move, just lay there with his eyes closed, breathing erratically. "Yeah?"

She'd been sitting here alone contemplating her life and watching the occasional glimpses of the moon through the slivers of clouds streaking across the midnight black sky. The moonlight did strange things to the world, leeching out the color so that everything seemed like nothing more than a web of shadows cast in silver. Maybe she'd hit her head when she'd taken a header out of the bathroom window.

Stupid panic.

But then again, she'd rarely thought clearly while

operating under high stress. And it seemed at the moment, she wasn't the only one.

Keane finally spoke again. "What the hell?"

"What the hell what?"

"What the hell are we doing on the damn rooftop?"

"I come up here when I want to be alone," she said, emphasis on *alone*. But then she took in the sheen of perspiration on his face, the way his chest was rising and falling like he'd just run a marathon. "Are you afraid of heights?"

"No," he said, still not moving a single inch.

"No?" Her gaze was glued to his lips, the ones she wanted hers on again now that she was thinking about it.

"No, I'm not afraid of heights." He paused. "I'm terrified of them."

This ripped a laugh right out of her. Her own troubles momentarily forgotten, she leaned over his big, long, tough body, the one she dreamed about at night. Every night. "And you still came all the way up here to save me?"

"At the moment, I'm the one that needs saving. Pretty sure I'm going to die of lack of oxygen."

Still leaning over him, she lowered herself until she nearly-but-not-quite touched him from head to toe. "Don't worry, I know CPR."

He kept his eyes closed but his mouth curved. "You're teasing me. And I'd make you pay for that but I can't because seriously, *dying* here."

Keane both felt and heard her laugh at him as she kissed one corner of his mouth.

"Take it from me," she whispered. "When facing your worst fears, all you need is something else to concentrate on." Then she kissed the other side of his mouth.

He liked where this was going. "Like a distraction," he said.

"Exactly."

He opened his eyes. "I like the sound of that," he said, knowing the logic was more than a little faulty but unable to concentrate with all sorts of dirty, wicked scenarios of how they might "distract" each other playing through his mind. "Maybe I've already died and gone to heaven."

She lifted her head with a smile. "You think this is heaven?"

"You're touching and kissing me," he said. "So yeah. I think this is heaven."

He felt the brush of her hair on his face and then her teeth sank into his earlobe, making him groan. The dilemma—let her continue, or stop her before they took this where she hadn't intended to go . . . ? Before he could decide, her hot, sexy mouth made its way back to his and her hands slipped under his shirt, landing on his abs, her fingers spreading wide.

"You're hard," she whispered against his lips. "Everywhere."

True story.

Her fingers danced up, up, up, teasing his nipples for a beat before heading southward, and he stopped breathing.

She shifted and then jumpstarted his heart by straddling him.

"Willa," he said but she was kissing her way down his throat and he was having trouble drawing air into his lungs. Fisting his hands in her hair, he tugged her face up so he could look into her eyes. "Willa—"

"That's my name," she agreed and bit his lower lip, tugging a little bit so that he mindlessly rocked his hips up into hers.

Jesus. He sat up and caught ahold of her hips, tightening his grip to keep her still. "What are we doing?"

"Oh, sorry, I thought you knew." She took his hands in hers and brought them up to her breasts. "Any further questions?"

She filled his palms perfectly, her nipples pressing through layers of clothing for his attention. Yeah. He was most definitely in heaven.

"I'm ready now," she said softly.

She had his full attention and he searched her gaze. For the first time he could see her expression clearly and it was filled with heat and need and banked anger.

She was looking to defuse that anger, on him. And he was okay with that. More than. She needed him and God knew he needed her. "Come here," he said, nudging her even closer, his hands taking over, cupping her breasts, his thumbs rasping over her tight nipples as she let her head fall back, a gasp escaping her.

"More," she demanded.

"We're outside, Willa, on the roof. Anyone could come up—"

"No," she said against his mouth, "that fire escape's nearly a hundred years old. No one'll use that rackety old thing but me and the gang, and they're all in the pub."

His life flashed before his eyes again. "You mean I could've died on that thing? Is that what you're telling me?"

"You're in heaven, remember?" Her hands were on the buttons of his Levi's, popping them open one at a time.

And he was rapidly losing the ability to think rationally. "What if someone uses the inside stairs access?" he asked.

She shoved his jeans and knit boxers out of her way and wrapped her fingers around him so that his eyes crossed with lust.

"Those stairs are noisy as hell," she murmured. "We'll hear anyone coming a mile away." She tipped her head down to watch what she was doing to him.

He looked too and at the sight of her hands on him, he groaned, not recognizing his own guttural voice when he spoke. "Willa, be sure—"

"Oh, I'm sure." Her own voice was soft and husky, sounding more than a little breathless now too. "But if you're worried, you could work faster."

He let out a low laugh—which was a first, laughing with his personal favorite body part in a woman's hands. "Fast isn't my style."

"It probably should be tonight—" She broke off on a breathy gasp when he unzipped her bright red sweater and nudged it off her shoulders, letting it catch on her elbows, pinning her arms to her sides. While she became preoccupied with freeing herself, he happily realized she wore only a bra beneath, a sexy, lacy, mouthwateringly sheer number. He tugged the cups down, and not wanting her to get cold, cupped one bared breast while he sucked the other into his mouth.

A shuddery sigh escaped her and she cupped his head, holding him to her like she was afraid he might try to escape.

Not a chance. "How much did you have to drink tonight?" he asked.

She thought about that for a minute. "Enough to know I want this, but not too much that I'll have to kill you in the morning."

He stared back but who was he kidding, that totally worked for him. Sliding his hands up her skirt, he palmed her ass. "You're wearing too many clothes."

She laughed breathlessly as fingers wriggled their way beneath her tights and panties, where he found her hot and wet, very wet. He spent a glorious moment teasing panting little whimpers out of her while her hips oscillated against his touch and her nails dug into his biceps. "You like this."

She moaned something inaudible but he got the gist. *More.*

With one arm banded low on her back, his mouth busy at her breasts, his fingers stroked her in the rhythm she wanted. Using her body as his compass, he rose up and swallowed her cries as she came for him, her body shuddering in his arms.

Brushing his lips over her sweaty temple, he held on to her, stroking her back until she finally lifted her head. "Not exactly how I saw my evening going," she said, still a little breathless as she slumped against him.

"Not sure who could've foreseen an orgasm on the roof."

"I meant you." She put a finger to his chest. "I didn't see *you* coming."

"That's because I haven't."

She laughed, and loving the sound, he pulled her in by the nape of her neck and kissed her. "Ditto," he said against her mouth. He hadn't seen her coming either, not until she'd hit him over the head, knocking him out with her vibrant, sexy, adorable self.

She flashed a smile at him, warm and also filled with trouble—which he really hoped boded well for him.

She went to work, wrestling off one of her boots. By the time she wriggled a leg out of her tights, he'd lent his hands to the cause. Then she wrapped her fingers around him and was guiding him home when he barely managed to catch her.

"Condom," he managed.

She stilled, eyes wide on his. "Oh my God, I can't believe I almost forgot," she whispered and fisted her hands in his shirt, going nose to nose with him. "Tell me you were a Boy Scout, that you're prepared, that you have a damn condom."

The thing was, he hadn't expected to need one and he still wasn't exactly one-hundred-percent sure he should even go there now. He met her gaze. "I wasn't a Boy Scout."

She groaned and dropped her head to his chest.

"But."

She jerked her head up, face hopeful. "Yeah?"

Sitting on the roof with her straddling his lap, he

somehow managed to pull his wallet from his back pocket, thinking *please have been smart enough to leave a condom in there* . . .

"Yes!" she burst out with when he came up with one.

Laughing, he tore the thing open and started to roll it down his length, but she pushed his hands away.

"Me," she said. "I want to . . ."

By the time she got him halfway covered, he was back to sweating and trembling like he was a seventeen-year-old kid with zero control. "I've got it," he said, putting his hands over hers to finish the job.

"Because we're in a hurry?"

"Because I'm about to lose it in your hands."

She snorted but the laughter seemed to back up in her throat with the sexiest little gasp when he pulled her closer so that the insides of her thighs snugged tight to the outsides of his.

"You're going to let me drive?" she teased.

"This rooftop's too rough for you to be on your back," he said, cupping her bare ass. "Up on your knees, Willa." And then before she could move, he lifted her himself, urging her to sink slowly onto him.

They both gasped, mouths locked on each other's, kissing deep and wet, hands clutching whatever they could reach, moving slowly at first, then faster and harder, until Keane completely lost himself. Winding his fist in her hair, he forced her head back, suckling on her exposed throat, marking her.

She came first, digging her fingernails into him, the combination of pleasure and sweet pain sending him skittering into the void right along with her.

Chapter 15

#HitMeBabyOneMoreTime

It was a very long time before Willa managed to catch her breath and her world stopped spinning out of control. Or started spinning again. She couldn't figure out which. In either case, she was completely dazed as she realized something shocking.

Several somethings, actually.

One, she was sitting on Keane, wrapped up tight in his warm, strong arms, arms that still quaked with the seismic rockings that came after some really great sex.

Really, *really* great.

And two, she felt both wildly alive and . . . *safe,* two things she'd most definitely never felt at the same time in her entire life.

Since that invoked some worrisome emotions, all of which tried to encroach on her momentary blissful haze, she shoved them all back and lifted her head.

Keane's dark eyes were on her, intense and yet

steady. God, she loved that. Her axis was tilted and she was in danger of losing her grip, but he had her. And just looking at him, she calmed. "So, that was . . . something."

His low chuckle reverberated from his chest to hers.

She smiled. "Was that a good enough distraction for you?"

His answering smile was slow and lazy and incredibly sexy. "If I say no, will you try to distract me again?"

"Maybe."

"I thought I'd seen and done it all," he said, "but this was a first for me."

She let out a low laugh and tried to right her clothing. "I can bring out the best or the worst in just about anyone."

"What would you call this?"

She didn't need to even think about it. "The best." She was failing at putting herself back together. Keane took over while she sat on his lap like a limp rag doll. Since she couldn't resist his delicious mouth, she leaned in, lingering—just for another moment, she told herself—kissing him one last time. But before she could break it off and get up, he banded his arms around her tightly and took over, kissing her long and deep and hard until she was back to a panting, needy mess.

When he slowly pulled back, she let out an unhappy moan of protest and her mouth chased after his.

This had him letting out a low laugh. The warm look in his eyes made her remember that she wanted things for herself. Things she'd never wanted before. Things she'd set aside because she knew he didn't want them. Suddenly more confused than ever, about the night, the holiday season, her damn life, everything, she crawled off of him and went back to her original pose, sitting, hugging her knees close to her chest.

He seemed happy to hold the silence as well, there in the dark beneath the half-ass moon.

"I could use some popcorn," he finally said.

She laughed a little and met his gaze. "That was some animal magnetism."

"Yeah," he agreed, tucking a lock of her hair behind her ear. "It was." He pressed a single soft kiss along her jaw. His breath was warm against her skin, sending a shiver through her, and she found herself leaning into him, closer to that calm aura that always surrounded him. "So. You kicked Santa out of the bar for me."

"How did you know?"

She smiled wryly and patted the phone tucked into her pocket. "A text came in from Elle before you got up here." Turning her head, she met his gaze. "You're a good guy, you know that?"

"Just don't let it get out." He took her hand and brought it up to his mouth, brushing his lips over her knuckles. "I'm not really much of a talker," he said quietly. "But you are."

She snorted. "Tell me something everyone doesn't already know."

"Exactly what I was hoping you'd say. So talk to me, Willa. Tell me about the Santa thing."

Well, she'd walked right into that one. She tried to pull her hand free of his but he held on, doing the same with her gaze. "Look," she said. "Just because we . . . did *that*," she said with a vague wave of her hand to the rooftop behind them, "doesn't mean we have make to small talk."

"What I want to talk about has nothing to do with *that*." He gave her a small smile. "Also known as the hottest rooftop sex I've ever had. Not to mention, the *only* rooftop sex I've ever had."

She let out a low laugh, but looked away.

With a hand to her jaw, he brought her face back to his.

"Okay," she said. "I agree the rooftop sex was very hot. But as per our previous agreement, we don't have to do this. I mean there's a me, and there's a you. And sometimes there's this crazy, stupid"—she waved her hand vaguely again—"thing. But it was just a one-time thing. And it's probably out of our systems now." She met his gaze with difficulty. "So really, you don't have to do the whole awkward-after with me."

"Maybe I'm a sucker for the awkward-after."

With a laugh, she dropped her head to her knees. "I'm trying to give you an out here, Keane." Hell, she was trying to give *herself* an out. Her heart needed it, bad.

Because she got it: he didn't get attached. But she sure did, and hard. And she was going to have to be very careful to protect herself.

"Humor me," Keane said. "Pretend I'm irritable to talk to."

Not much pretending required there . . .

"Tell me what happened tonight," he said.

"Well," she quipped in a last-ditch effort to lighten up this conversation. "It's about the birds and the bees—"

"You know what I want to know, smartass."

She sighed. Yeah, she did. He wanted to know why, if she was afraid of Santa, she celebrated Christmas like she was still five years old, and he wasn't going to accept the nonanswer she'd already given him.

But she rarely allowed herself to think about it, much less talk about it.

After a long beat of silence, he spoke. "When I was little, I was sent to a Catholic military boarding school one year, run by nuns and ex-marines."

She looked at him. "You were? How old were you?"

"Five. Actually, not quite five. But by the time I turned ten, I was back at home in the public school system. Let's just say, I didn't fit in at the private school."

She gasped, almost unable to fathom this, even though she'd gone into the childcare system at the same young age. "Your parents sent a four-year-old away? And then left you there until you were ten?"

He shrugged. "I was a pain in the ass. I did pay for that though."

"The school punished the kids?" she asked in horror.

"Only if you were an asshole punk." He tipped his face up to the dark night, a small smile on his lips. "I still twitch if I see a nun."

She fell quiet, mulling over the reason he'd shared the story. He'd wanted to be open so she would. Dammit. "I didn't twitch when I saw Santa," she said.

"No," he agreed. "You didn't twitch. You had a full-on seizure."

Keane watched as Willa fidgeted. He knew she wanted to move on from this subject, and she wanted that badly too. But he felt like they were on the precipice of something, something deeper than even their sheer physical animal attraction. He also knew that this was the point where he should be running for the hills, but he didn't want to end this here.

She still hadn't said a word and he resigned himself to that being it, this was as far as they went, when she finally spoke.

"I was sent away for the first time right about the same age as you," she said softly.

He turned and met her gaze. "What happened?"

"I was in the foster system on and off for most of the next fourteen years." She paused. "My mom's an alcoholic. She'd get it together for a little bit here and there, but not for long. Usually she'd fall for some guy, break up and fall off the wagon at the same time, and then go a little crazy, and I'd end up back in the system."

Christ, how he hated that for her. "Any of those 'some guys' dress up like Santa?"

"Just the first one," she said with a shudder. "After a few encounters, I finally got my nerve up and spilled his coffee on his lap. And that was that."

"Tell me it was fucking boiling hot," he said.

She smiled proudly. "Yep."

He hoped like hell she'd melted the guy's dick off but either way she'd been left with a scar too. Shocking how violent he could feel for something that had happened to her twenty years ago, but violent was exactly how he felt at the moment.

People had disappointed her. Hurt her. And damn if he hadn't put himself in position to do the same by making it clear that what they shared was in the moment only.

He'd never felt like a bigger dick.

Reaching out, she squeezed his hand. *Comforting him,* he realized and he actually felt his throat go tight as he held on to her fingers. "How many times did you go into the system?" he asked.

"At least once a year until I turned eighteen and was let loose."

His gut clenched thinking about how rough that must have been for her. "Not a great way to grow up."

She shrugged. "I got good at the revolving door. I'm still good at it."

"What do you mean?"

"You don't attach," she said. "And I don't tend to lock in. At my shop, customers come and go. The animals too. Even my employees. And men. The only constants have been my friends." She shifted as if uncomfortable that she'd revealed so much. "I should go—"

He tightened his hold on her because no way in hell was he crawling back over the edge of this building after her. "I'm going to call bullshit on the not-locking-in thing," he said gently. Oh yes, she was a flight risk now; he could feel her body tensing up. "You're smart as hell, Willa. You're self-made. You never give up, and the depth of your heart is endless. If you wanted to lock in, as you call it, you would."

She looked away. "Maybe you're giving me too much credit."

"I doubt that."

He couldn't even imagine what her early years had been like for someone like her, with her heart so full and sweet and tender. And then the foster care system, which must've been a nightmare. "Are you still in contact with your mom?" he asked.

"Yes. She lives in Texas now, and we text every other week or so. It took us a while to come to the understanding that twice a month is the right amount of time for us—halfway between missing the connection and wanting to murder each other in our sleep." She smiled, but he didn't.

Couldn't.

She pulled out her phone. "No really, mostly it's good now, or at least much better than it ever was in the past anyway. See?"

> Mom:
> Hi honey, just checking in. You're probably busy tonight . . . ?

"Translation," Willa said. "She's sober and also fishing." She tried to take the phone back but he'd gotten a look at her return text and smiled.

He read it out loud, still smiling.

> Willa:
> The daughter you're trying to reach will neither confirm nor deny that she has plans tonight since you're clearly trying to find out if she's seeing someone. This violates the terms of our relationship. If you continue to harass your daughter in this fashion, she'll start dating girls again.

Keane stopped and looked at her, and when he managed to speak, his voice sounded low and rough to his own ears. "Again?"

She squirmed a little bit and dropped eye contact. "It was a one-time thing," she said. "A phase. And I got over it real fast when I realized girls are crazy."

"Guys aren't much better," he said.

"No kidding."

He smiled as he rasped his thumb over her jaw, letting his fingers sink into her hair.

"Keane," she said softly. "Thanks for tonight." She rose. "For no strings, it was pretty damn amazing."

He didn't say anything to this. Couldn't. Because he was suddenly feeling uneasy and unsure, two things he didn't do well. Not that he said anything. No reason to reveal his own pathetic insecurities.

She moved to the edge of the roof and turned back. "Do you need help down?"

"Over my dead body."

She laughed. And with that, she vanished over the ledge.

Keane moved over there and looked over the edge, and then had to sit down hard while life passed before his eyes. "Fuck." It took him a moment to get his shit together, and by then Willa was long gone.

Perfect.

He moved in the opposite direction, toward the door that led to the inside stairwell, consoling himself with the fact that at least there was no one to see him taking the easy way down.

Chapter 16

#Legendary

The next morning Willa stood in the back of her shop shoving down a breakfast sandwich with Cara and Rory. It was midmorning and they'd been swamped since before opening.

Although not too swamped that she couldn't relive the night before, the way Keane's voice had been a rough whisper against her ear, the heat in his eyes as he'd taken control and moved knowingly inside her, his hands both protective and possessive on her body.

When a text came in, she was tempted to ignore it, but in the end her curiosity won. It was from Elle.

HeadOfAllTheThings:
I'm going to need a detailed report of what went down last night.

"Dammit," she muttered, and Cara and Rory both pointed in unison to the swear jar.

Willa pulled a buck from her pocket, shoved it into the jar, and moved to the dubious privacy of her office to stare blankly at Elle's text.

No one had seen her and Keane last night, she was certain of it. But when she'd climbed down the fire escape, she'd run smack into Pru in the courtyard.

Willa sighed and put her thumbs to good use.

> Willa:
> Going to have to kill her.
> HeadOfAllTheThings:
> Wear gloves, keep the fingerprints off the murder weapon.

Willa had to laugh as she responded.

> My favorite part of this is that you don't even question who I have to kill.
> HeadOfAllTheThings:
> The less I know, the less I can say during the interrogation.
> HeadOfAllTheThings:
> But seriously, where are my deets?

When Willa ignored, and in fact deleted, the texts, Elle simply called her.

"Houston, I have so many problems," Willa said miserably.

Elle laughed. "If you think having a hot guy want you is a problem, we need to talk. I'm at work right now and swamped, so I mean this in the most loving fashion I can deliver given how many idiots I've dealt with since dawn—did Keane screw your brains out on the rooftop last night, and if so, was he amazeballs or do I have to hurt him?"

Willa dropped her head to her desk and thunked it a few times. Because here was the thing about Keane. He was smart. Sexy. Incredibly handsome and virile. And when he looked at her, he sent a quiver through her body in all the best possible places . . . every time.

Being with him so intimately last night had been incredible—but in retrospect, it was a bit scary too because now her heart was invested.

And then there was the fact that Keane didn't intend to get invested at all.

At least she'd set the ground rules by saying out loud that it'd been a one-time thing. That helped.

Okay, it hadn't helped at all but she'd been the one to instigate what'd happened up on that roof, and she had no regrets.

"Well?" Elle demanded.

"It was a one-time thing."

"Great," Elle said. "Got no problem with that. But it isn't what I asked you."

Willa blew out a sigh. "Yes and yes."

There was a beat of silence. "If it was so great, why won't there be round two?"

"He's not round-two material," Willa said and had to bite her tongue because she immediately wanted to take the statement back. Keane was smart and funny and sexy, and well worthy of a round two. Which meant she'd just lied to one of her closest friends in the whole entire world.

But the truth was too hard to say out loud. The truth

hurt. The truth was . . . she wasn't sure *she* was round-two material.

"Honey," Elle said after another long beat of knowing silence. "Let me tell you something about yourself that you don't know. When you lie, you speak in an octave reserved for dogs."

"I can't do this." Dammit, her voice was so high that probably Elle was right, only dogs could hear her. She cleared her throat. "Not now."

"Fine," Elle said agreeably. "Girls' night. Does tomorrow sound good? Pizza and wine and a little chit-chat about believing in yourself, since you're one of the very best human beings I know and love."

"You hate most human beings," Willa said.

"Proof that I mean it then. Shit, I'm looking at my calendar. Can't tomorrow night, Archer needs my help on a job."

"Maybe we should have girls' night to discuss why you and Archer haven't—in your own words—screwed each other's brains out," Willa said. "Everyone knows it's going to happen sooner or later."

"Well then, 'everyone' should be watching their backs," Elle said grumpily. "It's not going to happen. Ever. I'm clearing my schedule for tonight. Pizza and wine and a heart-to-heart."

"I'm on a diet."

"Me too," Elle said. "It's a *fuel* diet. I eat whatever's going to fuel my soul, and tonight that's going to be pizza."

Willa opened her mouth to claim that she was busy but Elle had disconnected. "Dammit, I hate when she gets the last word," she muttered.

Keane was halfway through his morning laying out wood floor at the North Beach house, while playing last night repeatedly in his brain. The good parts, not the part where somehow he'd let Willa put them into the one-night-stand category.

No, he'd shoved that aside. Instead he kept going back to when Willa had come all over him, shuddering gorgeously in his arms, his name on her lips—

Someone knocked on the front door for the second time. He had a crew of ten today but no one stopped working.

"Sass," he called out.

Nothing.

"Sass!"

Looking irritated as all hell, she stuck her head in from the hallway, jabbing a finger to the phone glued to her ear, reminding him with a scathing look that she was here ordering the window treatments.

He blew out a sigh, dropped his tool belt, and moved toward the door himself. It couldn't be a subcontractor; they would've just let themselves in. He hoped it wasn't a neighbor complaining about the noise. He tried to keep it quiet but some things couldn't be helped.

Like the nail gun he'd been using on the flooring.

He pulled open the door, prepared to politely apologize and then continue doing exactly what he'd been doing. Instead he stared in shock at his Aunt Sally.

She was hands on hips. "I've had to chase you all over town. Do you have any idea how much I just paid in cab fares?"

He stuck his head out the door, looking past her for the cab. "I'll pay—"

"Already done." She sniffed with irritation. "You don't answer your phone. Which is rude, by the way. Your entire generation is rude with this whole twittering and texting ridiculousness. No manners whatsoever."

Keane pulled his phone from his pocket and saw the missed call. With a grimace, he shook his head. "I was using power tools and couldn't hear—"

"Don't give me excuses, boy. I've got one hour left before I have to be back. Where's Petunia? Where is my sweet baby girl? That thing is scared of her own shadow. All these people and the racket must be terrifying her."

If Petunia was a "sweet, little thing" or "scared of her own shadow," Keane would eat his own shorts. As for where she was, well that was going to be complicated. Knowing today would be loud as hell, he'd dropped Pita off at South Bark this morning.

And okay, so he'd been hoping to lay eyes—and maybe his mouth as well—on Willa. Yeah, he'd gotten her message last night loud and clear.

It'd been a one-time thing.

He got it. And actually, one-time things were his specialty. It was all he ever did these days. So the smart thing was to get on board and agree with her.

But he wasn't feeling all that agreeable, not that he wanted to think about *that*.

And in the end, it hadn't mattered. Willa hadn't been in the shop yet and he'd dealt with Rory, who'd been closed-mouthed on where her boss might be.

Worried that he might've had something to do with her absence, Keane had both texted and called Willa's cell, but hadn't gotten through. He could admit to feeling uneasy. Either she'd decided last night had been a huge mistake on top of a one-time thing, or . . . well, he couldn't think of an alternative.

But the thought of her regretting what had been the best night in his recent and ancient history didn't sit well with him. His big plan had been to rush through the day and get back to South Bark before closing so he could see what the hell was going on.

"Well?" Aunt Sally demanded.

He joined her on the porch and shut the door behind him, closing off the noisy racket from inside. Plus if she was going to yell at him, he'd rather she didn't do it in front of his crew and undermine his authority. "What do you mean you only have an hour left?" he asked. "Did you run away from the home? What's going on?"

"Oh no," she said, shaking a bony finger in his face. "You first. Where's my baby?"

"She's not here. I knew the noise would upset her so I—"

"What have you done with her? Oh, my God." She wrung her hands. "You did it, you sold her."

"No," he said. "She's with a friend."

"She's delicate, Keane. And I don't even think she knows she's an animal, much less a cat! I know that's what your parents did to you when you caused some ruckus, shipped you off, but that's not how to handle things." She sounded worried sick, which made him feel like a first-class jerk.

And a little shell-shocked. That's exactly what he'd done. He'd shipped the cat off rather than deal with her, just like his parents had always done to him. Jesus. *Was he like them?* "She's fine," he promised. "My . . . friend loves cats." Look at him trip over the word *friend*.

"Your friend?"

"Yes," he said and really hoped that was true, that at the very least he and Willa were still friends, that he hadn't blown that last night.

"Where is this person?" Aunt Sally demanded. "Take me to her right now."

Okay then. He stuck his head back inside and came face-to-face with an obviously eavesdropping and also obviously amused Sass. *"Chicken,"* he whispered.

"You don't pay me enough to lie to sweet old ladies," she whispered back.

In fact, yes he did pay her enough to lie to old ladies. He paid her enough to run a third-world country. But now wasn't a good time to point that out. "I'll be back," he said.

Sass smiled. "Want me to call ahead and warn Willa that you've lied to your sweet old great-aunt and ask her to lie for you as well?"

"Not lie," he said. "I merely omitted a few facts."

"Such as you pawned off her cat to day care."

"Just hold down the damn fort," he said and shut the door on her nosy nose.

He turned back to his aunt and took her hand. "I'll drive."

Ten minutes later he parked outside the Pacific Pier Building, right in front of South Bark Mutt Shop.

Sally eyeballed the shop and then turned and glared daggers at him. "If there's one little hair on Petunia's sweet little head harmed . . ."

"Death and dismemberment," he said. "I know." Just as he also knew that if anyone had been harmed, it wouldn't be that cat. She could slay anyone at a hundred paces.

Working her way through some dreaded bookkeeping on a break, Willa stopped and stared sightlessly out the window. Over the last few weeks there'd been a pattern of her cash drawer being short forty bucks.

Even more concerning, it only happened when one of her employees closed up. She hated the implication but she was now down one hundred and twenty precious dollars and she couldn't ignore it any longer.

Rory poked her head in. "Everything okay?"

Rory had been with Willa the longest. Willa didn't want her thief to be Rory, but she couldn't be sure so she said, "Yep."

"Okay," Rory said, clearly not buying it but not pushing either. "I'm going to groom Buddy. Can you listen for customers?"

"Of course." Buddy was a twelve-year-old cat who hated baths. But he did love being combed, so they had an ongoing love/hate relationship, though he was partial to Rory.

A few minutes later, the bell above the front door rang. Willa was heading out there when from the back came a startled scream, a growl, a yelp, and then a crash.

She raced back there and found Rory on her hands

and knees peering under their storage shelves, and Lyndie standing in the center of the room wringing her hands.

"What happened?" Willa asked.

"Something startled me and Buddy." Rory muttered this with a scathing glance in Lyndie's direction, and Willa knew there was a lot more to this story.

"*Something?*" she asked.

"Yeah, and then he bit me and I let go of him. He's under the shelves cowering. Come here, Buddy," Rory said in a singsong voice. "I'm not mad at you, I'd have bitten me too. I didn't mean to startle you."

Willa dropped to her hands and knees next to Rory and peered under the shelving to find two huge, terrified eyes staring back at her. "Aw, baby, it's okay. Come on out now . . ." She pulled a pupperoni treat from her pocket and waggled it enticingly. "We'll go right to the combing part, okay? You love that."

Buddy, always unable to resist food of any kind, crab-crawled his way out from beneath the shelf and very cautiously took the treat.

Willa gently pulled him into her body and cuddled him close, kissing him on top of his bony head. "You poor, silly baby." She craned her neck and eyed Rory's finger, which was bleeding profusely. "How bad?"

"I'm fine," she said and headed to the sink.

Willa had to believe that, at least for the moment while she dealt with Lyndie and the suspicions that had been churning in her own gut. "When did you get here?"

Lyndie sucked on her lower lip and exchanged a glance with Rory.

Willa bit back a sigh. She'd thought they were past this. "Lyndie," she said quietly, gently. "I know you slept here last night. I know you sleep here when you need to."

"No," she said, the denial instantly defensive. "I—"

"Stop," Willa said in that same calm voice. No judgment. No censure. Because she, more than anyone, understood the need to get out of a bad situation and yet have no safe place to go. "I want you to feel safe here. But on the nights you need a place to sleep, you just have to let me know. I've got a couch four flights up that's far better than the floor of this wash room. Ask Rory, she slept there on and off her entire first year with me."

Rory nodded. "She makes cinnamon toast late at night when you can't sleep and we watch Netflix."

Lyndie stared at Willa for a long beat and then swallowed hard. "You'd let me sleep in your apartment?"

"Yes," Willa said. "But there's something that I *won't* let you do. And that's steal from the till."

Lyndie's eyes shuttered. "I didn't steal anything." She backed up to the door. "You can call the cops but you can't keep me here to wait for them—"

"I'm not calling the cops," Willa said and rose to her feet. "I need you to listen to me, Lyndie, and really hear what I'm saying, okay? I love having you as an employee, I love how you treat the animals, but no one's holding you against your will. More than that, I don't want anyone here who doesn't want to be here, and I won't allow anyone to take advantage of me. Rory, what's my policy on stealing?" she asked without taking her eyes off Lyndie.

Rory had washed out her finger and was wrapping it in a paper towel to stanch the bleeding. "Two strikes and you're out."

"And why isn't it three?" Willa asked.

"Because you were born early and without patience," Rory recited.

Willa nodded. "Do you get what I'm telling you?" she asked Lyndie.

The girl swallowed hard. "I've had my first strike."

"You've had your first strike," Willa agreed. She was firm on that, always. Boundaries mattered with the animals and boundaries mattered with the kids as well.

"I'm sorry," Lyndie whispered.

"Thank you, and I know. But we both deserve better, okay?"

Lyndie nodded and Willa moved to the grooming station with Buddy. "You two go out front and take care of customers. I've got Buddy."

When they were gone, she cooed to the scared cat, "And you, you adorable little beast. Let's make some magic together."

"How about me, want to make some magic with me too?" asked an unbearably familiar, low, and sexy voice from behind her.

Keane, of course, because who else could make her heart leap into her throat and her nipples go hard while everything inside her went soft at the same time?

Chapter 17

#ReadMyLips

Keane was amused that he'd rendered Willa speechless. For once.

But there was no getting around the fact that she didn't exactly look happy to see him. Moving toward her, he picked up the comb she'd dropped and handed it to her, holding on to it until she met his gaze. "Hey."

"Hey," she said back. At first, she'd looked a little bit like a deer in the headlights, but now she was closing herself off, right before his very eyes.

"You okay?" he asked.

"Yes, just busy, so—"

"Not so busy at all!" Rory had stuck her head in the door and was grinning like a loon. "Lyndie and I've got it all handled out here so you two just"—she smiled guilelessly—"make magic or something."

And then she was gone.

"She's match-making," Willa muttered. "I was very

busy having a moment with them and now they're match-making."

"Want to talk about that moment you were having?" he asked. "Seemed serious."

"I've got it handled."

She always did. She was good at that, handling whatever came her way. "Okay, then let's talk about how even your employees can see how much you like me," he said.

She rolled her eyes at that, which made him laugh. He moved in and let his mouth brush her ear. "You telling me that you didn't have a good time last night?"

As close as he was, he felt the tremor go through her but before he could pull her in, she stepped free and glared at him. "Stop using your sex voice," she said, hugging herself. "And you know I had a good time." She hesitated, looking around like maybe she was making sure no one could hear them. "Twice," she whispered.

He burst out laughing. "You mean three times."

She stared at him. "You were counting?" she asked in disbelief.

"Of course not. Didn't have to." He leaned in. "And anyway, we both know it was four."

She pointed at him. "And that. *That's* why we're not doing it again. Because you want to talk about it. And I don't."

He caught her when she would've moved away. "We really not going to do that again?"

"One night," she said softly, holding his gaze. "You agreed. No strings attached. You agreed to that too."

"Yeah." He shook his head. "I might've been premature."

She choked out a laugh. "Now that's one thing you weren't . . ." She shook her head when he snorted. "I think we both know that we're better off as friends, Keane."

"Friends," he repeated, still unsure how he was feeling about this.

"Yes," she said. "Friends stick." She lifted a shoulder, as if a little embarrassed. "I guess I wouldn't mind if you . . . stuck."

He looked at her for a long beat, picturing the novelty of that, being friends with a woman he wanted naked and writhing beneath him. "I like the sticky part."

She pushed him but he caught her hand and got serious. "I'm in," he said.

Her mouth curved. "In as friends, or was that another sexual innuendo?"

"Both," he said just to see her smile go bright again.

When it did, his chest got all tight. It told him that this was something much more than the still sizzling chemistry between them, but given the look on her face, he didn't have to point that out. She already knew.

"So," she said after an awkward pause. "What brings you here? You done working for the day?"

"No, my great-aunt wants to see Pita."

Willa processed Keane's words and felt her spine snap straight as she rushed for the door.

Keane was right on her heels and she sent him a

glare over her shoulder. "You should've told me right away she was here!"

"I told you as soon as you stopped talking about magic and sticky."

"Oh my God." She was going to have to kill him. He was keeping up with her, his broad shoulders pushing the boundaries of his work T-shirt, jeans emphasizing his long legs, scuffed work boots on his feet, all combining to make her heart take a hard leap against her ribs.

Or maybe that was just *him* doing all of that to her.

She took another peek and their gazes locked and held. During that long beat, Willa forgot her problems with Lyndie, forgot the shop . . . hell, she forgot her own name because images from last night were flashing through her head again. The way his big, work-roughened hands had felt on her, the deep growl from his throat as he'd moved deep inside her, touching something no one else ever had. He'd taken her outside of herself and it'd been shockingly easy for him to do so, as if he'd known her all his life.

Then there'd been the sheer, unadulterated, driving need and hunger he'd caused. And fulfilled . . . And she'd put them in the friend zone.

She was an idiot, a scared, vulnerable idiot . . .

An older woman was making her way around the shop, walking slowly, maybe a little painfully, her face pinched with anxiety and concern.

"Aunt Sally, this is Willa Davis," Keane said, introducing them. "She owns and runs South Bark."

"Lovely to meet you," Willa said.

The woman narrowed her eyes. "You're the *friend* who has my Petunia?"

She slid a look Keane's way. "Yes. She's safe and sound, as always when she's here."

"As always?"

Ruh-roh, Willa thought, but before she could speak, Sally beat her to it.

"I want her back." Keane's aunt's white hair was in a bun and that bun quivered with indignity. "Right now."

"Aunt Sally," Keane said quietly, putting his hand over the older woman's. "Pita—er, Petunia really is very happy here, I promise you."

"Who's Pita?" Sally asked.

Willa laughed but when Keane sent her a pained look, she turned it into a cough.

"She wasn't meant to be crated all day," Sally said. "She hates being contained—"

"Oh, I don't keep the fur babies in a crate," Willa said. "I only take on a very select few in the first place and they stay with me or one of my employees all day. Petunia is one of those select few. And she's really wonderful, by the way. So sweet and loving."

This time it was Keane to choke on a laugh and then tried to cough it off.

Willa ignored him. "Petunia really enjoys being high up and viewing the world from a safe perch."

"Yes," Sally said with great relief, losing a lot of her tension. "She does."

Willa turned and gestured to the other end of the store, where she had a built-in shelving unit lining the wall with an assortment of animal beds for sale, ranging from Saint Bernard–size down to small enough for the tiniest of kittens.

Petunia was on the highest shelf in the smallest of beds, half of her body overlapping on either side—which didn't appear to be bothering her one bit, as she was fast asleep.

"Oh my," Sally breathed, cupping her own face, which had softened with pleasure. "She looks . . . ridiculous."

Willa laughed. "She chose the perch, and she's perfectly content. She just came back from a walk—"

"A walk!" Sally exclaimed. "Outside?"

"On a leash," Willa said. "One of my friends took her and two golden retrievers out together this morning. They all had a great time."

Sally whirled to Keane, eyes bright as she reached up and smacked him in the chest. "You're brilliant."

Keane looked surprised. And wary. "I am?"

"And here I've been thinking how sad it is that you never recovered from losing Blue enough to get another pet. Blue was his childhood dog," she said to Willa before looking back at Keane. "I thought when your mother and father gave that dog away without talking to you about it first that the loss had irrevocably destroyed your ability to love another animal."

Keane's expression went blank. "They didn't give him away," he said. "I left the back door open and he escaped. It was my fault."

Sally shook her head. "I always wondered what hokey-pokey bologna they fed you. Keane, you loved that dog beyond reason, you'd never have carelessly left the back door open knowing your yard wasn't fenced in."

"How do you know this?" he asked. "You weren't around."

"My sister and I share a best friend. And let's just say that Betty didn't turn her back on me like everyone else. She keeps me updated."

Keane still wore that blank expression, but there was something happening behind his eyes now that tugged hard at Willa's heart.

She'd bought his party line that maybe he was a guy who didn't feel deeply, who didn't have a sensitivity chip. A guy who couldn't attach. But she was starting to suspect it was the actual opposite, that he had incredible heart, he'd just been hurt. Badly.

"Petunia," Sally called softly, her voice cracking with age. "Baby, come to Mama."

Petunia immediately lifted her head with a surprised chirp. She leapt with grace to the counter and jogged straight to Sally, right into the woman's open arms.

Sally bent her head low, and cat and woman had a long moment together, the only sounds being the raspy purr from Petunia and the soft murmurs from Sally. "I have to go, Petunia," she whispered softly. "You might not see me for a while. You be a good girl for Keane, okay? He's male so he might not know much, but he's got a big heart, even if he doesn't know that either."

Willa's heart squeezed hard. She turned to Keane with worry and he gave her a very small smile, reaching for her hand. She gently squeezed his fingers.

His eyes were warm as they slid over her features.

Warm and grateful, she realized. Because she'd taken good care of Petunia? Or that she'd been kind to his aunt? Or maybe it was simply because she was there.

Sally lifted her head. Her eyes were dry but devastated as she turned away. "I need a ride back now," she said and snapped her fingers in the air.

Keane smiled grimly at Willa. "I've been summoned." Leaning down, he brushed a kiss across her mouth before looking into her eyes.

For what she had no idea. But wanting to give comfort however she could, she pressed into him and felt him let out a low breath, like maybe he was relaxing for the first time all day.

Pulling back, he kissed her once more, and then he was gone.

Chapter 18

#NoChill

Keane was good at burying emotions, real good. He was also good at compartmentalizing. But when he'd walked Sally inside her rehab center and she'd hugged him, whispering, "Be better than the rest of the family," and then patted his cheek and walked away, he'd had a funny feeling that he couldn't place.

That evening, just as he was leaving work to pick up Pita, his architect and engineer showed up for an impromptu meeting on the Mission job. Worried about making Willa work late, he quickly called South Bark. Willa was with a customer but Rory told him no worries, they'd take care of Petunia as late as he needed. Someone would just take her home if need be.

Relieved, he went into his meeting and when it was over an hour later, he realized with a hit to his solar plexus what the niggling feeling about Sally had been.

She'd been trying to tell him goodbye.

He left the jobsite and stopped to see his aunt on his way to South Bark—only to be told that Sally had been taken to the hospital.

When he got there, they wouldn't tell him a damn thing because she hadn't listed any contacts. Luckily Keane knew the nurse and in spite of the fact that they'd slept together twice before he'd backed off when he'd seen wedding bells and white picket fences in her pretty eyes, Jenny seemed genuinely happy to see him. They exchanged pleasantries and then he asked about Sally.

She shook her head. "I can't tell you anything about her condition—I could lose my job for that. You're hot, Keane, and great in bed . . ." She smiled. "Really, *really* great, but even I have my limits."

She did, however, let him sit in Sally's room.

Exhausted, he stretched out his legs and leaned his head back. He was half asleep when his aunt's cranky voice came from the bed. "You paid my rehab center bill."

And he'd pay her hospital bill too, if she needed. "Don't worry about it," he said.

"Worrying is what I do."

"Just get better."

"Huh," she said. "Is that out of concern for me or concern for you that you might get stuck with Petunia?"

"Both."

She cackled at that. "I might have to write you into my will."

He found a smile. "Look at you being all sweet. I knew you had it in you, deep, deep down."

"Just don't tell anyone," she said. "They'll think I have no chill."

He blinked. "What?"

"It's a term used when you act specifically uncool about something."

He laughed. "I know what it means, I'm just wondering how you know."

Sally shrugged. "My nurse keeps saying it about the doctors. Now stop stalling and explain to me what the hell you're doing here. I know I didn't have anyone call you."

He shook his head. "And why is that?" he asked, apparently still butt-hurt over it.

She closed her eyes. "You should be home with your girl right now."

Keane scrubbed a hand over his face. "Willa's not mine."

"Spoken just like a man who's never had to work for a woman in his life."

This wrenched another laugh from him. He stared at his clenched hands and then lifted his head. "I want to know what's going on with you. I want you to put me on as your next of kin and contact, and I'd like to have your power of attorney as well."

"Circling the inheritance already?"

"I want to be able to make sure you're being cared for," he said.

She stared at him, her rheumy eyes fierce and proud and stubborn as . . . well, as he imagined his own were. Finally, she blew out a rough breath. "I lived the past three extra decades without any family at all."

"Yeah and how has that worked out for you?" he asked.

She huffed and leaned back, closing her eyes. "It doesn't matter now. What matters is that you go."

"Not happening."

Her mouth went tight, her eyes stayed tightly closed.

He blew out a sigh. "Aunt Sally—"

"I'm dying," she said flatly.

He stopped breathing. "No." He stood up and moved to her bedside, covering her hand with his. "No," he said again.

She looked up at him. "You can stand as tall as a tree and scowl down at me all you want. I'm eighty-five years old. It's going to be God's truth."

"When?"

She shrugged.

"Soon?"

"Only if you keep drilling me."

He let out a low laugh and scrubbed a hand over his face. "Christ."

"Look, I could choke on my Metamucil tomorrow morning and go toes up just like that, you never know."

"And I could die from slipping and falling in warm cat yak getting out of bed," he said.

She laughed. "It's the warm that always gets me." She sobered. "I just want you forewarned. Since you seem so fragile and all."

"Yeah," he said dryly. "I'm as fragile as a peach."

"I want you to listen to me," she said, squeezing his fingers with surprising strength.

So he bent low, thinking she was going to tell him something important in regard to her wishes.

"If you take my cat to the pound after I'm gone," she said, "I will haunt you for the rest of your life, and then I'll follow you to hell and haunt you for all of eternity."

Chapter 19

#MischiefManaged

Keane drove straight to South Bark. It was past seven and he felt like a dick that he'd left Willa to deal with one of his problems. He could only hope Pita had been . . . well, *not* a PITA.

The shop was closed, locked up tight as a drum, and dark, except for the twinkle of the holiday lights strung across the glass window front. He took it as a good sign that there wasn't a note posted for him.

He pressed his face up against the glass but no one was inside. Turning, he strode across the cobblestone courtyard, lit by more strings of lights. The water fell from the fountain, the sound muted by the music tumbling out of the pub, which was still going strong.

Near the alley, Old Man Eddie was talking to two gray-bunned ladies. "Some beauty for the beauties," he said, handing them each a little spring of green held together by a red ribbon.

The ladies handed him some cash and smiled broadly. "Thanks for the . . . *mistletoe.*"

Mistletoe his ass, Keane thought with a reluctant smile. That was weed. He entered the pub and moved to the end of the bar. Rory was there, seemingly in a standoff with Max, who was minus his sidekick, Carl.

"No," she said.

"Look, you want a ride home to Tahoe for Christmas," Max said. "And I happen to be going that way. Why take two buses and a damn train when I could drive you?"

"Maybe I already have my tickets."

"Do you?"

She rolled her eyes.

Max just stood there, arms folded across his chest.

"What's your problem?" she snapped.

"You know what my problem is," he said. "It's you."

She pointed a finger at him. "You know what you are, Max? You're a hypocrite." And she whirled away from the bar, nearly plowing Keane over.

He put his hands on her arms to steady her.

She backed away from him, a scowl still on her face. "Sorry."

"No worries," he said. "You okay?"

"If one more person asks me that, I'm going to start kicking asses and taking names."

"Fair enough," Keane said, lifting his hands in surrender. "I'm just looking to relieve whoever is on Pita duty."

A small smile crossed her face. "I offered to be, but Willa insisted. She was here with her friends, it was girls' night, but I lost track of her."

"Try the back," Sean suggested from where he was serving behind the bar. "Pool table."

Archer and Spence were playing pool back there, and arguing while they were at it.

Seemed like it was the night for it.

"It's getting too cold. You've got to get him off the streets," Archer was saying as he shot the four ball and bounced it off the corner pocket.

Spence stood and pointed at the nine ball. "Bottom pocket," he said and made his shot before pointing at Archer. "And I've gotten him off the damn streets. Multiple times. Have you ever tried arguing with someone who literally fried their brain at Woodstock?"

"Man, that guy is *still* frying his brain," Archer said. "And speaking of, he hung some of his clippings in the alley entrance and is telling any woman who walks by that it's mistletoe."

"You talking about Old Man Eddie?" Keane asked.

Archer and Spence exchanged a look. "Yeah," Spence finally said. "We're trying to figure a way to keep him warm and healthy for the winter months that he'll agree to. So far all he agrees to is living in the fucking alley."

Keane nodded. "He's out there right now, selling some of that 'mistletoe' to a couple of older ladies."

Archer jabbed a finger at Spence. "Deal with him tonight or I will."

"Thought you gave up being a cop," Spence said.

Archer narrowed his eyes and the testosterone level in the back room spiked to off-the-chart. "Was that supposed to be funny?"

"A little bit, yeah." Spence turned to Keane. "You play?"
Keane eyed the pool table. "Some."

Archer's bad 'tude never wavered as he reset the balls.

"Never mind him," Spence said. "He's just pouting because he's a big, fat loser tonight. I'm already up fifty bucks."

"You whined so much when you lost last week that I felt sorry for you," Archer said. "I'm letting you win."

Spence shook his head. "Lying to make yourself look good is just sad. Especially since girls' night ended and Elle isn't even here anymore for you to show off."

Archer shoulder-checked Spence hard as he moved around the table to shoot.

Spence practically bounced across the room but he didn't look bothered in the least. In fact, he looked smug.

Archer slid him a hard look. "You know why I want Eddie cleaned up or gone. You fucking damn well know why."

Spence's easy smile slipped. "Okay, yeah. I do know." He waited quietly while Archer shot again, and then again, each time sinking multiple balls into the pockets. "I'll deal with it. I promised Willa the same thing because she doesn't want her kids tempted."

Keane choked on his beer. "Her kids?"

Archer looked up from the pool table and actually smiled. "She didn't tell you?"

Spence gave Archer a shove. "You're an asshole." He turned to Keane. "Not *her* kids. Her employees, the ones she so carefully collects to save, since there was no one to save her."

Keane prided himself on being cool, calm, logical. Emotions didn't have a place in his everyday life. But ever since he'd walked into Willa's shop that first time, he'd been having emotions. Deep ones.

Spence's words evoked a picture in his mind of what it had been like for Willa, leaving the foster-care system at age eighteen without anyone to take care of her. "She's got someone now," Keane said, surprising himself.

Archer shot again and sank the last of his balls. "Big loser, my ass." He pointed at Spencer. "You owe me fifty bucks. And also, if you keep opening your trap about Willa, she's going to kick your ass." He turned to Keane. "You mean what you just said? About Willa having someone now?"

Keane opened his mouth but nothing came out. Until this very moment he'd truly believed that a no-commitment policy was the best thing for him. No, wait. That wasn't exactly true. He'd been doubting his policy for a while now. Since Willa had plowed her way into his life.

He just had no idea what to do with that realization.

Spence laughed quietly at the look on Keane's face. "Give him a sec, man. I think he just shocked himself more than us."

Truer words . . . "I've gotta go," Keane said.

"Nice job," Archer muttered to Spence. "You scared him off."

"Nah, that guy can't be scared off. He's as bull-headed stubborn as you are. And hell, you still can't even admit what you feel for Elle, so . . ."

Keane didn't hear the rest of that thought because he walked out of the pub into the chilly night. He hit the stairwell and climbed to the fourth floor, not stopping until he was in front of Willa's door.

With absolutely zero idea of what he thought he was doing.

She opened after his knock wearing a tiny pair of flannel plaid PJ shorts just barely peeking out from beneath a huge hoodie. "Hey," she said and then frowned. "What's wrong?"

Not wanting to get into his aunt being in the hospital or his epiphany about Willa herself, he shook his head. "Nothing. Is it still girls' night? Are you guys having a pillow fight?"

"No," she laughed. "Pru wasn't feeling good. We cut it short before we even got to dinner."

Keane had learned to tell her mood by her hair. The wilder the strands, the wilder her emotions, but tonight her hood was up, falling over her forehead with the words *I Solemnly Swear That I Am Up to No Good* across it. "Sorry you got stuck with Petunia," he said.

"Oh, I didn't mind." She turned from him to look for the cat, or so he assumed, and saw the words *Mischief Managed* written across her sweet ass, making him realize the sweatshirt and shorts were a matched set. Nudging her aside, he let himself in.

Her place didn't surprise him. He'd seen her shop and he'd had an idea that her home would somehow look the same, cutesy and colorful.

"Mischief managed?" he asked.

She blinked like he'd surprised her. "You know Harry Potter?"

"Well, not personally," he said and smiled. "But I read the books."

"You mean you saw the movies?"

"No, I mean I read the books."

She didn't look happy about this. Color him completely lost. "And that makes me . . . ?"

She moaned and closed her eyes. "Bad for me. Oh so bad for me!"

Yeah, still lost. "Can I be bad for you over dinner?" he asked. "Because I'm starving."

Her eyes flew open and she stared at him.

He had no idea what she was thinking. "Are you hungry?" he asked.

"I'm always hungry. But it's getting late."

"And?"

"And . . ." She looked boggled. "Lots of reasons."

"Name one."

"Okay . . . Well, it's nearly Christmas. And Christmastime is usually for dear friends and family."

He just looked at her, not buying any of that.

"Keane," she said softly.

Was he going to tell her about his epiphany about wanting more from her? Hell no. One, he had no idea what that more was. And two, assuming he could figure that out, he then had to convince her to feel the same. No wonder he'd lain low on love. This shit was hard. "You told me family is where you make it," he said. "You told me your friends are your family. You told me we're friends. Was any of that a lie?"

"No, but . . ." She looked at him beseechingly. "I'm trying to resist you here, okay? I'm trying to tell myself we have nothing in common except this weird and extremely annoying chemistry that won't go away, not even when we . . ."

He went brows up, really wanting to hear her finish that sentence.

"Okay, when *I* jumped your bones on the roof," she finished, eyes narrowed, daring him to laugh. "But then you show up at my door, clearly exhausted and rumpled and looking . . . well, hungry, and it makes me want to do things."

"Things like . . . ?"

"Take my clothes off. Okay? You make me want to take my clothes off."

He started to smile but she poked him again. "Don't say it," she warned. "Don't you dare say that me stripping works for you."

"But, Willa, it does work for me. You stripping will always work for me."

This earned him an eyeroll. "Shock," she said. "But *friends* don't do that. They don't, Keane," she said when he opened his mouth. "And I was going to be okay with that. But then you went ahead and told me you've read Harry Potter." She hesitated and considered him. "Which one?"

"All of them."

She covered her face and moaned miserably. "All of them," she muttered. "I'm a dead woman. You've just killed me dead."

"I read a lot," he said, trying to improve his odds. "Not just Harry Potter."

"Making it worse . . ." She dropped her hands from her face. "Why are you here again?"

"To pick up Pita."

"Oh yeah."

"And to thank you for watching her." He paused. "With a meal because I'm starving and I want to buy you dinner. You look like the very best thing I've seen all day long, Willa. Can I tell you that without a disagreement?"

She eyeballed him for a long beat. "Dinner where?"

He bit back his victory smile. "Your choice."

"Sushi?"

He manfully held in his wince. He hated sushi. "Your choice," he said again.

"But you hate sushi."

"How do you know?" he asked.

"Because your eyes grimaced. Why would you agree to sushi if you hate it?"

He was starting to get a headache. "Because when I said your choice, I meant it. Are we going to argue about that too? And if so, can it wait until I get some food?"

"Sure. How about Thai?" she asked and studied his face carefully.

He gave her his best blank face. He wasn't crazy about Thai either but now his eye was full-out twitching. "Thai it is," he said. "You ready?"

She went hands on hips. "You don't like Thai either? What's wrong with you?"

"Many, many things," he said, wondering when

she'd come to be able to read him so damn clearly that he couldn't hide a thing from her. "Can we go now?"

"Italian. Indian. Taco Bell."

A laugh escaped him. "Yes."

"Which?"

"Willa, if you get your sweet little ass on the move, I'll take you to *all* of them."

She bit her lower lip and stared at him, her eyes bright.

Not moving.

"Babe," he said. *"What?"*

"I want to go somewhere *you* want to go," she said. "Can we make it your choice?"

What he wanted was to go to her bed. Directly and without passing Go. He wanted to strip her out of every stitch of clothing and feast on her.

For a week.

Some of that must have shown on his face because she blushed to her roots. "Pizza," she said quickly. "Pizza work for you?"

"Thank Christ, yes," he said.

She nodded and then hesitated.

"What now?" he asked.

"You ever going to tell me what's wrong?"

"I'm getting pizza and beer." *And you,* he thought. "What could be wrong? Come on." He reached for her hand, but she evaded with a low laugh.

"I can't go like this," she said. "I have to change first."

"I like what you're wearing."

She looked at him as if he'd lost his marbles.

"Okay, fine," he said. "Throw on sweats and call it good."

"Did you come through the pub?"

"Yes. Why?"

"Because then people saw you. People like Spence and Archer. Maybe Elle too, if she was still there. And trust me, they watched you leave and saw that you weren't leaving at all, that you came upstairs. They're going to gossip about it, and then tomorrow I'll be interrogated by the girls. Did I let you in? Did you stay? And what was I wearing? And I'll be damned, Keane, if I tell them that I was wearing sweats."

He blinked. He didn't quite follow. In fact, he needed to buy a vowel but he nodded gamely, willing to agree to anything to get food. "Okay."

"Okay." She vanished into her bedroom.

Chapter 20

#WithASideOfCrazy

Willa ran into her bedroom and startled Petunia, who was sleeping on her bed. "Sorry, don't mind me," she said to the cat and yanked off her clothes. She pulled on a pair of jeans that weren't comfortable but they gave her a good butt, and a soft green Christmas sweater that had a reindeer on the front, and fell to her thighs.

Which made the good-butt jeans unnecessary.

She peeled them off and tried a pair of black leggings instead.

Now she just looked a little lazy.

"Shit." She stripped again and started over.

And then over again.

Ten minutes later she'd tried on everything in her closet—which was now in a pile on her bed in front of Petunia—and she was in her bra and panties and starting to panic.

Nothing worked.

She swore a bunch more and started pawing through everything she'd already discarded on her bed, telling herself it was silly to be hung up on this. Silly and ridiculous and asinine and stupid—

"Willa," Keane called out, his voice shockingly close, like maybe he was heading down the hall toward her bedroom. "What are you doing, sewing a brand-new outfit?" His voice was right outside her door now.

With a squeak, she grabbed up her huge sweatshirt and held it in front of her. "Don't rush me!"

He poked his head into the room, eyes half amused, half male frustration. There was at least a day of scruff on his jaw and it was sexy as hell, damn him.

A fact that only served to annoy her.

He rubbed his belly like it was hollow. And hell, with those ridged muscles and not an ounce of fat anywhere on him, it probably was hollow.

"I've been waiting for hours," he said, petting Petunia when she meandered over to him for a scratch.

"It's been ten minutes," Willa said.

"Feels like hours." Keane pressed his thumb and forefinger to his eyes like he was trying to hold them into the sockets. "You ready?"

She tore her gaze off his lifted arms and the way his biceps and broad shoulders and back muscles strained the material of his shirt. "Almost," she said a little thickly.

Or not even close.

Reading her expression, he groaned and then looked around her room. "Did a bomb go off in here?"

She eyed the mess. "Maybe."

"You've got a lot of clothes and"—his gaze locked and snagged on a lacy bra and undies—"stuff." Then he saw the secondary pile on the club chair in the corner. "Holy shit," he said. "How many clothes have you tried on?"

"All of them!" she said. Maybe yelled. And then glared at him to see if he so much as dared to crack a smile. "I've got nothing to wear."

He once again took in the huge piles of clothing all over the place. "Okaaaaaay . . ."

She sighed.

He cut his eyes to hers, rubbing his jaw. The sound of his callused fingers against the scruff gave her a zing straight to her good parts.

And she'd had no idea she had so many.

"It's just pizza," he said.

"And here I'm scrambling to look hot enough to ruin you."

He smiled at that. "Willa, I fantasize about you. A lot. And I'm good at it too. You should know that you and your daily hotness have already ruined me."

And in turn, he was ruining her as she stood and breathed, not that she was about to admit it. "So you're saying I look hot to you right now," she said.

His gaze slid slowly over her. She was covered—mostly—by the sweatshirt she was holding to her front, but by the flash of heat in his gaze, he had X-ray vision. His expression softened. "You look batshit crazy and frustrated and hot as hell," he said. "Never doubt it."

She felt a reluctant smile pull at her mouth. "Turn around."

"I've already seen it all."

"Only once, and it was dark."

He smiled. "I have good night vision."

"Do you want to eat?" she asked and he turned around. She pulled back on her good-ass jeans and picked up a white sweater that was a little tight and gave her some impressionable assets, if she said so herself. "And you usually do too," she told him. "Look hot as hell."

He had his back to her, hands on his hips. He had a really great build, and if she was being honest he also had the best ass she'd ever seen, and she spent a few seconds taking in the sight. "Usually?" he asked.

"Well . . ." She eyeballed her room, which looked like a survivor of a category five hurricane. "Sometimes you look hotter than hot," she admitted. *Like now, with those jeans stretched across his buns . . .*

He turned to face her, taking in her outfit in a way that told her he appreciated the white sweater very much. "When?" he asked.

"I'm not telling you. It'll go to your big head."

"Already did," he said and looked down at himself.

Her eyes followed suit, landing on his crotch, and at the obvious hard-on there, she snorted. "I meant your other big head, you pervert."

He grinned at her, charming her effortlessly, damn him. "Now you're just throwing out the compliments left and right," he said. "Let's talk about the *big* part."

She laughed. "You know exactly how big you are . . . *everywhere*. You almost didn't fit. And why are we even having this conversation?"

"Because I like to talk about sex," he said.

"See, *pervert*."

"Well, you should know . . ." His smile dared her to remember exactly how it'd been between them last night.

But here was the thing—she didn't have to drum up the memories; they were burned in her brain. *Combustible*. They'd been—and were—combustible together.

He smiled cockily at her and that was it. She pointed to the door. "Out!"

"Okay, okay!" Laughing, he told Petunia he'd be back for her and left the room, his stomach growling, the sound reaching her across the room.

"Have you really not eaten all day?" she asked.

"It was a crazy-busy day."

Taking pity on him, she shoved her feet into boots with a three-inch heel so she could pretend to be tall and took a quick peek in the mirror.

Her eyes were bright, her cheeks were flushed.

All thanks to her mad dash, she told herself, and absolutely not the man waiting in her living room.

As to why her heart was racing, she decided it was best not to speculate.

"Mischief managed?" he asked hopefully when she came out, like maybe she was a live hand grenade.

"Mischief managed," she assured him, and hoped that was true.

They walked. The night was chilly but clear. They headed into the Marina. With the streets lined with restaurants, bars, galleries, and shops, there were a lot of people out walking, threading their way into the eclectic mix of mom-and-pop places mixed in with high-end stores. In a single square city block, you could eat any kind of food from just about anywhere in the world, not to mention buy anything you wanted.

They got pizza and she told him how a customer had walked into the shop earlier with his parrot on his shoulder. The bird had taken one look at Petunia and fallen in instant love. He'd flown to the edge of the bed Petunia had been snoozing on and begun to garble his love song to her but the cranky cat had smacked him in the face with her paw.

The parrot had left brokenhearted.

They talked about his day too. How Mason had stapled his own hand to the ceiling and then superglued the ensuing slice in his hand rather than go to the doctor.

"Oh my God," Willa said. "And you were okay with that?"

"Cheaper than an ER trip," he said and laughed at the horror on her face. "It's actually what we do. A lot." He showed her a couple of scars on his hands and arms that had been "treated" by superglue.

She shook her head. "Boys are weird."

"I'll give you that," he said.

She laughed and so did he. And the shadows in his eyes faded away a little bit and she felt about ten feet tall.

After dinner, they walked some more. They stopped to watch through the window of a candy shop as a woman pulled her dough through a complicated machine, turning the red and white lines into candy canes.

A crowd had gathered and Willa wound her way to the front, practically pressing her nose to the window in awe. Smiling, she stood there mesmerized when Keane pressed up close behind her, giving her a different kind of yearning altogether.

"Hey, little girl, want some candy?" he whispered in her ear.

"Ha-ha, but yes," she said, not looking away from the window. "I really do."

She felt him smile against her jaw. "Wait here," he said. "I'll be right back."

Not ten seconds later, she felt him brush up behind her again and she laughed. "That was fast."

"Oh, sorry. I got jostled."

Not recognizing the male voice, Willa's smile froze in her throat. She whipped around and faced a guy about her age. Same height, he wore glasses that kept slipping down his nose and an awkward smile.

"Hi," he said. "You should watch on the nights they make chocolate candy canes. Have you ever had one? They're better than *anything*."

"Sounds delicious," she said, but couldn't help thinking *I bet it's not better than sex with Keane Winters . . .*

"They're using chocolate tomorrow night," he said. "I'll be here." He paused and looked at her with a hopefulness that made her want to give him the pupperoni treat in her pocket and pat him on the head. She'd just opened her mouth to let him down gently when she felt a presence at her back. A tall, built, warm, strong presence with testosterone and pheromones pouring off of him, and since her nipples went hard she didn't have to turn this time.

Keane settled in close, not saying anything, just being a silent, badass presence. Craning her neck, she found him giving the Chocolate Candy Cane Guy a death stare that would've made most people pee their pants.

Chocolate Candy Cane Guy gave a little start, cleared his throat and looked at Willa again, an apology in his eyes. "I'm sorry," he said. "I didn't realize you were . . . on a date."

"No worries—" she started but he spun on a heel and vanished into the crowd. She turned to face Keane. "Seriously?"

"What?" he asked innocently.

"Oh no, you don't get to '*what*' me like that," she said, saying the word *what* in an imitation of his own much lower timbre. "What the hell was that?"

"Me getting you candy." He held up the bag.

"No, you just peed on me in public."

His mouth twitched.

"You did!" she said, tossing up her hands. "You totally intimidated that poor guy and all he was doing was talking to me."

Keane looked after him. "You think I was intimidating?"

"Enough to make him go crying for his mama." She jabbed him in a rock-solid pec. "You can't dominate me like that. I don't like it at all."

He smiled, but it was a little bit like the Big Bad

Wolf's smile as his hands went to her hips. And right there, surrounded by a crowd of people, none of whom were paying them the slightest bit of attention, he hauled her into him.

"I'm not done being mad," she said.

"I know. It's okay." His hands slid up her arms and cupped her jaw, warm and strong. "You just tell me when you're done." And then his eyes went dark and heated as he lowered his head. "I'll wait . . ." And then he kissed her.

The air around them crackled and in spite of the cold night, the heat between them pulsed and ebbed. Willa felt the rumble of his rough groan as he palmed the back of her head to hold her to him. And just like that, everything around them faded away to nothing more than a dull murmur in the background. There was nothing past the feel of Keane's strong arms around her, the steady beat of his heart thudding against the erratic pace of her own.

Eyes closed, she felt herself melt into him, their bodies seeking each other as if they'd been together for years. It actually scared her and she clutched at him.

In response, he slowed the kiss down, soothing her until they stilled entirely, mouths a breath apart but sharing air. The night breeze caressed her face along with his fingers and she opened her eyes.

His face was shadowed but she wasn't afraid anymore. Feeling almost like she was in a dream, she went back up on tiptoe and lifted her hands to the nape of his neck, the silky strands of his hair slipping through her fingers as she pulled his face back to hers. "When," she murmured against his mouth.

The last thing she saw before her eyes drifted shut again was his smile.

She parted her lips for him eagerly, desperate for another taste, and felt a heat wash over as his hand fisted in her hair. Unable to get close enough, she paused, moaning at the feel of him hard against her.

When he finally lifted his head, she was breathing like a woman who needed an orgasm.

Bad.

She did her best to look unaffected, but he laughed at her. *Laughed.* And then he took her hand and they walked back to her place.

As they got off the elevator, Keane felt Willa squeeze his hand and look at him as she unlocked her door. "What?" he murmured.

"You okay? You seemed a little off when you first came over, and it's back now."

He was a stone wall when he wanted to be, or so he thought. But apparently not with her, because she put a hand on his chest. "Tell me what's wrong?" she asked softly.

It'd been a damn long time since someone had asked him that question and meant it. But he didn't do this, he didn't unload. Ever. She didn't need the burden of his aunt's illness, or the odd sense of limbo his life had become as he sat in his big Vallejo Street house night after night making up reasons not to sell it and move on, so he shook his head.

Her hand slid up his chest, her palm once again

settling on the nape of his neck, her fingers sinking into his hair.

Clearly she also knew just how much he loved it when she touched him like that.

"Keane, when you ask me if I'm okay, you expect honesty, right?"

His brain was more than a little scrambled by her touch, which was arousing as all hell and took away his power of speech, but he did manage a nod.

She nodded back, as if to say *good boy,* as her guileless eyes met his. And then she moved in for the kill.

"So why would I expect anything less from you?" she asked softly. "Tell me what's wrong."

"You first," he said.

"Me? What about me?"

"You could tell me about this morning, when I walked in on you and your employees having what seemed like a pretty serious confrontation."

"Lyndie screwed up," she said. "She then 'fessed up, the end."

"Not the end. What you did, letting her off the hook like that, it was really generous. Incredibly so. Anywhere else, anyone else, would have fired her, and you know it."

"Everyone deserves a second chance," she said. "Now you."

Letting out a low laugh, he pressed his forehead to hers, stepping into her so that they were toe to toe, letting his hand come up to cup her face. Knowing her better now, knowing the incredible woman she was, she truly amazed him. She'd overcome a rough and dark past, and yet she was an incredible light.

One that drew him in.

Neither of them had been given much love, but she hadn't been stymied by that. Instead she'd turned it around, giving it back wherever and however she could. And what had he done? He'd blocked himself off. Yes, he'd made a life for himself too, and a damn decent good living while he was at it, but he was still closed off. It was hard for him to open up but he wanted to try, friend zone or not. "Now me," he repeated softly.

She nodded. "Now you. Tell me what's wrong, and what I can do to help."

"What's wrong is that I need you," he murmured, dropping his head to kiss the underside of her jaw. "What you can do to help is let me in."

She was ego-strokingly breathless from his touch. "You're already in," she panted.

Was he? Testing that theory, he nudged her inside her apartment, kicked her front door shut, and gently pushed her up against it.

She stared up at him as he lowered his head, not closing her eyes until the last second, but when his mouth covered hers, she moaned and wrapped her arms around him tight enough to hurt in the very best possible way.

Chapter 21

#TurnDownForWhat

Willa lost herself in Keane's words . . . *"I need you,"* in the feel of his hard, heated body up against hers, in the taste of him as he kissed her in the way only he could. He made her ache and yearn and burn. She'd told him that he was in, and she meant it.

Like it or not, he was definitely in her heart. What she wasn't sure was what it meant, to either of them. She'd said they weren't going to do this again, and she'd said that out of self-preservation, but now with his hands on her, she couldn't remember why exactly.

"I'm not usually this easy," she said out loud, hoping to make him laugh and relieve some of this tension, because she didn't know about him but *she* felt strung tighter than a bow.

"Willa." He did indeed laugh, sexy low and gruff as he pressed his face into her hair. "Babe, you're many, many things. But easy isn't one of them."

When she tried to shove him away, he tightened his grip and lifted his head to meet her annoyed eyes with his laughing ones. Then his smile faded. They watched each other for a beat, his gaze suddenly heated and unwavering. "I know you said one night was all you wanted," he said. "But I'm thinking two is better than one."

She nodded, happy to be on the same page. "Two is always better than one, right?"

Letting out a very sexy, very male sound of agreement, he kissed her again, his hands both rough and arousing as they slid up to fist in her hair, holding her still for his kiss. With one tug he bared her throat, scraping his teeth along her skin, making her shudder and press even closer if that was possible. Then his hands skimmed beneath her shirt. She managed to get hers into the back of his jeans and—

"Mew."

Breathless, they broke apart and turned in unison to find Petunia, head low, butt raised in the air and wriggling.

"Watch out," Keane said. "Attack mode initiated."

"Petunia," Willa said softly and the cat lifted her head. Ice blue eyes were narrowed in disapproval.

"I didn't know that she's a kiss blocker," she said on a laugh.

"In two more minutes she'd have been a cock block—"

Still laughing, Willa put her fingers over Keane's lips. "No swearing in front of the children."

He nipped at her fingers and heat slashed through her from her roots to her toes, setting fire to some special spots along the way. "So," she whispered, staring at his mouth. "Where were we?"

He slid his hands up her arms and back into her hair. "Right here." And he kissed her again, a slow, melting nuzzle of lips; warm, comforting.

Tempting.

Her body moved of its own volition, shifting closer, seeking his heat. With a groan, he pulled her in, those wide shoulders blocking out the light, everything but him. One of his big, warm hands settled at the nape of her neck, holding her steady as he continued to kiss the ever-loving daylights out of her.

She cupped his strong jaw, stroking the two-day stubble that she wanted to feel scrape over her body. When her jacket fell from her, she startled. He'd unzipped and nudged it off her shoulders and she hadn't even noticed.

"Shh," he whispered, his mouth on her throat. "I've got you."

And he did. Supported between the wall and his big, delicious body, it was okay that her legs felt wobbly.

Because he had her.

They had to break the kiss for a single beat when he lifted her shirt over her head and then his warm hands were on her bare breasts.

He'd unhooked her bra, letting that fall away as well.

Lifting his head, he looked down at her and let out a long, slow exhale, like he was struggling with control. He watched as she arched into his touch, begging without words for his mouth, for him to find her irresistible, pretty.

"I can't take my eyes off you," he murmured, lips at her ear. "You're so beautiful, Willa."

"Mew!"

"*Quiet,*" they both said at the same time, holding each other's laughing gaze.

"I thought it was kids that were supposed to act like birth control," he said.

Petunia actually sighed and stalked off, legs stiff, tail twitching.

"Don't go away mad," Keane told her. "Just go away."

"Keane."

"Only for a few minutes," he called after the cat. And then he lifted Willa into his arms, the muscles of his shoulders and back rippling smoothly under his shirt. Mmm. Pressing her mouth to his jaw, she wrapped her legs around his waist as he carried her down the hall to her bed.

Where he tossed her.

A surprised squeak escaped her but before she'd bounced more than once he was on her, pressing her down into the mattress, covering her body with his.

"What did I say about dominating me?" she asked with a laugh.

He raised his head, his eyes as dark as the night. "I was hoping that didn't apply to sex." His mouth left her lips, heading toward her ear, taking little love bites as he went. "Cuz I'm feeling a little dominant here, Willa."

Each nibble, each scrape of his teeth seemed to melt her bones away. "That's okay," she panted. "Maybe we could take turns."

"Maybe." His movements over her were sensual,

slow, and dreamlike, and so erotic she writhed for more. He worked his way south from her neck to her collarbone—who knew that was an erogenous zone?—making her gasp when he got to her breast. His tongue worked her nipple over, teasing and tormenting along with his talented, knowing hands, and the sensations drove her right to the edge of a cliff and left her hanging there. *"Keane."*

"I know." He slid further down her body, divesting her of the sweats as he went. Then he made himself at home between her legs, spread wide by his broad-as-a-mountain shoulders.

"Um," she said. "I—"

He scraped her panties to the side, pressed a kiss to the hot, wet flesh he exposed, and she promptly forgot what she'd been about to say. She heard a shuddery moan and was shocked to realize it was her. "Off," she demanded, pushing his shirt up his ridged abs, not wanting to be the only half-naked one, but also wanting to see his gorgeous bod.

Without skipping a beat or taking his mouth off of her, he reached one hand up and tugged his shirt over his head. This did momentarily rip his mouth from her heated skin, but the moment he was free of the shirt, he went back to loving her with his mouth.

She could feel him now, *all* of him. "When did you lose the rest of your clothes—Oh my God," she cried out, eyes crossing with lust when he did something in combination with his teeth, his tongue, and his fingers. "Don't stop doing that."

"Never," he promised as he played with her, teasing

her to the very edge. But just as she felt her toes start to curl, he stopped and she cried out.

He only flashed a wicked smile, not at all concerned that he was a fraction of an inch from certain death for leaving her hanging like that. Leaning up over her, he gave her one hard kiss and then hooked his long fingers in the sides of her panties, tugging them down her legs, sending them sailing over his shoulder without taking his eyes off of her.

And what he'd exposed.

"Oh, Willa. Christ." His big hands held her thighs open. "You're so gorgeous." Surging up, he kissed her mouth, his hands still tormenting her, the sensations skittering down her every nerve ending with a little *zing*, driving her back to the edge she'd never really left. She dug her fingers into his biceps.

"If you stop again—"

"I won't." And true to his word, he continued the assault, the sexy bastard, slowly kissing his way south, stopping at her belly button to take a little nibble out of her, making her squirm.

Laughing softly against her, he tightened his grip on her hips, holding her still so he could drive her crazy. This involved his mouth taking the scenic route, where he alternately dragged his tongue along her heated skin and stopped once every other breath or so to take a little love bite.

"Keane!"

He lifted his head, his eyes dark, so dark she nearly drowned in them. "Last time we did this your way," he said. "It's my turn now. My way, Willa."

She swallowed hard at the heat and fierce intensity of his low voice. "And your way is to torture me?"

He flashed another wicked grin. "To start."

With a groan, she flopped back to the bed, arms over her head.

"Yeah, I like that," Keane said and reached up, stroking his hands along her arms to her fingers, which he wrapped around the bottom rung of the headboard. "Don't let go." Then he held her open, groaned at the visual, and licked the length of her center.

Willa got a little fuzzy on the details after that but they involved her moaning his name nonstop and fisting her hands in his hair, and after a shockingly short time, coming apart for him.

Completely.

His body was hard and muscular and felt amazing against hers and she forced her eyes to open to take in as much as possible because this was absolutely going to have to be it. She couldn't do this again with him and not hopelessly fall. In fact, she was only half convinced that she could resist doing so *this* time.

Braced on his forearms on either side of her head, he looked down at her. A lock of hair fell over his forehead, his eyes dark with heat and sexy concentration, his mouth still wet. The sight of him took her breath.

God, *he* was the beautiful one, she thought dazedly. Simply beautiful. Reaching up, she traced his bottom lip with a fingertip and then tugged him closer so she could suck that lower lip into her mouth.

He gave a half groan, half growl as she slid her tongue into his mouth, sliding it along his.

"Love the taste of you," he said and thrust inside of her.

She cried out and arched up to meet him, unable to figure out when he'd put on a condom, but grateful one of them was thinking with something other than their pleasure buttons.

Above her, Keane's eyes drifted shut, his expression uninhibited pleasure.

He took her breath.

He had one arm beneath her shoulders to anchor her, the other gripping her ass as if he needed to be as close as possible. When he began to move, it was in a slow, lazy grind, like he had all the time in the world to love her.

But he didn't. Given the lump in her throat, they were on a time crunch now, before panic hit. So she shoved him, rolling him to his back. To his credit, he went easily, flashing a wolf smile.

"Your turn?" he asked huskily, his voice pure sex.

Not wasting her breath with words, she rocked her hips, fast and hard.

"Yeah," he murmured, filling his hands with her breasts. "Your turn."

Then he became the backseat driver, reaching between them, touching her intimately, knowingly, causing her to explode all over him.

While she was still dazed, she felt his hands shift her, snugging her inner thighs tighter to the outsides of his, causing him to fill her even more, taking her on an out-of-body experience. And this time when she began to convulse around him, he followed her over the edge.

Early the next morning, Willa came awake all warm and toasty, her face smooshed into the crook of Keane's neck. He was flat on his back, out cold, and she . . . well, she was all over him.

Petunia was no better, having made herself at home on his feet.

Willa put a finger to her lips and very carefully eased away and dashed into her bathroom. She caught a look at herself in the mirror and blinked at the flushed, dazed expression on her face. Was she . . . smiling? Damn, she was. She tried to turn it into a frown but couldn't. She literally couldn't.

That's when she noticed the duffel bag on the floor. Keane must've brought it in last night when he'd run out to his truck to get his phone charger somewhere around midnight.

The bag was unzipped and she accidentally-on-purpose took a peek inside. Extra clothes. A toothbrush. Deodorant.

In her hand, her phone beeped and scared her half into an early grave. "Hello?" she whispered.

"Hey," Elle said. "I—"

"He's got a one-night-stand kit!" she whispered.

Elle paused. "Who has a what?"

Willa shut the bathroom door, leaned back against it, and let her weak legs collapse, sliding down the door until she was sitting on the floor. "Keane," she said. "He showed up here last night to pick up Petunia and now I'm in the bathroom looking at a duffel bag full of his stuff that—"

"Whoa. You can't just go from last night to this morning without more details than that! What's the matter with you? I want the good stuff. You slept with him again?"

Well, technically, there'd been very little actual sleep involved both on the roof *or* last night, which had been one round after another of torrid, erotic, sensual sex such as she'd never known.

"You're holding out on me," Elle said.

"Forget that!" Willa whispered. "He has a *one-night-* stand kit!" Okay, technically last night made night two, so it was really a two-night-stand kit.

"Honey, that just makes him a smart man."

Willa rolled her eyes so hard they nearly fell out of her head and she disconnected. Things were fine. She was fine. She could do this. One-night stands turned into two-night stands all the time. In fact, she stared at Keane's stuff and could admit that maybe Elle was right. Not that she was about to admit it because Elle already knew she was right.

Elle was always right.

Willa slipped into the only clothes she had in the bathroom—yesterday's work clothes. She did this because she could think better when she wasn't naked. A quick peek in the mirror confirmed she was still smiling like an idiot. She took a deep breath and opened the door.

Keane stood there propping up the doorjamb with a beefy shoulder, expression slightly wary. "Hey."

"Hey."

He gave her a half smile. "Gotta be honest. I figured you'd be long gone when I woke up."

"It's my place."

"You know what I mean," he said. He wasn't playing this morning.

So she wouldn't either. "I'm working hard at being a grown-up," she said. "And that would have been rude anyway."

His smile spread and sent warmth skittering through her. "God forbid you be rude." He tugged her into him and nuzzled at her neck. "Mornin'."

Since her knees wobbled, she clutched at him. "Mornin'. Um, Keane?"

"Mmm?" His mouth was busy at her throat and he was big and warm and shirtless, and her eyes nearly rolled back in her head.

"I really do have to get to work," she managed. "It's later than I usually get started. You can stay, of course, use my shower, whatever. Just lock up when you go."

He lifted his head and met her gaze. Searched it. And then apparently decided she was indeed to be trusted being a grown-up because he nodded.

Relief that they were handling this without hurt or hard feelings, and even better yet, a discussion that she wasn't ready to have, she leaned in and kissed him, going for short and sweet.

But he tightened his grip, changed the angle of her kiss and took over in Keane fashion. By the time he let her go, she had to search her brain for what her game plan had been.

"Work," he said with a smile. "We both have to get to work."

"Right." She blinked. "Um . . ."

With a low laugh, he put his hands on her hips and turned her toward the living room, adding a light smack on her ass to get her moving. "Have a good one."

She'd had so many orgasms the night before that she couldn't count them. She was wearing a perma-smile. What could go wrong?

Chapter 22

#ThrowingShade

When Willa was gone, Keane looked down at Pita, sitting calmly near his bare feet.

She regarded him from down the length of her nose and gave a little sniff.

"Yeah, yeah," he said. "You're stuck with me again."

His phone was having a seizure on the nightstand, full of texts and emails from Sass and Mason. He scrubbed a hand down over his face and swore when the phone went off again, this time a call from Sass. He hit ignore.

"Mew," Pita said, going for pathetic.

"I know. Food. Pronto." He pulled on his jeans and searched out his shirt, finding it hanging from a lampshade.

Normally this would've given him a smile because it meant the night had been suitably down and dirty and sexy hot.

And it had been those things.

It'd also been a helluva lot more. Which he figured was the real reason Willa had taken off so early for work. She was feeling it.

But she didn't want to.

Not the best feeling in the world. Pulling the shirt over his head, he turned in a circle looking for his shoes.

Petunia was sitting in front of them looking very smug and happy with herself.

"Move, cat."

For once in her life, she did as he asked. She moved—revealing that she'd once again used his shoes as her own personal kitty litter.

Willa sat on the counter of her own shop in yesterday's clothes, stuffing her face with Tina's out-of-this-world muffins.

The muffins didn't fix anything that was wrong with her life, but they did make her feel better.

It was still early, way before opening time, a fact for which she was grateful. At some point she'd have to figure out how to eke an extra hour out of her day in order to get upstairs to her apartment and out of yesterday's clothes. She'd also have to figure out how to lose the ridiculously sated, just-laid expression still all over her face, but so far it was refusing to go away.

Damn orgasms.

Rory and Cara showed up and took one look at her and smiled. "Are you making the walk of shame in your own shop?" Cara asked.

Yes. "Of course not."

Rory eyeballed Willa up one side and down the other. "Actually," the girl said, "the true walk of shame is when you take all the mugs and plates you've been hoarding from your nightstand to your kitchen."

They both laughed.

Willa ignored them and popped the last muffin into her mouth. She took a moment to close her eyes and moan as the delicious pumpkin spice burst onto her tongue.

"She's not talking," Cara said to Rory. "That's weird. I've never seen her not talk."

"As soon as the caffeine kicks in she'll come back to life." Rory nudged Willa's coffee closer to her and then backed away like Willa might be a cocked and loaded shotgun.

"But she doesn't look tired," Cara said, staring at Willa. "She looks like how my sister looks when her boyfriend's on leave from the Army and they boink all night long."

Willa choked on her muffin.

Rory pounded her on the back, flashing a rare grin as Elle and Haley and Pru knocked on the back door.

Willa came to life with sudden panic. "Don't let them in!"

So of course Rory let them in. "Watch out," her soon-to-be-dead employee said to her best friends. "She's not fully caffeinated and I think she's also had a lot of sex."

Willa choked again. She glared at everyone, but her best friends were in possession of more muffins and coffee, so she held out her hands. "Gimme."

Pru handed everything over. "Sorry I had to bail on girls' night, but I'm feeling much better." She studied Willa's face, head cocked. "Hmm. Keane's good. He even got rid of the stress wrinkle between her eyes."

"Wow," Haley said, peering in close to see for herself. "You're right. Sex works better than that ninety-buck wrinkle lotion we all bought that doesn't work worth shit."

Willa glanced at Elle, who was standing there quietly assessing the situation. "I'm going to need you to say something here, Elle. You know, be your usual voice of reason so I don't murder anyone."

"There's no Netflix in prison," Elle said.

"Okay, that'll do it, thanks."

Elle tipped her coffee to Willa's in a toast of solidarity.

Willa drank her coffee and let out her biggest fear. "Am I being stupid? Letting another guy in? Is this a mistake?"

"Is he as good a guy as he seems?" Pru asked.

Willa thought about it. "He doesn't like cats and yet he's taking care of Petunia. He's financially taking care of his sick aunt even though he barely knows her. He's got an incredibly demanding career going but he always makes time for me. And . . ."

"What?" Elle pressed quietly when Willa broke off.

"He makes me feel good," she said. "Special." She felt a little ridiculous even saying it and her face heated.

But Elle smiled and it was the kind of smile that reached all the way to her eyes. Rare and beautiful. "Well then," she said, squeezing Willa's hands. "There's your answer."

"But I think I blew it," Willa said. "He stayed over last night and I woke up and . . ."

"Panicked," Elle said helpfully.

Willa blew out a sigh and held up her finger and thumb about an inch apart. "Maybe just a very little bit."

Elle held up her own two hands, two feet apart. "Or a lot." She looked at Willa. "I still don't get why you can't just enjoy a hot man and hot sex. You can always bail when and if it fizzles out."

"But what if it doesn't fizzle?" Willa asked. "What then?"

"You enjoy it," Elle said gently.

Right. Why hadn't she thought of that?

"What did you do?" Haley asked. "Kick him out?"

"Worse," Elle said, looking amused.

Willa put her hands to her hot cheeks. "I ran out of my own place like the hounds of hell were on my heels."

Haley bit her lower lip.

Pru didn't have the same decorum. She didn't bother to try to keep her laugh in; she let it out and in fact almost fell over she was laughing so hard.

Elle shook her head. "I tried to tell her—*never* leave a hot man alone in your bed."

Well, technically he hadn't been still in bed when she'd left but why had she left again? Willa honestly couldn't remember her justifications for that, which left the only possible answer.

She was running scared and that just plain pissed her off about herself. Since when was she a scaredy-cat?

She hopped off the counter, pointing at Pru. "You're off today?"

"Yes."

"You're officially an employee. Rory will tell you what to do. We're having a big sale and she'll need extra hands on deck. I'll be back!"

"But why me?" Pru called after her.

"Because you laughed the hardest."

"Well, shit," Pru said.

It was still early when Keane got out of his truck, jogged up the stairs to the Vallejo Street house, and quietly shut the door behind him. Coast clear. All he had to do now was get up the stairs to his shower without being seen and—

"Whoa," Sass said from behind him.

Fuck.

"Mas!" she yelled. "Come look at this."

Keane turned to face her, eyes narrowed.

She smiled sweetly as she looked at her watch. "How nice of you to show up for work today. We've been calling you."

"I've been busy."

She ran her gaze down the length of him and came to a stop at his bare feet. "Where are your shoes? Under her bed?"

Actually, they were in the Dumpster, not that he was about to tell Sass that. He thrust out Petunia's carrier. "Take this," he said. "I'm going to shower. I'll meet you in the office for the morning meeting in ten—"

Someone knocked on the door and grateful for the interruption, Keane hauled it open.

Willa stood there chewing on her lower lip, looking a little bit unsettled that he'd opened the door so quickly.

He didn't know why he was so surprised. She'd been surprising him continuously from the moment she'd let him into her shop that first morning three weeks ago now and saved his ass by taking Pita.

"Hey," she said quietly. "I—" She broke off and looked beyond him.

Keane turned and realized that Sass was watching avidly. Mason walked into the foyer as well, eyes on his phone as he spoke. "It's about damn time, boss. You ignored my calls all morning—which is a huge infraction of the rules, as you like to remind us every other second—" He raised his head from his phone and eyed the situation. He winced, turned on his heel, and walked back out.

Not Sass. She stood there smiling wide. "Hi," she said, reaching out a hand to Willa. "I'm Sass, Keane's admin. And you're Willa, or as we like to say around here, The Amazing Person Who Makes the Boss Smile. We love you, by the way."

"Thanks," Willa said. "I think."

"I've seen you before," Sass said. "At O'Riley's Pub. You were up onstage doing karaoke with two of your friends, singing Wilson Phillips's 'Hold On' like it was your job."

Willa grimaced. "Oh boy."

Sass smiled. "Yeah, you guys were a lot of fun. If you ever get Keane up there to sing, I'm going to need it recorded."

"Okay," Keane said, pulling Willa inside before turning to Sass. "I'm sure you have to go back to work now."

Sass smiled. "Yes, with you. We're not done with our morning meeting. We were just getting to the why you've been ignoring phone calls, texts, and emails, but I'm guessing the reason just showed up."

Keane pointed down the hall. "I'll be there in a minute."

"Oh, don't postpone a meeting for my sake," Willa said hurriedly. "You're busy. I'm just going to go—"

Keane grabbed her hand. "Wait. It'll only take me a minute to kill Sass—"

"If I had a dime for every time he said that," Sass quipped.

Keane didn't take his eyes off Willa. "Please?" he added quietly and was relieved when she nodded. He then turned to Sass. She was still smiling at him, the kind of smile that said she was getting a lot of mileage out of this. Reluctantly letting go of Willa, he nodded at Sass to follow him.

"Don't start," he warned as they moved down the hall, hopefully out of hearing range. "I know damn well that if it'd been an emergency, you'd have let me know. You were snooping just now because I'm never late. I don't pay you to snoop, Sass, so get your ass to work."

She kept grinning.

"Don't pay you to grin at me either."

"Well, honestly," a woman said. "That's no way to talk to the people you care about."

Keane glanced over into what would eventually be the dining room but at the moment was a blueprint room. Meaning there were several pairs of sawhorses set up with large planks of plywood as makeshift tables. Covering these tables were the blueprints of the building.

The woman was standing amongst the sawhorses, glaring at him.

He blew out a sigh. "Mom, it's called sarcasm. That's how we show we care."

"Well, it's hurtful," she said. "I taught you better than that."

No, actually, what she'd taught him was to show no feelings at all. He looked at Sass, who'd clearly let his mom in.

Sass smiled. "Meet the emergency."

Keane turned back to his mom. She'd not stopped by any of his jobs for a long time, and in fact, they'd talked just last month, so . . . "What's wrong?"

His mom straightened and came toward him. If she noticed his bare feet or the fact that he was still carrying a cat carrier because Sass hadn't taken it from him, she gave no indication.

"I wanted to tell you that we're all done with the rental," she said. "Which I assume you know because you deposited money into our account. We don't want money from you, Keane. That wasn't part of the deal."

His parents had both retired two years ago. And

because they'd assumed they were the smartest people they knew, they refused his advice for years regarding getting a financial planner. So when they'd invested their funds with a "friend who knows what he's doing" and that friend took off with all their money, they hadn't wanted to admit it.

In fact, Keane had only found all this out when he'd inadvertently learned from a mutual acquaintance that they'd gotten an eviction notice. They'd finally admitted that they were broke and because of that might soon be homeless, but they still refused to take money from him.

So he'd been forced to let them "work" for him instead. He'd put them up in an apartment building he owned in South Beach. In return they insisted on helping him renovate the place in lieu of paying rent. Just until they got on their feet.

It'd been a serious pain in his ass because he and his mom had butted heads on every single renovation the building had required.

But at least they weren't in the streets. "You could have just called me," he said.

His mother nodded. "I did. Your admin said you weren't taking calls and suggested I stop by."

Sass slid him a . . . well, sassy look. He returned the volley with a "you're fired" look but she just smiled at him serenely.

She knew as well as he did that she was the glue. His glue. It would be comforting if he didn't want to strangle her more than half the time.

"Anyway . . ." His mother made a big show of holding out a set of keys. "Wanted to give these back to you."

He didn't take them. "Mom, you can stay there. You don't have to go."

"But we're done with the work."

"Stay there," he repeated. He didn't want them out on the streets. He didn't want to have to worry about them. "It's no big deal."

"No big deal?" she asked, looking as if he'd just suggested she murdered kittens for a living. "You giving us a handout is *no big deal?* Well, I'm glad to know we mean so little to you then."

"You know that's not what I meant."

"I'll have you know we have plenty of other options," she said stiffly. "Your sisters, for one. Janine wants us in her house with her. With her child, so that we could be a *part* of their lives. Rachel would have us as well."

Okay, so he stood corrected. She absolutely *could* make this more difficult. And he knew firsthand that his sisters were just making noise with the offer to host them. Janine's husband would probably run for the hills if that happened. James was a decent enough guy but he was smart enough to have hard limits, and living with the elder Winterses was definitely a hard limit.

"By all means," Keane said. "If that's what would make you happy. But the offer to stay in my apartment building stands."

Her lips tightened.

And because he wasn't a complete asshole, he

sighed. "Listen, I really could use someone to manage the place, to keep up with the building and the renters' needs."

She stared at him for a beat, clearly torn between choking on her own pride or calling his bluff calling hers. Finally she snatched the keys back from his held-out palm and shoved them in her pocket.

"We'll keep a careful accounting of our work, crediting it back for rent," she said.

"Mom, I trust you."

"Expect monthly reports," she said.

The equivalent of a hug and kiss and an "I love you, son."

She turned to the door and then stopped. Still facing the door, she said, "And I know that's Sally's cat. You're helping her too."

"She's family," he said and then he lied out his ass. "And the cat's no problem."

"You're doing more than just taking care of her cat," his mom said. "Sally called me yesterday and told me everything."

Keane let out a low breath. "Then you know that me helping her is the least I can do."

She didn't say anything for a long beat, did nothing but take a small sniff that struck terror in his heart.

Was she . . . crying? He'd never seen her lose it and truthfully, he'd rather someone ripped out his fingernails one by one than see it now. "Mom—"

"I'm fine." She sniffed again and then still talking to the door softly said, "I was the teacher, for twenty-five years. But sometimes you teach me things I didn't expect."

He stared at her, stunned.

"Well," she said with a nod. "I'm off. I'll call you, keep you updated."

"You don't have to—"

"I'll call you," she repeated and he realized that she was trying, in the only way she knew how, to stay in his life.

"That would be nice," he said. "I'll call you too, okay?"

Her voice was soft and there was an unmistakable sense of relief in her voice. "Okay."

And then she was gone.

He turned and caught the flash of someone ducking behind a doorway. A petite, insatiably curious redheaded someone. Slowly she peeked back out and winced when her eyes locked on him.

She was cautious of getting in too deep with him and besides the fact that he'd come right out and told her he didn't do deep, she was right to be wary. Giving in to this thing between them would be insanity, and having his mother remind him of the way he was wired, how the entire family was wired—with an utter lack of the giving-someone-your-heart gene—had been a wake-up call. Willa was dodging a bullet here and she didn't even know it.

"You okay?" she asked quietly.

Was he? He had no idea, not that he was about to admit it. "Yeah." He thought maybe he could see some pity in her gaze and he pretty much hated everything about that so he gave a vague wave at the place around him. "I've really got to get to work."

She nodded, but didn't move. Instead she clasped her hands tight together and held his gaze. "I wanted to explain my abrupt departure this morning. It's just that when I woke up wrapped around you like one of those amazingly delicious warm pretzels at AT&T Park, I . . ."

"Panicked?"

"No," she said. "Well, okay, yes, but only for a few minutes. I don't regret last night, Keane. I just wanted you to know that. I'm sorry—"

"Willa, stop," he said, interrupting her. Both this morning with her on top of the visit with his mom had left him feeling a little hollow and far too raw to deal with any more heavy emotions. "Forget it, okay? It was nothing."

She looked a little stunned at that and it took him a second to realize she thought he was saying what they'd shared was nothing. "Not what I meant," he said, but since he didn't know what he *did* mean, he fell silent.

She nodded like she knew though, which he was glad about. Someone should know what the fuck was going on here. His tool belt was lying on one of the sawhorses and he put it on, hopefully signaling he was good with no further conversation.

She took a deep breath. "If this is about me hearing that conversation with your mom—"

"It's not."

"Because it's not your fault how she treats you," she said.

"Yes, it is. I was a rotten kid, Willa. I was," he said firmly when she opened her mouth. "I get that some of it was because I didn't get a lot of positive attention, but that's no excuse."

She was arms crossed now, defensive for him, clearly not willing to believe the worst of him, all of which did something painful and also a little wonderful inside his chest.

"What could you possibly have done that was so bad?"

"For one, I was a complete shit. Even after I graduated high school. They gave me tuition money to complement a partial football scholarship for two years, until I got injured and blew the scholarship. I hated every second of school, by the way. So when they gave me tuition for year three, I quit and used the money for the down payment for my first renovation project."

"I take it they didn't approve."

"I didn't tell them for several years," he admitted.

Her eyes widened.

"See?" he asked. "A complete shit. I paid them back with interest, but the point is that as a result of my own actions, they don't trust me very much."

"Not everyone is made for the academic life."

He shook his head. "Don't make excuses for me, Willa."

"Well someone has to give you a break," she said, tossing up her hands. "You've worked pretty hard to help your aunt and your family. You've worked hard to make something of yourself and—" She broke off and looked at him as if she'd never seen him before.

"What?"

"Oh my God," she whispered. "I just realized something. I accused you of not being able to attach. But clearly you can, and deeply."

He started to shake his head but stopped because given his growing attachment to her, not to mention some extraordinarily deep emotions on the same subject, she was right.

"And not only can you obviously love and love deeply," she said slowly, putting a hand to her chest like it hurt. "You can even hold on to it. Maybe even better than me. Hell, *definitely* better than me."

His chest got tight at the thought of her believing that about herself. "Willa—"

"I know, right? Not a super comfortable feeling." She paused when from inside his pocket, his phone went off.

It'd been doing so for the past half hour. Subcontractors, clients . . . probably Sass as well. And even as he thought it, a well-dressed couple parked out front.

Clients with whom he had a meeting with in . . . he looked at his watch. Shit. Right now.

"The real world calls," Willa said and took a step back.

"This is my real world," he said. "They can wait."

"Keane," Marco Delgado, a longtime client, called out with a smile. "Good to see you, my man."

"It's okay," Willa said as she moved farther away.

Kind of the story of his life really.

"You understood this morning when I needed to get to work," she said, "and I understand this."

And then she was gone.

Shit. Whelp, he was happy to know she understood. He just wished he knew exactly what she understood and if she would explain it to him.

Chapter 23

#SquadGoals

Willa went to the shop. The shop had always been her escape, her joy, her first and only love.

But as she walked in with all the Christmas lights sparkling and a customer's dog barking at her stuffed Rudolf the Red-Nosed Reindeer sitting on the kitty-litter display, and Rory smiling and handling customers from two different corners of the place, she didn't feel the usual calm wash over her.

She hadn't felt calm since she'd woken up that morning but especially not after overhearing the conversation between Keane and his mom. Because now she knew an uncomfortable truth about herself. She'd been cruising along with Keane, secure in the knowledge that he wasn't interested in love, but there was a fatal flaw with that.

It was all on her. *She* was the one with the issues.

She hadn't seen that coming.

Luckily her day was long, not allowing her much time to think or dwell. And at the end of it, she looked around for more to do but there wasn't anything. And yet she didn't want to go home. Going home alone would remind her that she was . . .

Well, alone.

So she went to the pub, where Finn immediately caught her eye and gestured her over. "Try this," he said, handing her a mug. "Homemade whipped cream over the best, most amazing hot chocolate ever invented."

"How many ways are there to make hot chocolate?"

"Only one way," he said. "My way." He gestured to the mug. "It's a new recipe, a surprise for Pru. Tell me what you think."

She sipped and he was right. It was the most amazing hot chocolate ever invented. "Oh my God."

He smiled. "Yeah?"

"Oh yeah. It's orgasmic."

He grimaced and took the mug away from her. "Not in my pub."

She could see Spence and Archer in the back arguing over the darts and knew she could go back there and join them. Knew too that Finn would make her his famous chicken wings if she wanted. But for the first time in as long as she could remember, she didn't want to be here either.

Finn's smile vanished. "Hey. What's wrong?"

"Nothing."

"Willa." He leaned in. "Don't bullshit a bullshitter. I know you better than just about anyone. Something's wrong." He studied her a minute. "Is it Keane? Do I need to beat the shit out of him?"

She choked out a laugh. "You think you could?"

"No, but I could get Archer to do it. Archer could make him disappear and no one'd ever be the wiser. Just say the word."

"No!" She laughed again, but it faded fast. "No," she repeated firmly and shook her head. "This one's on me."

"Fine. We'll help you bury the body. Just name the time and place."

"You're not even going to ask me why?"

"I don't need to know why."

That was the thing about Finn, and the others as well. They loved her like family should. Unconditionally. Without question. No doubt. No hesitation.

No qualifiers.

And even though Finn was just teasing, she knew if she ever needed something, anything at all, he'd be there for her.

Always.

Her throat tightened because she loved knowing that, but at the moment it wasn't what she needed.

He caught her hand as she slid off the barstool. "Seriously, what can I do?" he asked quietly.

"You've already done it." She brushed a kiss over his jaw. "Thanks."

She took herself to the rooftop. She climbed the fire escape and then stilled as she was bombarded with flashes of the last time she'd been here. Keane's hands holding her over him, his mouth at her ear whispering dirty sweet nothings, his hard body driving hers . . .

The breath escaped her lungs and her knees wobbled.

She'd come here to be alone to wallow, but now all she could do was ache . . .

When the stairwell door opened and a pair of obviously women's heels clicked their way across the rubber composite, she sighed. "Unless you have food with you, go away."

"Who do you think I am?" Elle, of course. "I've got food *and* wine," she said. Always prepared, she stopped next to where Willa sat right on the rooftop without anything to protect her clothing and shook her head. "Clothes deserve respect, honey. Serious respect."

"I'm in Levi's," Willa pointed out.

"Levi's deserve respect right along with Tory Burch." Elle searched her bag and came up with a *Cosmo* magazine. She tossed this to the ground and then carefully sat on it. "This is how much I love you. I'm sitting on the ground in a dress and heels." She handed over a box of Finn's wings.

"What's this?" Willa asked.

"A bribe."

And that's when Pru popped her head up over the ledge from the fire escape. "Is the coast clear?"

Elle waved her over. Willa knew Elle hadn't used the fire escape herself because one, climbing it in heels was a death sentence, and two, she only did things where she could look cool and gorgeous, and no one looked cool or gorgeous climbing the fire escape.

Pru climbed over the ledge, followed by Haley.

"I'm not in the mood to talk," Willa warned them.

"I remember a time when I said the exact same thing to you," Pru said and sat on Willa's other side.

"And I respected your wishes and left you alone."

Pru laughed good and long over that. "Hell, no, you didn't. You sat right next to me and held my hand while we marathoned *Say Yes to The Dress*. Elle got drunk."

"I did not," Elle said.

"Right," Pru said. "That was me. My point is, we're not leaving you alone."

Haley was beaming at them. "You know what this is right here? It's squad goals."

Elle pointed at her. "You need to cut back on Instagram."

Willa took the box of wings and dug in. "You guys don't have to stay. I'm not sharing the wings and there's nothing to watch."

"Well now that's just an insult to the universe," Haley said and pointed to the sky.

Which was a glorious blanket of black velvet littered with diamonds as far as the eye could see.

It was gorgeous, Willa could admit. "I'm pretty sure the universe is feminine. A male would've messed that all up."

Haley snorted in agreement.

"So men suck," Elle said. "What's new about that?"

Pru, the only one of them in a sturdy, stable, loving relationship, shook her head in disagreement. "Men are just flawed, is all. And that's a good thing."

"How?" Willa asked. "How in the world is that a good thing?"

"Hello, have you never heard of makeup sex?"

Willa thought about sex with Keane and sighed. It was pretty amazing. Off-the-charts amazing. She could only imagine what makeup sex would be like . . .

"They don't mean to be dumbasses," Pru said. "But sometimes they just can't help it. That's just how they're wired. But I've gotta say, Willa, Keane seems like a really good guy."

"You're certainly glowing like I've never seen you glow," Haley said.

Everyone looked Willa over closely and she swallowed a bite of delicious chicken wing and rolled her eyes. "If I'm glowing, it's from sweating in the shop all day."

"You haven't done anything for yourself in far too long," Haley said. "You should do Keane."

Everyone burst out laughing and Haley shook her head. "Okay, not what I meant. But hey, whatever works."

"I think I need a moment from . . . doing Keane," Willa said.

"Why?" Pru asked.

Wasn't that just the question? She knew she was giving off wishy-washy vibes but she wasn't being wishy-washy so much as she was going after one desire while protecting the other.

Meaning she wanted Keane in her bed. Oh how she wanted that . . . while somehow also keeping her heart protected.

The ship might have sailed there, she thought . . .

Yeah, it was too late. And if she'd been smart, she would have cut her losses before now. But she so loved being intimate with Keane, loved everything about it, and she'd had this fantasy that she could somehow keep the goodness of that separate from her growing emotions for him.

That ship had sailed too.

"It's a new development," she admitted. "See, in the beginning it was him who didn't want anything too serious, while I was ready to find a partner."

"And now?" Elle asked.

"And now . . ." Willa closed her eyes. "I want to keep sleeping with him but I don't want to call it a relationship. What does that make me?"

"A man," Elle said.

"Honey, I don't see the problem," Pru said over their laughter. "He's not going to get attached, you just said so. Go for it. But I have to warn you that sometimes really great sex turns into really great intimacy, which can then turn into a really great relationship before you even realize it."

Willa shook her head. She'd never been in a really great relationship; no need to start believing in that now. "I don't think we can move forward without a conversation. I think he wants to define things. We were on the brink of that this morning but luckily his work got in the way."

"Hey, I've got an idea," Haley said. "Call him over and then take off your top and distract him from talking. What?" she said when everyone just stared at her. "Willa has great boobs."

Elle eyed Willa's boobs critically. "It's true. Women pay big bucks for a rack like that."

Willa looked down at herself. She was short. A more polite word was *petite*. But in height only because everywhere else she wasn't dainty. She had curves. Hips. The aforementioned boobs. Even her stomach was a little too curvy to suit her but no amount of sit-ups or exercising seemed to help that.

Or at least she was pretty sure sit-ups and exercise wouldn't help. "He's too smart to fall for that. He'll see right through the distraction technique." She dropped her head to her knees. "Damn. I was so sure this wasn't in danger of going anywhere, that *he* wasn't relationship material . . ."

"And now?" Elle asked.

"And now . . . I'm realizing *I'm* the one who isn't relationship material." There. She said it. Admitted her biggest failing out loud.

Her friends gasped in instant denial, but Willa knew she was right and her heart felt heavy with it. "I'm not sure what to do here," she said softly. "I think I'm . . . broken."

"No," Elle said adamantly and everyone else piped in with equally emphatic *no*s.

"Please," Willa said. "Let's just move on to another topic, okay? How about those Niners, right?"

"You can't just ignore this," Pru said. "At least go back to having great sex!"

Haley nodded vehemently.

Willa had to laugh. "Just tell him right out that all I want is sex?"

"*Great* sex," Pru corrected.

"Agreed," Elle said. "Men do it all the time so why not?"

Willa looked at them. "So you honestly think I should just show him my boobs."

"Always works for me," Pru said. "When Finn and I get in a fight, I flash him and he forgets what we're fighting about. Boobs are magic."

Willa shook her head. "Nothing's ever that easy." At least not for her.

"Hang mistletoe and lure him in," Haley said. "Put it up in a convenient place, but not *too* convenient because you don't want to have to kiss any toads by accident."

"Oh, and lose your bra," Pru said. "He'll be so preoccupied, he'll never know what hit him. Guaranteed."

Haley was nodding. "So see, you have your plan. One, shave all the way up past the knee. Two, hang some mistletoe. Three, lose the bra. Four, call him over and let the good times begin. And then after the good times, when he doesn't quite have all the blood back to his brain, tell him you're okay with being just friends with benefits. It's every guy's dream come true. Just make sure to spell out what exactly the benefits are so he doesn't think you mean a threesome or anal. Tell him preapproved benefits only."

Pru choked on her wine and Elle had to beat her over the back.

Haley smiled. "I think it's perfect. Honestly, he'll never know what hit him. *Wait!*" She wore a small backpack as a purse and pulled it off to paw through it. "And these, take these!" She held up a set of spiked handcuffs.

This time they all stared at her, agog. Well, except for Elle, who took them and looked them over. "Nice."

"They were a Christmas gag gift," Haley said. "Office holiday party last night."

"From that pretty brunette temp receptionist?" Elle asked.

Haley blushed. "I wish. No, which is why I'm willing to give them up to Willa for the cause."

"Thanks," Willa said dryly. "Your sacrifice is duly noted, but not necessary. I do *not* need handcuffs."

"Oh, I don't need handcuffs to enslave a man either," Elle said, slipping them into her purse. "But it never hurts. The key?" she asked Haley. "Because it's all fun and games until someone loses the key . . ."

Haley handed over a small key.

Pru snorted wine out her nose again, and it was mayhem after that but somehow, after another few glasses of wine, The Plan suddenly seemed totally and completely feasible.

Friends with benefits . . .

What could go wrong?

Chapter 24

#ThatsWhatSheSaid

The next day Keane ran from jobsite to jobsite putting out fires. By the time he got back to his office and dropped into his chair at his desk to catch up on paperwork, he was done in.

Which was a good thing. Being this tired made it difficult to think about what had happened between him and Willa.

Or more accurately, what wasn't going to happen between him and Willa.

Shit. Opening his laptop, he froze when something brushed against his legs.

Pita was winding herself in and around his calves, rubbing herself all over his jeans and leaving a trail of hair as she did so.

"You must be desperate if you're willing to be friendly to me," he said.

At that, she leapt into his lap, turned in a circle, and then plopped with zero grace to lie all over him.

"Okay," he said, awkwardly patting her on the head. "We're doing this then."

A rumbly purr filled the room and she began to knead with her paws. When one of her needle-sharp claws caught on his crotch, he yelped and jumped to his feet, unceremoniously dumping her to the floor.

Paws spread wide, hunkered low to the floor, she looked up at him from slitted eyes.

"Well then, watch the damn claws, Jesus."

She turned away, tail straight up in the air, quivering with temper. And he knew—she was *so* going to take a shit in his shoes tonight. "Dammit, wait." He caught up with her and scooped her back up, sitting in the chair again, setting her next to him. "Stay," he said.

She shot him a look that spoke volumes on her opinion of being commanded to do anything, but she did indeed stay.

He was knee-deep into the engineering notes on the Mission project when he got a text.

Willa:
Can you come over after work? Need your help with something.

He stared at the words and felt an onslaught of emotions that he wasn't equipped to deal with. Hunger. Desire. Aching desire. How was it possible that a month ago he'd thought his life was just fine, but now he had this person in it who added color and laughter, one he had an amazing connection with, such as he'd never felt before, and he couldn't remember what he did without her?

He couldn't imagine what the woman who never asked for help could need, but it didn't matter. He'd do anything she needed. He got up and looked at Pita. "Behave."

She gave him a look that was a firm "maybe but probably not."

Shaking his head, he moved to the door.

"Whoa," Sass called from her desk in the next room over. "Whatcha doing?"

"Gotta go."

"There's a stack of stuff here for you to go over and—"

"Gotta go," he repeated.

She searched his gaze a moment. "So it's like that, is it?" She shook her head. "You poor bastard."

He drove to the Pacific Pier Building, parked, and walked through the courtyard.

Eddie was standing by the fountain, watching the water. Someone had given him a down parka with fur hood and he looked warm and happy.

"Found my cheer," he said to Keane.

Keane noted the flask in the guy's hand and smiled. "Good."

"You find yours? Cuz I got some mistletoe if you need."

"I'm good," Keane said. "But thanks."

"Understood." Eddie nodded. "There can be a lot of trouble with mistletoe . . ." He paused. "Or women."

Amen to that . . .

Keane took the stairs to Willa's door—which was ajar.

"Come in," she yelled from inside.

Frowning that she'd left her door not only unlocked but open, he walked in. Willa was high on a ladder next to the biggest tree he'd ever seen stuffed inside an apartment this size. She was looking festive and gorgeous in a short black skirt, black knee-high boots, and a bright red hoodie sweater snug to her every curve.

He looked his fill, loving the way the skirt clung to the sweet curves of her ass, enjoying the look at her legs. He loved them best wrapped around him but this was a good view too.

"I made a special holiday drink and I needed a taster," she said, backlit by the strings of lights across her faux mantel. When she turned to face him, he got the full impact of her front view. The strings on her hoodie sweater were weighted by tassels that bounced around right at breast height, drawing his gaze there. Four words were embroidered across her chest—*Dear Santa, Define "Naughty."*

And Keane realized something else he loved about the sweater—she was braless.

"What's going on?" he asked.

"I was hoping to bribe you into helping me hang some decorations."

He laughed. "You're putting up *more* decorations?"

"You know, I can sense the sarcasm there but I'm going to ignore it." Twisting, she met his gaze. "I've got some mistletoe."

This took his brain down Dirty Alley and he had to
clear his throat to speak. "Your tree is different than
the one you had before."

"That one's in my bedroom now."

"How did you get this one up here?"

"Archer helped me stuff it into the dumbwaiter." She
smiled down at him. "Thanks for coming."

"Anytime," he said and realized he absolutely meant
it. No matter that what was best for him seemed to be
some distance, he still wanted in her life. He'd take
whatever he could.

They stared at each other some more and then started
to speak at the same time. He had absolutely zero idea
of what he'd been about to say, but Willa looked like
she had no idea either so there was a beat of awkward
silence. Then they both started again.

Shaking his head, he pointed at her. "You first," he
said at the exact second she said the same thing.

She started to laugh and shifted her weight and he
had no idea how it happened, but in the next beat she
was in free fall. He managed to catch her but they both
went down.

He landed flat on his back with her over the top of
him, an elbow in his sternum, a knee uncomfortably
close to his nuts.

"Oh! Oh my God," she cried, all aflutter as she
pushed upright—using his gut for leverage. "Are you
okay?"

He wasn't sure, a feeling he was starting to get used
to when it came to her. Wrapping his hand around
her leg, he cautiously moved it from the danger zone.

Hoping to avoid any other damage, he caught her wrists and rolled, pinning her beneath him.

There. His body was safe, she was safe, and maybe, just maybe, he was going to manage to keep his heart safe as well.

But then she let out a throaty little "mmm" and spread her legs to make room for him between them.

"Oh," she breathed and then wriggled a little bit, making his eyes cross with lust. With a low laugh, he dropped his forehead to her shoulder.

She was killing him.

"Keane?"

"Yeah?"

She gave him a little push.

Thinking she'd come to her senses he shifted off of her but before he could get up she pushed again so that he fell to his back.

And then she claimed the top for herself. "Mmm," she said again.

Stunned, he put his hands on her hips, his fingers digging in a little bit in a desperate attempt to get reined in. "You did that on purpose?"

"No. Well not totally anyway." And then her mouth swooped down and covered his in a kiss meant to annihilate every single operating brain cell.

And it did.

When they broke apart for air, she was sprawled over the top of him, her pretty breasts smashed into his chest, her forearms flat to the floor on either side of his head, her legs straddling his hips so that not even a sheet of paper could have fit between them.

With a groan, he thunked his head onto the floor.

She slid her hands under the back of his head to protect it and he slid his gaze to hers. "Willa, what are we doing?"

She stared at him for a beat, chewing on her lower lip. "I was hoping it was obvious."

"Nothing with you is ever obvious."

"How about this—does this help?" She wriggled right over his erection and he groaned.

"You don't seem opposed," she murmured.

Hell no, he wasn't opposed. But there was something in her eyes behind the hunger and desire, something just out of his reach, something she wasn't saying. But before he could try to figure it out, she kissed him again, deeper, wetter, her sweet tongue chasing his. And either he'd just given himself a concussion or she was that good because he got lost in her. Given the breathy little pants and how her hands fought his for purchase on each other's bodies, he wasn't alone. She was just as lost as he.

They rolled several more times, jockeying for the driver's seat, but finally he pinned her to the floor, his hands once again capturing hers, a thigh spreading her legs, making himself at home as all his confusion about his feelings for her vanished. They always did when they were together like this.

He wanted to believe that she felt the same, that maybe that was what she hadn't been able to say, and he told himself she'd get there.

"Keane," she whispered throatily, arching to him. "Please . . ."

Yeah. He intended to please. He'd please her until she cried out his name in the way she did when she came. It took less than two seconds to discover that she was indeed not wearing a bra and that her sweater was soft and stretchy, so much so that one tug exposed her perfect breasts.

Another discovery—he was incapable of logic when he had her panting and writhing beneath him like this. He had a sweet, hard nipple trapped between the roof of his mouth and his tongue, and a hand inside her panties—where he discovered with a heartfelt groan just how into him she was—when one of their phones went off with the Muppets version of "Jingle Bell Rock."

"Ignore it," he murmured into her mouth, his fingers slowly caressing her hot folds.

She moaned out some wordless agreement and tightened her grip on his hair, doing her best to make him bald before his next birthday, and he could care less. Her panties were cutting into the back of his hand so he gave a quick tug and accidentally ripped them right off her. He stilled. "I'll buy you more," he said in apology. "I—"

"I liked it," she whispered.

Oh Christ, he was such a dead man. Rearing up, he kissed her hard and then slid down her body, pushing her skirt up as he went, groaning at what he'd exposed.

On the coffee table near his head, her phone buzzed again. He glanced over at it automatically, not meaning to invade her privacy. But then he saw the first line of the incoming text.

Haley:
Did the no-bra thing work on Keane?

"What is it?" Willa murmured.

He pushed off of her and came up on his knees. "You tell me."

She accessed the text and grimaced. "Well, crap." She sighed and sat up. "Okay, so I realized that I wanted to see you but not to talk, and—"

"And instead of being the promised grown-up about it and just telling me you were horny, you went back to high school and told your friends?" he asked.

"Worse," she said with a guilty wince. "I took advice from them on what to do."

He stood and stared down at her.

"I know!" she said. "I'm sorry! But they're deceptively sweet and really nosy, and very bossy and convincing!"

He tried to take it all in. "So the sexy sweater, the mistletoe, the text . . . all of it was some sort of plan to seduce me?"

"And the no-bra thing," she said. "Don't forget that part."

He pulled her up to her feet. "I really liked that part," he admitted. "But Jesus, Willa, I'm an easy lay when it comes to you. You could've just told me."

"I'm sorry," she whispered again and stepped into him, her eyes on his, warm and worried. "But for all my big talk, I'm not very good at . . . well, talking."

Her phone went off again. "Oh my God," she said. "Give it to me so I can tell them to knock it off." She stretched to reach it and Keane tried to not enjoy the mouthwatering view of her bent over the table. He wanted to reach out and push the skirt up, biting back a groan at the thought of the view *that* would give him.

And then he realized that she'd taken a call, not a text, and her voice was off. Scared, and urgent.

"Rory, where are you—" She broke off, her body unnaturally still and filled with tension. "Are you hurt?"

Keane went to her bedroom and grabbed her new undies from her dresser.

"On my way," she was saying in her phone. "Text me with the exact address. I'm coming for you." She disconnected and whirled in a circle, clearly looking for her things.

Keane held out the undies and then picked up her purse and keys for her.

"Always one step ahead of me," she murmured, stepping into the panties. "I'm sorry, but I've got to—"

"I'll drive."

"No, Keane, I'm not going to ask you to—"

"You didn't ask," he said and nudged her out the door.

Thirty-eight agonizing minutes later, Willa glued her face to the passenger window. "This one," she said, rereading the address she'd gotten from Rory. "Dammit."

"What?"

"This is her ex-boyfriend Andy's house." The pit of anxiety in her gut grew. "The one who put that bruise on her face all those weeks ago now."

Keane turned down the street. It was narrow, lined with apartment buildings that had seen their heyday decades ago.

There were no spots available on the street.

"Just stop here," Willa said, unhooking her seatbelt, leaping out before Keane could get the truck into park. She heard him swear behind her. "I've got this," she said over her shoulder. "I've got her. We'll be right back out."

"No, Willa. Wait—"

But she couldn't wait, not another second. She ran up the walk and into the building. She'd never been here before but she knew from the text that Andy lived in apartment 10.

With her phone in hand and the knot of fear in her gut growing, she knocked on the door.

It swung open, revealing a dark, cavernous room she couldn't see into. "Rory?" she whispered.

A soft whimper was the only reply. Anxiety and worry drove Willa forward, hand out to combat the fact that she couldn't see. *"Rory?"*

A light came on further inside the place, illuminating a kitchen. Rory appeared in the doorway, giving Willa a frantic "come here" gesture.

Willa rushed toward her through the still dark living room, her relief short-lived when she tripped over something on the carpet and went sprawling.

Rory gasped and ran forward, helping her to her feet. "Hurry! Move away from him!"

The anxiety and worry had turned into bone-melting fear. Ignoring the burning in her hands and knees, Willa let Rory pull her into the kitchen. "Please tell me I didn't just trip over a dead body."

"Not dead." Rory paused. "I'm pretty sure."

Willa gripped Rory's arms and looked her over. There were no noticeable injuries. "Are you okay?"

"I think so."

"What happened?"

Rory bit into her lower lip. "Andy got a job and said he was making bank. He said his boss had offered me a part-time job too and that he'd pay cash, a lot of it. All I had to do was show up and be, like, the receptionist or something. Only when I showed up, there was no office. Turned out it wasn't an office job at all. The boss takes people out for bungee jumps off the bridges and Andy assists. I was supposed to greet the 'clients' and take their money. But that's illegal, I know it is, and when I said so, the boss fired both me and Andy on the spot. And then Andy took me here instead of home and we got in a big fight about it."

"Still waiting on the part that explains his prone body on the living room floor," Willa said.

"It turned out we disagreed about other stuff too," Rory said, averting her gaze. "Like on the definition of the word *no,* so . . . I showed rather than told." She paused. "With a knee to his balls."

Willa's heart stopped. "Did he touch you?"

"Only a little," Rory said. "And that's when I dropped him to the floor. But he hit his head on the corner of the coffee table going down." Her face fell. "Which is my fault, right? Am I going to go to jail?"

"No," Willa said firmly, grabbing Rory's hand. "It was self-defense—" She broke off when Rory let out a startled scream but before Willa could react, a hand wrapped around her ankle and tugged.

For the second time in as many minutes, she went down and then blinked up into Andy's menacing, pissed-off face.

Damn, those spiked cuffs would have come in handy about now . . .

"You," he grated out, staring down at her with a frown like maybe his head hurt. And given the wicked slash across his eyebrow, it probably did.

"Let me go, Andy." Willa said this with a forced calm that she absolutely did not feel. In fact, it took real effort to speak at all with her heart thundering in her throat. "The police are on their way."

"I didn't do anything wrong."

Willa struggled, but it was futile so she went with Plan B and jammed her knee up between his legs.

Andy's eyes widened as he let out a squeak and slowly fell off her, curling into a fetal position.

"Well if I didn't break his nuts, that sure did," Rory whispered.

Willa rolled to her hands and knees, but before she could stagger upright she was yanked to her feet by a large shadow of a man who moved with the silent lethalness of a cat.

Keane.

He had a dangerous, edgy air to him as the harsh kitchen light hit his taut, tense features, his eyes filled with temper and concern.

"I'm okay," she said.

He didn't speak until he'd made sure for himself, looking over both her and Rory before hauling Willa in close to his side and reaching for Rory's hand.

The girl grabbed on to it like it was her lifeline and Willa knew the feeling.

Because he was her lifeline too.

"What happened?" he asked.

Willa gave him the short version and after hearing it, Keane called the police.

Behind them, Andy stirred and groaned. Keane let go of Willa and Rory and moved over him. "Get up."

"Fuck you."

Keane shook his head, like he couldn't quite believe what an idiot this guy was. Then he hauled Andy to his feet and pinned him against the wall so that they were nose to nose.

Andy closed his eyes.

Keane gave him a little shake until he opened them again. Keane didn't raise his voice or give any indication of being furious, but the air fairly crackled around him. "Let's get something straight."

"Fuck you," Andy said, repeating himself.

Keane put a forearm across his throat and leaned in a little, which appeared to get Andy's full attention. "So, a couple of things," Keane said calmly. "You're not going to touch Rory ever again. You're not going to talk to her, see her, or even think of her."

Andy hesitated and Keane pressed harder, which had Andy suddenly nodding like a bobblehead.

"Same for Willa," Keane said, still quiet. Deadly calm. "In fact, you're not going to get within a hundred feet of either of them. Do we need to go over what will happen if you do?"

Andy shook his head.

"Sure?" Keane asked.

More wild nodding.

"Keane," Willa said softly, setting a hand on his biceps, which felt like solid granite.

Keane let him go and Andy slid to the floor, hands protectively cupping his goods.

That's when the police showed up.

Two hours later, Keane finally led Willa and Rory into his truck. They'd had a few tense moments when the police had first arrived before getting everything sorted out.

Meaning keeping Rory out of having to take a ride to the station.

"I'm such a screwup," Rory said quietly from the backseat. "I have no idea what I'm doing with my life."

Before Keane could say a word, Willa twisted from the front seat and reached for Rory's hand. "Honey, no one knows what they're doing with their life."

"They seem like they do," Rory mumbled. "On Instagram everyone has normal pics of family and boy-friends and . . . really great-looking food."

"Trust me," Willa said. "Even your most perfect Instagram friend has an asshole ex and eats chocolate cereal for dinner once in a while, okay? You're not alone and you're not any more screwed up than the rest of us."

Rory choked out a laugh. "Was that supposed to be comforting?"

Willa gave her a small smile that tugged at Keane's heart. "Yes." She glanced over at him. "Right?"

"Right," he said. "But for the record, I don't like chocolate cereal. My jam is Frosted Flakes."

At this, Rory managed a second laugh and so did Willa, both of which warmed him. He didn't know how and he didn't know when, but the walls guarding his heart had fallen and he'd been conquered. Hard.

Chapter 25

#DontStopBelievin

Willa's brain was on overdrive as Keane walked them upstairs to her apartment. At the front door, Rory gave Keane a hug and vanished inside.

Willa quietly shut the door to give them privacy and looked up at the man quiet at her side. "I'll keep her here with me tonight. It won't be the first time she's slept on the couch." She paused. "I wanted to thank you," she said softly. "For tonight."

He smiled. "You mean when you lured me here under false pretenses pretending to need help with the mistletoe when really you wanted to take advantage of my body?"

She felt herself blush. "I meant with Rory. I wish I hadn't needed to be rescued by my . . ." She broke off.

He arched his brow, clearly waiting to hear how she intended to finish that sentence, but she'd talked herself right into a damn corner.

"By your what, Willa?" he asked softly. "The guy you're just fucking? Your friend? Someone you care about maybe too much? What?"

Overwhelmed, and also short of air because there was a big ball of panic in her throat, she looked away.

She heard Keane draw in a deep breath. "I'm going to give you a pass on that right now," he said. "Because we both know you have some shit to figure out. But I want you to know something and I need you to really hear it." He tipped her face up to his. His expression was serious and just about as intense as she'd ever seen it, including when he'd had Andy pinned against the wall.

"This thing between us?" he asked. "There's no price. I needed a cat search and rescue and you came running. You need a ride and maybe a little muscle backup to deal with some asshole, I'm going to come running. You following me?"

She chewed on the inside of her cheek, trying to figure out if the math really worked out. "I'm pretty sure I get more out of this than you do."

He shook his head. "Has anyone ever told you that you're stubborn?"

"Don't forget obstinate," she said. "And yeah, I've heard it a time or two." Or hundred . . .

"I'm not looking to rescue you," he said with quiet steel. "This, between us, has nothing to do with anything like that."

"What does it have to do with?"

He looked at her for a long beat, clearly weighing his words. "You let people in," he finally said. "I've seen you."

She wasn't sure where this was headed but she could tell she wasn't going to like it. "Okay . . ."

"Your friends, you'd give them the shirt off your back. Same with the kids you hire and keep safe." He stepped even closer so that they were sharing air. "You give them a safe haven, you let them into your life. You do the same with all the animals that come your way." He planted his big palms on the wall on either side of her head and let out a low laugh like he was more than a little surprised at himself. "I'm saying I've changed my stance on relationships and commitment. I want in your damn life, Willa."

While she was still reeling from that, he pulled something from his pocket.

A key.

"What's that?" she asked, her heart starting a heavy beat.

"A key to the Vallejo house."

"Why—why would you give me a key?"

He shrugged. "For the next time you and any of the girls need to all crash together since I have extra beds. Or if there's a leaky sink . . . or hell, say you buy a pizza and need someone to eat half of it." He smiled. "I'd be happy to be that someone."

She stared at him. "I can't just let myself into your house," she said.

"Why not?"

Yeah, her body said. *Why not?* "Because that's a big step," she said carefully.

"It doesn't have to be." His expression was leaning toward frustration. "It's just a damn key, Willa."

She stared down at it and nodded. And then shook her head. "It feels like a lot more."

"What it is, is up to you."

She stared at it some more, shocked at how much one little key could weigh. And then a low oath came from Keane and suddenly the key was gone from her palm as fast as it had appeared.

"You know what?" he said, jamming it back into his pocket. "Never mind—"

"No, you just took me off guard—"

He shook his head. "Forget it. Another time maybe."

Chest tight, unsure of what the hell had just happened and which one of them was to blame for the sudden chasm that had opened so wide between them that she couldn't possibly cross it, she hesitated. She had no idea what to say. "'Night," she finally whispered.

"'Night."

Well, she'd walked herself right into a corner now, hadn't she, leaving her no choice but to go inside and shut the door. She immediately turned to it, palms on the wood. Her heart felt heavy, and scared.

She didn't want to end the night like this.

She hauled the door open again, Keane's name on her lips, and there he still stood, hands braced up above him on the doorjamb, head bowed.

He lifted his head, his expression dialed to frustrated male.

"Um," she said. "I think I might have overreacted about the key."

He just looked at her. Not speaking.

She had that effect on men.

"I really am all sorts of messed up," she admitted in a soft whisper.

His eyes warmed a little but his mouth stayed serious. "Well, you're not alone there."

She didn't want to, she really didn't, but she let out a small laugh. And then she tipped her head down and stared at her feet and felt her eyes sting.

For so long she had been just that. Alone. Yes, she had friends, dear friends who were more like her family than . . . well, than any of her blood family had ever been.

But friends didn't sleep in her bed and keep her warm and make her heart and soul soar. Friends didn't give her the best orgasms of her life, even better than her handheld shower massager.

Now she had this guy standing right here in front of her, a smart, loyal, sexy-as-hell guy whose smile took her places she'd never been before. He wasn't into messy emotions but even so, and even knowing she was, he was still standing there. Baffled. Irritated. Frustrated.

But still standing there.

For her.

"You're thinking so hard your hair is smoking," he said.

She was surprised she hadn't gone up in flames. All she could do was stare at him, more than a little shocked at the intensity shining from his eyes.

He really did want more.

And if it was true, if he really wanted in her damn life as he'd so eloquently said, then . . . well, then there wasn't anything holding them back. Not a single thing.

Except, of course, herself.

Her heart had started a dull thudding, echoing in her ears. "You're not ready for this," she whispered.

He smiled, but it was filled with grim understanding and not humor. "You don't get to tell me what I am or am not ready for, Willa. And in any case, what you really mean is that you're not ready, isn't that right?"

She sucked in some air, but she shouldn't have been surprised that he called her out on this. He wasn't one to hide from a damn thing. "I want to be—does that count?"

"For a lot, actually," he said. "You know where to find me." He brushed a warm, sweet kiss across her mouth and then he was gone.

Keane walked down the stairs of Willa's building, not sure how to feel. This wasn't how he'd seen the evening going. If things had gone his way, he'd be stripping Willa out of her clothes right now.

He thought about how they'd taken each other to places he'd sure as hell never been, and he wanted to go there again. He'd thought, hoped, Willa was coming to feel the same way.

Crazy, considering that until a few weeks ago he could never have imagined that he'd want a relationship. The irony of the fact that he and Willa had mentally changed positions didn't escape him.

Damn. He'd known better than to get attached but he'd gotten sidetracked by a pair of sweet green eyes and a smile that always, *always,* put one on his lips as well.

Willa made him feel things and he'd gotten swept

away by that. But her entire life had been one big Temporary Situation; foster care as a kid, working at the pet shop where animals came in and out of her life but didn't stay, men—when and if she let them in, that was.

And for a little while at least, he'd been in, but was starting to realize that had all been an illusion, just hopeful thinking on his part. Because though it was true he'd not done permanent any more than she had, he at least wasn't fundamentally opposed to trying. Apparently, it only took the right person.

Problem was, that person had to want it back.

With a gnawing hole in his chest, he went home to Vallejo Street. Yeah, dammit, home. He'd gotten attached to this place every bit as much as he had Willa.

Both had been bad ideas.

He looked around at the big, old, beautiful house that reflected back at him some of the best work he'd ever done. He could sell it in a heartbeat and make enough of a profit from the sale to slow his life way the fuck down. He'd have time for the things that he'd never had time for.

Playing pool.

Sitting on rooftops star-gazing.

A woman in his bed every night, the *same* woman.

Things he'd never wanted before, but wanted now. *Craved* now, the way he used to crave only work. In fact, for long years in his life, the physical aggression of his job had kept him calm. Pounding nails. Carting hundreds of pounds of drywall up and down flights of stairs.

That was no longer the case.

He was a guy who prided himself on staying true to himself. He'd always known that he wasn't the guy who wanted a white picket fence, a woman wearing his diamond, and two point five kids. He'd never seen himself craving any of that.

But there was no longer any solace in the thought of being on his own for the rest of his life. And if he was being honest with himself, he could also admit he'd changed his mind about love and commitment as well.

Shitty timing on that . . .

Restless, determined to go back to his original plans, he strode through the rooms and headed into his office, where he called Sass.

"Somebody better be dead," she answered sleepily.

"I need you to get Vallejo on the market."

This got him a load of silence.

"Sass?"

"You're calling me at"—there was a rustling, like she was sitting up in bed—"midnight to tell me you want to sell your house?"

"I was always going to sell this place," he said. "You know that."

"Noooooo, you weren't. I mean yes, you *pretended* you would," she said, sounding far more awake now. "But we all knew . . ."

"What?"

"That you'd finally found yourself a home you wanted to keep instead of living like a vagabond. Especially now that you and Willa are a thing. She loves the place too—"

"You're wrong," he said flatly. "On all counts. Get the place on the market."

This time the beat of silence was shorter. "It's your life," she said and disconnected on him.

"It is," he said to the cat who was sitting at the foot of his bed, eyes sharp and on his face, tail switching about. "My life."

Pita stopped twitching her tail, said her piece with a simple but short and succinct "mew," and stalked up the bed toward him.

"We've discussed this. I don't share my bed with cats."

Not giving a single shit, she walked up his legs and then leapt to his chest, where she sat, calm as you please.

"No," he said. "Absolutely not."

She lifted a paw and began to wash her face.

"Cat, I'm serious."

She changed things up, washing behind her ears now.

"If you start going at your lady town, it's all over," he warned.

Still on his chest, she lowered her paw, turned in a circle, daintily curled up in a ball, and closed her eyes.

"Not happening," he said.

She didn't move.

And neither did he.

Chapter 26

#MagicallyDelicious

The next morning Willa lay in bed staring at the ceiling feeling the entire weight of her heart sitting heavily in her gut.

No regrets, she told herself. She'd done the right thing being honest with Keane, for both of them.

Trying to believe that, she got up and realized with some shock that it was the day before Christmas Eve. Normally this was her favorite time of the year. She loved the renewed sense of energy and anticipation the city of San Francisco put off, loved the smiles on the faces of everyone who came into her shop, loved the magic of the holiday, loved everything about it.

But her cheer was definitely missing as she quickly and quietly got ready for work.

Rory was still asleep on the couch. After Willa had entered her apartment last night to find Rory waiting up for her, she'd had to set aside the feeling of devastation about pushing Keane away and paste a smile on her face.

Rory had needed that of her. They'd sat together and talked. Rory'd had a little meltdown, admitting she missed her family, that she wished she hadn't so completely messed it up with them.

Willa had asked her to pretty please consider going home for Christmas and make peace with them. When Rory said she couldn't get a ride to Tahoe on this short of notice, Willa had once again promised to work it out for her. The girl didn't have much in the way of family, but there was a lot of love and forgiveness there if she would only reach out.

Her own heart had squeezed hard at that, almost as if the poor organ was desperately trying to tell her that there was something in there for *her* to think about as well.

Now in the light of day, she knew she wasn't caffeinated enough to go there. She tiptoed past the couch, thinking she'd handle the morning shop rush on her own today.

An early Christmas present to Rory.

Her first grooming client was a feisty little pug named Monster who had terrible asthma. He whistled on the inhale and snorted on the exhale, making him sound like an eighty-year-old man smoking and climbing stairs at the same time.

As soon as she got Monster in the tub, Elle and Haley showed up with coffee and muffins.

"Whoa," Haley said, stopping short, eyes on the pug. "That's the homeliest dog I've ever seen."

Monster tipped his head up, his huge black eyes on Willa as he snorted for air. She kissed him on the top of his wrinkly head. "Don't listen to her. You're adorable. And don't ask me how last night went," she warned the girls.

"Don't have to ask," Elle said. "You're not wearing your just-got-laid smile."

"It's because you didn't take the handcuffs," Haley said. "Isn't it?"

Willa lifted her hands off Monster, his signal to shake. Water flew all over them. Well, all over herself and Haley. No water dared to hit Elle.

Haley squealed and Monster seemed to grin with pride as he shook again.

"You're only egging him on," Willa warned, laughing.

"Dogs can't be egged on like that."

"He's a male," Elle said, still completely dry. "He was *born* to be egged on. Now talk to us," she said to Willa.

Willa sighed, and leaving out the part where she'd let Keane walk away, told them about the Andy portion of the previous evening.

Both Elle and Haley were suitably horrified, but when Rory walked in they pretended they'd been discussing the weather.

Looking surprisingly well slept, Rory stared at them suspiciously. "Willa told you about last night, didn't she?"

Elle and Haley 'fessed up and fussed all over Rory. The girl pretended to hate every minute of it but no one was fooled; she soaked up every drop of love and warmth that came her way.

When the door in the front of the shop rang, Willa left her friends to continue spoiling Rory and, holding a towel-wrapped Monster tucked in the crook of her arm, headed out there.

And then nearly tripped over her own two feet at the sight of Keane, looking deadly sexy in a pair of dark jeans, an aviator jacket, and sunglasses.

He smiled at Monster. "Cute."

Just looking at him made Willa ache so she very carefully didn't look right at him. "You need me to watch Pita?" she asked.

"No."

When he didn't say anything else she finally met his gaze. A huge mistake, in the same way looking directly into the sun was a huge mistake. It was painful. Even more painful was the apology she owed him. "Keane?"

"Yeah?"

"I'm sorry I had a little freak-out about your key."

"Key?" came a low whisper from behind them. Pru. "Holy cow, what did we miss?"

When Willa turned to look, Pru was indeed there; she must've come in the back door. Now all three of her friends plus Rory were crowded in the doorway, eavesdropping like a bunch of little boys.

"Whoops," Haley said, wincing when she caught Willa's gaze. "Excuse us, we're just . . ." Looking a little panicked, she turned to the others, eyes wide. "What are we just?"

"Um . . ." Pru said.

Elle shook her head in disgust at them. "Amateurs. We're eavesdropping, and shamelessly. And it'd be helpful if one of you would actually repeat whatever happened last night so we know what's going on."

Willa stared at them. "Are you kidding me?"

"Honey, you know I don't kid," Elle said.

Rory was looking horrified. "Ohmigod. I think they're fighting because of me. I ruined their night."

Willa's mad turned to guilt. "No, honey, that's not it. It has nothing to do with you."

"No, but it must," Rory insisted. "Because everything was fine between you two—until I got stupid and needed you, needed you both because Andy would've hurt you, Willa, I know it, and . . ." Her voice cracked. "That would have been my fault."

Elle wrapped an arm around Rory and hugged her close, but her eyes never left Willa and Keane. "Not your fault," Elle said firmly. "Not last night, and not whatever's happening here. In fact, these two silly kids are going to take their little discussion to Willa's office and not come back out until everything's fine and everyone's smiling because it's Christmas Eve Eve, dammit."

"Will you?" Rory asked Willa, looking heartbreakingly unsure. "Will you two go work it out?"

She was asking because nothing in her life had ever worked out before. Willa knew this and felt the air leave her lungs in one big whoosh. No way was she going to let Rory give up on emotions. On love. No way would she be the one to make her lose faith. "Of course," she said, knowing she could pretend with the best of them, and she'd make Keane do the same. Then she'd also make him promise to give her some space until her heart didn't threaten to burst at the sight of him. With that plan in mind, she handed Monster off to Pru and gave Keane a nudge toward her tiny office.

But Keane, of course, couldn't be nudged anywhere. He was big and strong and as hardheaded as . . . well, as her. He slid her a gaze that was partial amusement that she thought she could push him, and part challenge.

He wanted to be asked.

God save her from annoying, big, badass alphas. She blew out a breath and, very aware of Rory's concerned gaze on her, smiled through her gritted teeth. "Will you please come into my office so we can"—she glanced at Rory, even sent her another smile—"work things out?"

"Would love to," Keane said easily. He even took her hand and led the way.

She allowed it, but the moment they crossed the threshold over her office door, she shut it and opened her mouth. "Look, I know I don't have the right to ask but I'm going to need you to pretend for Rory that we're fine—"

Keane didn't answer. Instead, moving with the speed and agility of a caged leopard, he pressed her up against her desk. Then he sank his hand into her hair, tilted her face up, and crushed his lips to hers.

And damn. All the swirling, boiling emotions abruptly shifted, turning into something else altogether. With a moan, she threw herself against him, almost knocking him right off his feet.

He simply readjusted his stance and yanked her harder up against him. Somehow that worked for her and she continued to mindlessly climb him like a tree, desperate to get him even closer, her hands splaying across his strong, wide back. Which was how she felt the tremor wrack his body. She felt other things too, like how he was pressed up between her legs, hard and insistent.

There wasn't air for words, not then and not when he cupped and squeezed her ass in his big, callused palms. So hot. So perfect. So—

The door opened.

"Oh, sorry," Cara said as she stuck her head in. "I just wanted to tell you I'm subbing for Lyndie today and . . ." She broke off at the look Willa gave her. "Okay, so they sent me back here to find out if you guys are fighting," she admitted. "Rory wants to know."

Shit. "No one's fighting," Willa said, trying to be casual. "We're just . . . discussing cat care," she said, trying not to sound breathless or look as if she'd just had the daylights kissed out of her. "For Petunia."

Cara nodded. "Kitty care," she repeated. "Got it. I'll tell Rory."

When she was gone, Willa turned to Keane. "So about pretending to be fine for Rory . . ."

He hit the lock on the door with one hand and hauled her back into him with the other, covering her mouth with his. He grabbed the string on the blinds to the courtyard window and lowered them, all without letting her mouth free. It was quite the feat really. She might have suggested they turn the light off too because there was plenty of light filtering in through the shades, but she knew that request would be futile.

Keane liked the visuals.

She broke the kiss. "You need to stimulate her," she managed. "That's important in kitty care."

Keane arched a brow.

She gave a head jerk to the door, signaling that they were probably being eavesdropped on.

He looked at her for a long beat, his eyes dark and unreadable. "Kitty care," he repeated and before she could blink, he'd lifted her up and plopped her ass onto her desk and then stepped between her legs. His mouth was at her ear now, his voice so soft as to be almost inaudible. "You want me to stimulate your pussy."

She choked out a laugh and tried to shove free, but he tightened his grip. "You know that's not what I meant!" she whispered. "Rory's fragile right now and we have to make her feel safe."

"She is safe," he said in her ear. "And so are you." And then he smiled again, a very naughty smile as he raised his voice a little, to a conversational pitch. "Okay, so talk me through this . . . stimulation." He pressed his mouth to her ear again, using his bad-boy voice in a barely audible whisper. "Tell me slowly, and in great detail."

She shoved him again but he still didn't budge.

"I miss your body wrapped around mine," he said softly, serious now. "I need you wrapped around me again."

Her heart softened. There was a problem with this, she knew it way in the back of her head, but God help her, she couldn't articulate anything with his hands on her to save her life. Tightening her fingers in his shirt, she tugged.

He fell into her and his big body shook with laughter as he set a warm palm on either side of her hips and lowered his face to hers.

"Keane—"

"I know the rules now. This doesn't mean anything, it's just a one-time turned three-time thing, etc., etc. . . ."

She snorted and he smiled. "Hush now, Willa," he murmured, setting a finger over her lips. "Not a sound." His hands slid into the back of her jeans to cup and squeeze her ass. She started to moan and Keane bit her lower lip.

Right. Not a sound.

But the brutal strength in his embrace had her breathless as she twined her arms around his neck, pressing her breasts against his chest, because if they didn't get skin to skin in the next few seconds, she was going to spontaneously combust.

Somehow he managed to wrestle her boots off. And then popped open her jeans. When he slid a hand between her legs and stroked her over her panties, she had a moment's panic.

"What?" he asked when she froze.

"You have to promise not to look. I'm not in cute undies. In fact . . ." She grimaced. This was going to be embarrassing. "I'm wearing my ugliest ones. They're my willpower panties. I wear them so I won't show them to anyone. In this case, you. You're the anyone."

He stared at her and then tossed his head back and laughed. He looked so utterly sexy she lowered her guard, which was how he got her jeans halfway down.

"I know I'm totally sending mixed signals," she managed. "But it's not like I stopped wanting you—"

"Good."

"But . . ."

He groaned. "It's always the *but* that gets you."

"But," she continued, needing to get this out. "I'm . . . a little mixed up—"

He slid her a wry look. "A little?"

She tried to close her legs, not easy with a hundred and eighty pounds of muscle standing between them.

"Shh," he said again, somehow both gentle and badass at the same time. "I've got you, Willa. I get you. For now, this works. You always work for me, however I can have you."

And on that emotionally stunning statement, he dropped to his knees, tugged her jeans the rest of the way off, and looked. And he took his sweet-ass time about it too. He was grinning when he rose to his full height again. "I like them."

"You're a sick man," she managed.

"There's no doubt," he agreed and kissed her some more, until she was back to squirming, in the very best way now.

"Hurry," she murmured breathlessly against his mouth and together they freed each other's essentials.

And good God, there was nothing like Keane's essentials . . . She was very busy filling her hands with him when his stubbly cheek rasped across her bare nipples and she nearly came on the spot. His mouth was everywhere, wild, fast, and she kissed him back as best as she could while still trying to get him inside her.

He laughed low in his throat but before she could kill him for that, he managed to drop to his knees again and get his mouth on her.

A minute ago he'd been in a huge rush and *she* still was, but now he held her down and took his time driving her insane with his tongue, and when she lost it, when she began to come, he rose up and covered his mouth with hers, swallowing her cry as he protected them both and then thrust inside her.

Their pace was frantic, desperate. Hungry. It didn't matter how many times they were together like this, Keane never failed to steal the very air from her lungs. She felt herself come again, or still . . . she had no idea. With Keane it was always one endless and erotic beat in time.

When she could finally see and hear again, she realized his face was snuggled into the curve of her neck, his breath puffing against her skin like a soft caress. One hand was drifting up and down her back, slowly, gently, helping her to calm, his other hand cupping her jaw, his thumb on her lips reminding her to be quiet.

Oh, God. Had she been quiet? She couldn't remember!

He grinned and she bit his finger. Hard.

Laughing softly, he straightened and then helped her off the desk. Her damn knees wobbled and he tightened his grip, pulling her into him, cuddling her into him.

She felt his lips brush her temple, and his hand stroked the hair from her eyes. Then that hand took hers and brought it to his mouth. She could feel the warmth of his breath on her skin and the gesture felt so . . . intimate, even more so than having him buried deep inside her. "That was . . ." She paused, searching for the right word.

"Kitty care at its finest?"

She tried not to laugh and failed. "Keane," she said softly. "What the hell are we doing?"

He slowly shook his head. He didn't know either. "I just needed to see you," he said simply.

"And I needed to see you," she said. "But what does it mean?"

"That you needed me bad."

She choked on another laugh.

"You don't think so?" He turned and lifted up his shirt. He hadn't refastened his jeans so they were sagging a little, enough to reveal the ten fingernail indentions, five on each perfect butt cheek.

She slapped her hands over her eyes in tune to his soft laugh.

Great. He was invigorated by sex and she . . . well, she'd lost another chunk of her heart. She straightened her clothes, swearing when she couldn't find her panties. Being a sex fiend was getting expensive.

Keane came close and buttoned up her top for her, his hands lingering to cup her face, gently tilting it up to his for a soft kiss. "Okay," he said. "Tell me. Tell me what you want me to know. Do you still need space? Because I'm thinking eight to nine inches should do it."

She huffed out a soft laugh and rubbed her temples.

"It's just that when we do this"—she gestured vaguely at her desk—"it makes me feel things. More each time."

"Good."

She tipped her head back and stared at the ceiling as she let out another low laugh. She felt his hands slide up and down her arms.

"Willa, look at me."

She hesitated because she knew damn well she got lost in his eyes every time, but she did meet his gaze.

"You get that you're not alone in this, right? I'm right here in this with you, and just as unnerved by what's going on."

She shook her head. "Are you? Because you seem so at ease with it. You move in and out of the intimacy without even blinking an eye, like it's not hitting you."

He studied her for a long beat. "You think I don't have emotions?"

"I think you're better at managing them than I am."

"You've got to have faith," he said. "In me. In us."

"That's hard for me."

"So are you ending this then?"

"No." Her stomach quivered at just the thought. "No," she said again more firmly and actually clutched at him.

"Okay," he murmured, pulling her in, holding her tight. "Okay, I'm not going anywhere."

She was too choked up to do anything more than nod as she sought comfort in his embrace for a long moment before pulling back, making sure they were both decent.

"I'm not going to pretend anything," he warned her

when she turned to the door. "Not even for Rory. Don't ask me to."

She shook her head. "I won't."

Her entire crew was hanging close by, clearly trying to eavesdrop. When they saw her, they all scattered wildly.

Except for Elle, who studied Willa for a long beat and then Keane.

Willa ignored her the best she could and gestured for Keane to make his escape. Instead, he came close to her and kissed her. Not a deep kiss but not a light one either. It was the kiss of a man staking his claim. When he lifted his head, the barest hint of a smile crossed his lips. "Still your ball and your court," he said.

And then he walked away from her without looking back.

When Willa finally got home that night, she had a raging headache from the thoughts she'd managed to block all day. A raging headache and some deep gouges courtesy of an extremely pissed-off cat who'd been brought in for grooming after a run-in with a rose bush.

The cat had been so wild that Willa had refused to let Rory or anyone else work on her, which meant she'd handled the situation alone.

And had paid the price.

Rory had wanted to treat Willa's deep scratches but Willa had told her she was fine.

But really, she was as far from fine as she could get. Feeling much more alone than she could remember feeling, she strode through her dark apartment without bothering with lights. Outside, rain was battering the building and inside, all she wanted was a PB&J sandwich—triple-deckered—and her bed. She was halfway through making the sandwich when she was driven crazy by her leaky kitchen faucet. "Shut up," she told it.

Drip. Drip. Drip.

Dammit. She used to love being alone. When had she stopped loving it?

Drip. Drip. Drip . . .

"Fine. I'll shut you up myself," she muttered and crawled under the sink with a wrench. She gave the loose bolt a twist and then screeched in shock and surprise when icy water burst all over her.

Sputtering indignantly, she sat on her kitchen floor and stared down at herself.

She was a mess.

Fitting, given her day. Refusing to cave to it and lose her collective shit, she was back at spreading peanut butter when she heard a knock at her door. Because it was past midnight and that kind of a night, she brought the knife with her to look out the peephole. Her good parts tingled and she told them to shut up too.

Keane stood on her doorstep looking dark as the wet, cold night and just as dangerous.

Chapter 27

#WhatYouSeeIsWhatYouGet

Keane hadn't been able to fall asleep to save his life. Feeling oddly weighted down, he'd gotten up to run, figuring pushing himself to exhaustion should straighten his shit out.

As he pounded the sidewalks, he ticked off the positives in his life. One, his great-aunt Sally was back in her rehab facility and doing well. She'd even left *him* a message for a change, telling him that an old friend had offered to take Pita off his hands. Two, his real estate agent was officially accepting bids for the Vallejo Street home over the next week.

He was in a good place. Hell, he was in a great place, so he should be over the moon.

He wasn't. None of it felt right.

Not giving up Pita. Not selling the Vallejo Street home. Not giving Willa space to figure her shit out, none of it worked for him on any level.

He ran harder, until his muscles quivered with exhaustion. And that's when he'd realized he'd ended up in front of Willa's building.

The simple truth was that he'd been drawn here like a moth to the flame. He loved her smile, loved her laugh, loved the way she made him do both of those things with shocking regularity. He loved the way she brought him out of himself, not letting him take himself too seriously. He loved . . . everything. Absolutely everything about her.

She opened to his quiet knock and he drank in the sight of her; hair wild, eyes flashing bad temper, her shirt drenched and just sheer enough that she could have won any wet T-shirt contest the world over.

She looked him over as well. "A water pipe spray you too?" she asked.

"No, I've been running."

"On purpose?"

He was surprised to hear himself laugh. "Can I come in?"

"Sure," she said so agreeably that he was suddenly suspicious.

"So what do you know about plumbing?" she asked.

"Everything."

"Then you're my man," she said. "I've got a leaky faucet you can fix."

He was so tired he could hardly hold himself up. "Now?"

"I tried to fix it myself and nearly drowned." She waved at herself with a knife that looked like it'd been dipped in peanut butter. "I had a shitty afternoon and evening, and all I wanted was a PB&J and some sleep, but the drip-drip-dripping is killing me . . ."

Since she sounded far too close to tears for his liking, he wrapped his hand around her wrist to stop her from waving her knife around. "I've got it," he said quietly and then took her knife because he might be a sucker when it came to her, but he wasn't stupid.

He shut and locked the door and moved past her into the kitchen. The makings of a peanut butter and jelly sandwich sat on the counter. There was water all over the floor and the cabinet beneath the sink was open. "You could have called me," he said.

"I know how to fix a damn leaky sink for myself."

He might have argued that she didn't or they wouldn't be having this conversation but he'd had a long day too, extremely long, and he wasn't that far behind her in the bad-mood department. Eyes gritty with exhaustion, he grabbed the wrench and went to work.

It took him two minutes. He set the wrench aside and still flat on his back, took a look at Willa.

She was sitting on the counter licking peanut butter off her thumb with a suction sound that went straight to his favorite appendage. "Done," he said, voice a little thick as he got to his feet and moved to stand in front of her.

"So it's not going to drip all night, forcing me to kill it?" she asked.

"There's no killing on your to-do list tonight."

She sighed deeply. "Thanks," she said softly. "Really."

"You're welcome. Really." He stepped in closer so that her knees pressed against his thighs.

She fisted her hands in his shirt and tried to tug him closer but he resisted.

"I want my eight to nine inches," she whispered.

Somehow he managed to resist. "I need a shower, Willa."

She tugged harder. "Not for me you don't."

"I ran over here, so yes I do."

She choked out a laugh. "And they call me stubborn and obstinate." She stared at him and her smile faded as she slowly dragged her teeth over her bottom lip. "I can't sleep," she murmured.

Her hair was in her eyes. Her mascara was smudged. Her shirt was still wet and she shivered as she pressed close, and again he had to hold her off. "Careful, I'm all sweaty."

"Don't care." She snuggled into his chest and when she tilted her face to his, it was the most natural thing in the world to kiss her. She tasted like peanut butter and heaven.

"Why can't you sleep?" he asked against her lips.

"I was grooming a geriatric cat and got complacent but she taught me. She got my back and shoulder pretty good trying to claw her way out of town and it's all burning like I'm on fire, which means I'll have to sleep on my left side or my stomach and I'm a right-side sleeper." She huffed out a sigh, then sucked in a sharp breath and flinched away from his hands as he tried to turn her away from him to get a look. "No, it's fine—"

Ignoring her protests, he put his hands on her hips and forced her to turn, and then began to peel her shirt gently upward.

"Seriously, I—"

He stopped short at the sight of the raw, red, angry gouges deep across her back and shoulder. "Willa, these have to be cleaned."

"I know, I will." She tried to pull her shirt back down, but he held firm and then finally just pulled the thing over her head, tossing it across the room.

"Keane!" she gasped, crossing her arms to cover herself, trying to turn to face him, but he held her in place while he surveyed the wounds.

"First aid kit?"

"Hall linen closet," she said.

He went to hunt down the supplies he needed and when he came back, she hadn't stayed. *Shock.*

He found her in her bathroom, holding a towel to her breasts, twisting, trying to see the gouges in the mirror.

The curve of her bare back was smooth and delicate, and so damn sexy to him. He wanted to run his hands down her spine to her ass, bend her over and—

The fantasy was cut short when she reached to touch one of the scratches and winced in pain.

"Hold still," he said and went to work.

She didn't speak while he cleaned the scratches. She didn't breathe either it seemed, but by the end her muscles were quivering, giving away her pain. Leaning forward, he placed his lips at the base of her neck.

A sigh shuddered out of her as she let her head fall forward, giving him better access, and he was a goner.

"Keane . . ."

"Tell me to go and I will," he whispered against her

beautiful skin and then it was him holding his breath, waiting on her response.

Willa turned to face Keane, and caught the same hunger and desire on his face that she knew was all over hers. Going up on tiptoe, she gently brushed her mouth over his. *"Don't go."*

With a rough groan rumbling from his chest, he carefully wrapped her up in his arms and took control of the kiss. And oh God, how he kissed her, like she was the sexiest woman on the planet. It was addicting.

He was addicting.

When they were both breathing like lunatics, he raised his head. Eyes dark on hers, he ran his fingers along her temple, tucking a strand of hair behind her ear, letting his thumb brush her jaw, her lower lip.

Melting into him she closed her eyes, but that only made it seem all the more intimate, the way their bodies had sought each other out, pressing close.

Around them, her apartment was still dark beyond the kitchen, the rain drumming against the side of the building the only sound.

Except for her accelerated breathing.

Because she had no idea if she'd fooled him even a tiny bit but she could no longer fool herself. This wasn't just sex.

"Willa."

She dragged her eyes open, raising her eyes to meet his, hoping he couldn't see the truth in her expression. Something dark and unreadable moved deep in his eyes but she didn't want to go there. Instead she took his hand to lead him to her bedroom.

But he stopped her. "Shower," he said firmly and turned on the hot water.

"But—"

"Don't worry, I give good shower."

He had them both stripped down to skin in a blink and nudged her into the hot, steamy water. Soaping up his hands and running them all over her body, he proved his statement.

He was good in the shower.

Twice.

When she was sated and shaking from the aftermath, he propped her up against the tile wall and quickly and efficiency washed himself up. Just watching him, she got hot and bothered all over again.

When he caught her staring at him like a voyeur, he smiled. "See something you like?"

"You know I do." She reached for him, but he turned off the water, dried her off first, and then finally allowed her to drag him off to her bed. She tried to push him down to the mattress but he took her with him so that they tumbled together in a tangle of limbs. Wordlessly he rolled her beneath him, his mouth on hers for a deep, bruising kiss.

She wasn't the only one feeling desperate tonight.

He had her stripped of her towel in a blink and she pressed herself close to all those hard, hot muscles she hadn't gotten enough of. Wasn't sure she *could* get enough of.

Slowing her down, Keane let his hands roam, heating every inch of her skin until she was begging for more. When he finally rose above her and thrust in deep, the world stopped.

He made her look at him and that was new for her. Eyes open. Heart open.

New and terrifying.

And in that moment, she knew the truth. She'd fallen irrevocably, irreversibly in love with him.

Closing her eyes against the onslaught of emotion, she tried to take it all in. His scent. The rough rumble of his sexy groan. The way his arms banded around her, one hand fisted in her hair, the other at her hip holding her, grounding her so that she could let go of everything but this. Because he had her.

He always had her.

Remember, she told herself desperately, remember how his body felt thrusting into hers, his muscles clenching, his skin hot under her hands. "Keane," she whispered, his name falling from her lips without permission.

He groaned, and knowing he was close she wrapped her legs around him and met his thrusts with an intensity of her own, forcing her eyes to meet his, reaching one hand to lay flat against his chest, needing to feel the beat of his heart.

Afterward, she lay pressed against him, feeling her pulse pounding, thinking that had been the most real, most erotic experience of her life. "Thanks for tonight," she whispered.

His huff of laughter brushed her temple. "No, thank *you.*"

"I meant for the plumbing rescue," she said. "I didn't want to need you to come in and wave your magic wand and fix my life."

"Babe, I didn't wave my magic wand until after I fixed the plumbing."

She lifted her head and stared at him in disbelief. "Did you really just say that?"

His mouth twitched. "Trying to avoid having a deep, meaningful conversation that probably won't end well for me. Thought charm might help."

"That wasn't charm, that was pure cheese."

He smiled. "But you laughed. I love your laugh, Willa."

She felt herself soften. "You're changing the subject."

"Trying," he said and rolled off the bed. Bending to his jeans, he began to pull on his clothes.

"Are you leaving?"

"Yes."

"Are you tiptoeing around my crazy and trying not to crowd me, or are you running away as fast as you can?"

He gave a low laugh and grabbed his phone off her nightstand.

He really was leaving. She got up and wrapped her arms around him from behind. "Keane."

Turning, he met her gaze. "I'll never run from you."

This stole her breath and she just stared up at him.

He stared back. Not exactly patient, but one hundred percent attentive and willing to hear whatever she said next.

"I'm just in deeper than I meant to be," she said softly.

"And again, you're not alone there."

Her heart squeezed. "I don't know what any of this means, what to feel."

"I know." He pressed his jaw against the side of hers. "I'm trusting you to figure it out and get back to me."

"Do *you* know?"

"I'm getting there," he said, as always brutally honest and unapologetic.

A part of her was deeply grateful for that. But another part of her was terrified because she was pretty sure she knew too.

It was just that her heart had two speeds: asleep or foot-to-the-metal. She'd been in relationships where she'd gone full throttle, feeling some of what she felt like when she was with Keane. Excited. Happy. *Alive.* Except that in each of those relationships, she'd been the only one all in. And then she'd stayed all in, past the warning signs. Past the recommendation of her friends. Past logic and common sense.

And she'd been burned.

Oh so burned.

"Willa." Keane's voice was as heartbreakingly gentle as his hands, which came up to her arms. "Don't rush yourself, not for anyone and especially not for me." That said, he kissed her, a devastatingly perfect kiss.

And then he was gone.

Chapter 28

#TheTribeHasSpoken

Willa woke up on Christmas Eve morning with her toes frozen. So was the rest of her. She thought about how much nicer it'd have been to be wrapped around Keane's big, warm body right about now.

And not just to climb him like a tree, but because she didn't like mornings. Because she thought that with him in bed with her, looking at her in that way he did that said she was the prettiest, smartest, funniest, sexiest thing he'd ever seen, she might learn to like waking up after all.

It was just that he had a way of making her feel special. Like she mattered. *Really* mattered. When she was with him, she felt like a better version of herself. So why the hell did she need space again? The answer was simple.

She didn't.

She blinked at the ceiling. Wow. She really was in

love with him. And damn, if she'd only figured that out last night, he might still be here.

With a sigh, she sat up in bed and checked her phone. Shockingly, there was nothing. No missed calls, no texts.

Nothing.

She set the phone in her lap as an odd emotion drummed through her, one she couldn't put words to.

Liar. She had words, several of them. She was feeling unnecessary because no one had needed her.

She swiped her finger over the screen of her phone and let her thumb hover over Keane's name. "Don't do it," she whispered to herself. "Don't . . ."

But then her finger swiped. "Whoops," she said to the room.

Keane answered her FaceTime call wearing sweatpants and nothing else, and her breath stuttered in her chest. His hair was wet and she could only imagine how delicious he smelled.

He took in the shirt she was wearing and his eyes darkened.

"You left your T-shirt here," she said and then bit her lower lip. "I slept in it."

His smile went hot. "Commando?"

"Yes," she admitted. "You owe me a trip to Victoria's Secret, by the way."

"I'll buy you whatever you want, and also thinking of you without panties is making me hot."

"Everything makes you hot," she said.

"True story." He cocked his head and studied her. "So whatcha doing up so early? Making a list, checking it twice? Tell me it's full of your deepest, darkest sexual fantasies."

She choked on a laugh. "No!" Then she bit her lower lip, but the question escaped anyway. "Do *you* have a list of fantasies?"

"Absolutely," he said, no hesitation.

She blinked. "About . . . me?"

He just looked at her, eyes molten-lava hot, and she felt herself go damp. "Written down?"

He tapped the side of his head. "All in here, babe." He smiled. "Unless you want me to write them down. We could mix our lists up and take turns picking out one at a time, and—"

"You want to act out our fantasies together?" she squeaked.

He just smiled and she nearly had an orgasm on the spot. "I . . . I don't know if I can write them down," she admitted.

"Sure you can. Close your eyes, think of something you've always wanted to try, and write it down." He waited expectantly.

She stared at him. *"Now?"*

"I will if you will."

Ten minutes later when her morning alarm went off, she had five fantasies written out. So did Keane.

"Time to get up," she said.

"Babe, I'm already up."

She rolled her eyes. "What's it called when you sext over FaceTime?"

He flashed a grin. "Sex-Time?"

She laughed. "You just made that up."

"No." He smiled. "Yeah. Show me under the shirt, Willa."

She wasn't going to admit that his soft demand gave her the very best kind of shiver. "Keane."

"Come on, show me yours and I'll show you mine."

"Is there anyone there with you?" she asked.

He turned his phone so she could see that he was in his bedroom at Vallejo Street, alone except for Pita sleeping on his pillow.

"I thought she wasn't allowed on your pillow."

"She's not," he said. "But apparently she's the ruler and I'm just her bitch." Then his face was back in the screen. "Show me," he said.

She lifted the hem of the shirt high, did a little shimmy, and then dropped the material back down.

Keane's eyes were so hot she was surprised her screen didn't melt. "That's going to get me through a very long day," he said, voice low and reverent.

She laughed. "You could get porn up on your phone anytime you want. Hell, you could probably get any woman in your contact list to send you nudie pics."

"I don't want any woman. I want you."

Her heart skipped a beat at that. "The feeling's mutual."

He smiled. "Have a good day, babe."

"You too." And with her heart lighter than she could remember feeling, a burgeoning hope blooming in her chest, she disconnected and went to work.

Willa did think of Keane, but not about the sexual fantasies.

Okay, she thought about those. A lot.

But mostly she thought about the man he'd grown into and how much that man had become such an integral part of her life in one short month.

When an older couple came into the shop to buy treats for their miniature schnauzer, finishing each other's sentences and holding hands like they were newlyweds, she had to ask. "How long have you been together?"

They grinned in unison. "Fifty years," the man said. "Fifty of the best years of my life."

"When you find the right one, honey," the woman said, her eyes on her hubby, "don't ever let go."

"Ever is a long time," Rory noted thoughtfully when the couple was gone.

Which was funny because ridiculously, Willa was suddenly thinking how much comfort was in the thought of forever . . .

She almost called Keane to tell him she thought maybe she'd figured some things out, namely that she realized she wanted in.

She wanted him.

But she didn't trust herself not to mess it all up over the phone so she sent a short text inviting him to the gang's private Christmas party at the pub that night, ending it with a *please come*.

By the time she closed up the shop and changed for the party, she hadn't gotten a response from him, and wasn't sure what that meant.

She walked into the pub a little off her game, but she'd made Keane wait for her to figure things out— she could certainly do the same for him.

The pub was closed to the public; tonight was just a family thing. Spence, Finn, Archer, Elle, and Haley, Pru, and Sean, Finn's younger brother, who was doing his best to adult these days now that he'd hit the ripe old age of twenty-two.

Finn poured Willa a glass of wine. The rest of the gang was at least a round ahead of her, everyone greeting her with hugs and cheer, and she felt her throat go tight with love. She was so damn lucky to have these people in her life.

"Where's Keane?" Pru asked. "You invited him, yeah?"

She nodded. "I left him a text."

"Does that mean you've decided to stop fighting yourself and your heart and go for it?" Pru asked.

Willa never thought the admission would be difficult but she was still surprised when her eyes filled as she nodded.

"Alcohol!" Elle called out. "Stat! Another one of us is about to go down the rabbit hole."

Finn and Pru, the first ones "down the rabbit hole," grinned wide.

Then Finn and Sean served them a feast that—no surprise given the fearless and competitive nature of the guys—turned into a chicken-wing-eating contest.

Spence won, though Willa had no idea how he did it. He was as tall as a tree with the lean muscled build of a runner, not a single ounce of extra meat on him.

And yet he put away twenty-five wings.

"Twenty-fucking-five," Archer said in awe as he counted the pile of bones on Spence's plate. "Ten more than your closest competitor." He looked at Finn. "That's you, man. You going to keep going, or forfeit so we can crown him?"

Finn looked down at his place and inhaled as if he was fortifying himself.

"Forfeit," Pru said for her man. "What," she asked at Finn's look. "None of *them* have to sleep with you tonight. As the lone person who does, I vote you're done, before you explode."

"Yes!" Spence thrust a fist in the air triumphantly and then let out an impressive burp. "'Scuse me."

Willa had been sneaking covert glances at the door, hoping to see Keane, but he was still MIA.

They moved on to their annual Christmas Karaoke Championship, first fortified by another round of heavenly spiked eggnog. And if Willa kept looking to the door every few minutes, no one called her on it—although she caught Elle and Archer exchanging more than one worried look, which she ignored.

The prize for karaoke was the same as for the wings—bragging rights for the entire next year.

And everyone wanted those bragging rights. Bad.

The girls got up and did "Moulin Rouge."

Spence and Finn did "Purple Rain."

But then Archer, seeming unaffected by the alcohol they'd consumed—although the Santa hat sitting askance on his head was clear evidence that he was very relaxed—sang "Man in the Mirror" and brought down the house.

Afterward, he came back to his seat, tipped back his chair, and gave them all a rare grin.

Elle was staring at him oddly. "How much have you had to drink?"

"He's drinking virgin," Finn said. "He said he's our DD tonight."

Elle's eyes widened. "So you're completely sober," she said to Archer. "And you can sing like that? How did I not know you can sing like that?"

"You don't know a lot about me."

He said this mildly but Elle blinked like he'd slapped her.

Ignoring this reaction, Archer reached past her to grab a handful of cookies that Haley had baked herself. "Are these as good as they look?"

"Better," Haley said while Willa rubbed the kink in her neck, the one she'd gotten by taking too many peeks at the damn door.

"We do karaoke all the time," Elle said to Archer, apparently unable to let it go. "You've never sang like that before."

"Sure I have."

"Never," she said adamantly. "You could go on any singing show in this country and win."

"No shit," he said easily. "But I don't want to sing for a living. I want to catch the idiots and asshats of the world for a living."

"Why would you choose such a dangerous job when you could literally stand there and look pretty and sing?" Haley asked.

Archer shrugged. "Because I'm *good* at catching the idiots and asshats of the world," he said. "I'm not all that good at looking pretty."

"You just like wearing at least three weapons at all times," Elle accused.

"That too," he agreed and went for more cookies. "Isn't it time for gifts yet?"

He was referring to their annual White Elephant/ Secret Santa gift exchange. The rule was simple—the gifts had to be under twenty bucks, not that this stopped them from competing like it was for a pot of gold.

It all started out very polite, with each of them setting their wrapped present in a pile. Then, like calm, civilized adults, they took turns choosing and unwrapping one.

But in ten minutes flat—a new record for them—it turned into a wrestling match when Haley jumped on Archer's back and bit his ear to keep him from getting the *Star Wars* shower curtain that she wanted so badly.

"Okay," she said ten minutes later, the shower curtain safe in her hands. "That didn't happen."

"Spence already put it on Instagram," Elle said.

"Dammit!"

There was another scuffle over some bacon toothpaste and then they all shared another round of eggnog.

Willa drank her third and took yet another glance at the pub doors.

"You okay?" Pru asked her.

"Yes." She shook her head. "Actually, no, I'm some distance from okay. I mean I thought I was fine, you know? I was alone and I was good at that. I'd given up men and that was working for me—until, of course, the sexiest of all the men in all the world named Keane made me forget my no-man decree, and now . . ."

She shook her head. "And now I'm not good at alone anymore."

"You could switch things up and come to bat for my team," Haley suggested. "But you should know, women are even harder to deal with than men, trust me."

"I don't want a team," Willa said. "No more sexy times, which really sucks because me and Keane were good at it, *really* good. Okay, so *he* is the one who's really, really, really, *really* good—"

"Uh, honey," Elle said and drew her finger across her throat signaling Willa that she should stop talking now.

But she wasn't done. "You know what? I think I'll be my *own* team. I've got a good shower massager, I'll take care of my own business."

Normally this would've gotten her a big laugh, but instead each of her dearest friends in the world was looking at her with varying winces and grimaces on her face. *Oh shit.* "He's right behind me, isn't he?" she whispered.

"Little bit," Spence said.

She didn't look. She couldn't; someone had glued her feet to the floor.

Finn topped off her drink and hugged her tight. "It's not as bad you think."

No. It was worse.

Elle leaned in. "Hey, guys *like* women who can take care of their own business."

Archer appeared to choke on his own tongue.

Pru smacked both him and Finn upside the back of their heads and pulled Finn away. *"Kitchen,"* she said firmly.

Haley quickly stood. "I'll go with you. Spence?"

"Yep." Spence's gaze slid past Willa for a beat and then he lowered his voice. "You let us love you, Willa. But maybe it's time to expand your horizons beyond the core group, you know?"

"But *you* haven't," she said desperately.

"Trying and failing isn't the same as not trying," he said. And then he walked away, nodding at the man behind her.

Willa could feel Keane, but she wasn't ready to look.

"Whatever you do," Elle said quietly, "do it from your gut and take no prisoners." She watched Spence walk away. "I'm going after him," she said. "You know this is a rough time for him. Unless you need me to stay and kick ass and take names . . . ?"

"I'll be okay," Willa said bravely.

The only one left, Archer set his beer down and looked at her. It was hard to take him seriously with the Santa hat. "Let me guess," she said miserably. "Follow your heart or something Hallmark-y like that, right?"

This had Archer letting out a rare laugh. "Fuck, no."

She let out a low laugh too in spite of the panic choking the air from her lungs. Of all her BFFs, Archer was the most closed off. King of his own island and no one had a set of the laws but him.

"I was going to say run like hell," he said, "but Keane looks like he can catch you with no problem at all." His smile faded and he ducked down a little. "But if you've changed your mind and don't want to be caught, you give me the bat signal and I'm there, okay?"

She looked into the eyes of the man who would do anything, and she meant anything, to keep his friends safe. "Okay."

And then she was alone in the bar with the only man who'd ever really snagged a piece of her heart. Slowly she turned and faced him.

He looked utterly exhausted. It must be raining again because his hair was wet, his long dark lashes spiky. He hadn't shaved that morning. And probably not the morning before either.

"I'm sorry," he said.

She blinked. "For what?"

"A lot of things but let's start with tonight. I wanted to be here earlier, I intended to be, but . . ." His eyes were dark, his expression was dark, and her heart immediately stopped.

"What's wrong?" she asked, thinking *please don't let it be Sally . . .*

"Pita's gone again, but this time I think she got out of the house."

She gasped. "What?"

"There were people going in and out all day and I was working in the attic and . . . shit." He shoved a hand through his wet hair, leaving it standing on end. "I fucking lost her."

"Why didn't you call me sooner?"

"I did. You didn't answer. I figured you were pissed that I hadn't shown up. I came here to beg you for help—"

"I didn't hear my phone—" She slapped her pockets.

Empty. She turned in a slow circle looking for her purse, which she'd left on the bar unattended. She ran over there and pulled out her phone and saw the missed calls. "I'm so sorry." She headed for the door. "Let's go."

Chapter 29

#MakingAListAndCheckingItTwice

Keane drove them to Vallejo Street, his mind filled with worry about Pita but still having enough room to enjoy the way Willa looked tonight, which was smokin' hot. "I'm sorry about taking you away from your Christmas party." He slid her a lingering look. "I like the dress."

She looked down at her little red dress. Emphasis on *little*. "I wore it for you."

He felt a knot loosen in his chest and met her deep green gaze. "The invite. Was that just to the party? Or into your life?"

She nibbled on her lower lip but held his eyes prisoner. "Both," she said.

The rest of the knots fell away as he pulled up in front of his house. Rain pelted the truck as he turned to her, one hand on the steering wheel, the other going to the nape of her neck.

She leaned across the console and kissed him, short

but not sweet. "Petunia first," she said quietly. "The rest later. We have time."

He cupped her jaw, his thumb stroking her soft skin. "I like the sound of that," he said. "I'll go check with the neighbors. See if anyone saw her."

"Can I use your office to make some posters?" she asked and, if he wasn't mistaken, shivered while she was at it.

"Posters?" he repeated in question, peeling out of his sweatshirt and pulling it over her head.

"Missing Cat posters." She hugged his sweatshirt to herself, inhaling deeply as if she liked his scent.

He reached into his pocket and held out the key he'd tried to give her the other day. He smiled. "You're going to need this to get inside."

Her fingers closed over his and their gazes met and held. "Thanks," she said. "For the key and the patience." Then she was gone, running up the steps, letting herself inside the house.

He watched her go and then grabbed his spare jacket from the backseat. A minute later he was going up and down the street asking about Pita while the woman he was pretty sure had just agreed to be his gave up her Christmas Eve helping him, simply because he'd asked.

Half an hour later, he had to admit defeat. No one had seen or heard the cat.

The streets were quiet, traffic was low to nonexistent, but that was because of the storm. Earlier, during rush hour, there'd been heavy traffic. For all he knew, Pita had gotten scared and run off, and then ended up lost. Or she'd been taken by someone.

Or worse, hit by a car.

He stood under a tree whose roots had cracked the sidewalk, only half protected from the rain, wet as hell, trying to figure out how he was going to ever face his aunt again when his phone vibrated.

"Well, finally," Sharon, his real estate agent said. "I called your office line first and your new girl answered."

"I don't have a new girl."

"Then your new girlfriend. She offered to take a message for me but after I told her the fabulous news—"

"What news?"

"Well now see, that's what I'm trying to tell you," Sharon said. "After I gave her the message, I realized I wanted to tell you myself so I tried your cell and hit pay dirt. You ready?"

"Just spit it out already."

"Okay, Mr. Grinch, you're not in a partying mood, I get it. But that's going to change because . . ."

"Sharon, I swear to God—"

"We not only have an offer, it's *The* Offer. Fifteen percent over our asking price! Merry fucking Christmas, Keane!"

He went shock still as conflicting emotions hit in a tidal wave. No, more like a tsunami. Over the past two days plenty of offers had come in, but nothing to write home about. He'd told himself the relief he'd felt was simple exhaustion.

But now that relief turned over in his gut because an offer for fifteen percent over his already inflated asking price was insane and more than he'd hoped for, way more. There was no reason not to jump on this offer, none. He'd told himself he wanted out, had wanted that badly enough to make it happen, and now here he was.

Wishes of his own making.

"Keane?"

"Yeah." Where was the elation? Or the sense that this was the right thing? "I'm here," he said, squinting as the wind kicked up, rain slapping him in the face.

"Tell me I'm accepting this offer," Sharon said.

If this was my home, I'd never leave it . . . Willa's words floated in his brain.

"Keane," Sharon said, suddenly serious. "I'm not going to lie, you're scaring me more than a little bit with the whole silent act here. Tell me we're selling. Say it out loud before I have the rest of this stroke you're giving me. I mean it, Keane. If I die from this, and it feels like I might, I want you to know I'm leaving my five cats to you. *Five.*"

"Yeah," he said. "I hear you."

"So can I accept this offer?"

He tipped his head up, looking through the branches of the tree at the wild, stormy sky. When he'd put the house on the market, he'd done so because he knew he wasn't cut out for the stability this house would provide. He couldn't even keep a damn cat. And yeah, things were looking good with Willa but there were no guarantees. There were never any guarantees. "Accept the offer," he said.

Sharon wooted and whooped it up in his ear and then disconnected, leaving him standing there in the storm, the icy rain slapping him in the face.

He should feel good. Instead, a pit in his stomach

warned him that maybe he wasn't thinking this all the way through, that maybe he was letting his lifelong, string-free existence rear its head and take over, ignoring how things had started to change deep within him.

Taking a deep breath, he turned back to the house, stopping in surprise when he found Willa on his porch. "Hey," he said. "Why are you out here in the rain?"

"I tried calling you," she said. She was hugging herself. And no longer wearing his sweatshirt. He started to take his jacket off to give it to her, but she held up her hand.

"I found Pita," she said.

"Seriously? Where?"

"You put a grate over the vent she went down last time, and then a chair over that, probably to dissuade her from another adventure." She held his gaze. "Or maybe it was for aesthetic value so that the room looked good when real estate agents paraded their clients through here."

Oh shit. He hadn't told her. Why hadn't he told her? *Because you hadn't really believed she could ever be yours* . . . He opened his mouth but she spoke quickly. "Petunia somehow squeezed herself under the chair, snagged the grate up with a claw, and down she went." She lifted a shoulder. "She was filthy so I cleaned her up in the bathroom sink. No worries, I cleaned up after, good as new for your new buyer." Her eyes were fathomless. Unreadable. "Congratulations, by the way."

"I was going to tell you about the offer," he said quietly.

She nodded, which was kind of her since they both

knew he hadn't even told her when he'd put the place up on the market. "Willa, I—"

"No," she said. "You don't owe me an explanation. Not for that, and not for the fact that you're giving Petunia away." Her mouth was grim. "I'm sorry, your phone was ringing off the hook, I thought maybe it was an emergency so I answered. Sally's friend's coming tomorrow morning to pick up Petunia."

Actually, Keane *did* owe her an explanation because it wasn't what she thought. It wasn't him trying to keep from getting attached, to the house or Pita. Or her. Because that ship had sailed. He *was* attached. He couldn't get *more* attached.

He hadn't told her about putting the house on the market because he'd been postponing doing that for so long he'd just assumed he could keep on postponing, never having to make the conscious decision to keep it.

As for Pita, he'd regretted that decision from the moment he'd so readily agreed. He'd thought being free of the cat and the house would simplify his life.

Turned out he didn't want simple. "Sally's friend wants to adopt Pita for her grandkids."

"So you're really giving her up?"

"Not me," he said. "Sally's friend wants her long-term."

"And you don't."

Recrimination and disappointment were all over her face.

"It wasn't my idea, Willa."

She stared at him for a long beat. "Well then," she finally said. "I'm glad for the chance to say goodbye."

He shifted in closer, reaching for her but she took a step back.

"Willa," he said quietly. "We all knew it was hopefully a temporary situation. There's no choice here."

She met his gaze. "There's always another choice."

Keane had thought admitting that he wanted her in his life was difficult but the joke was on him. The hardest part was still in front of him. How was he going to maintain a relationship when he had no idea how to even start? He'd never been successful at true intimacy.

But to be with Willa, he was most definitely up for the challenge. He started to tell her just that but a car came toward them, the lights shining through the downpour as it slowed and then stopped in front of the house.

Willa started down the steps but Keane caught her. "Willa—"

"I'm leaving, Keane. I called an Uber."

His other hand came up, holding her still as he stared down at her, his heart pounding uncomfortably. "Why?"

"You know why," she whispered. "This isn't going to work."

The Uber driver honked and Willa started to move but Keane held on to her, lifting a finger to the driver to signal they needed a minute. "Okay," he said, attempting to find his equilibrium here, not able to will his hands to let loose of her. "I fucked up but—"

"No, that's the thing," she said. "This isn't on you. It's all on me for thinking we could do this. The guy who doesn't need anyone or anything, and the girl who secretly dreams about love but doesn't know how to hold on to it." She put a hand to her chest like it hurt. "The mistake's mine, Keane. I let myself fall for the fantasy. Hell," she said on a short laugh. "I let myself fall period, even when I knew better."

The driver honked again and she turned that way but Keane blocked her. "I never meant to hurt you," he said, swiping a lone tear from her cheek with his thumb. "You believe in second chances, remember? Well give me one."

"It's not about second chances, Keane. It's that, as it turns out, we're *both* pretty damn good at being temporary specialists and leaving ourselves an escape clause."

Her shimmery smile broke his heart and he laughed mirthlessly. "I certainly didn't plan for an escape clause when I fell in love with you."

She stilled and stared up at him. "Wait—what?"

Jesus, had he really just said that, just opened a vein here when she had one foot out the door?

"Keane?"

Yep, he'd said it. Later he'd think it was like getting a brain freeze after gulping down a Slurpee too fast. There was nothing but the burn for a long beat as his mind went into a free fall. He loved her. Holy shit, *he loved her.*

But by the time he managed to gulp some air into his deprived lungs and kick-start himself again, Willa had given up on him and climbed into the Uber, leaving him alone in the cold, dark night.

Chapter 30

#TakesALickingAndKeepsOnTicking

Willa walked through the courtyard, soggy footsteps muted as she crossed to the fountain. It was as empty as her heart.

The water hitting the copper base was a familiar soothing sound and she stopped, hugging herself. She wished she'd kept Keane's sweatshirt, but his body heat had lingered in it along with his scent, and she was a junkie.

Time to go cold turkey.

"Hey," Rory said, coming around the fountain toward her.

"Hey. What are you doing out here this late, it's freezing."

"I'm fine," Rory said. "Just making a wish. World peace and all that."

Willa smiled. "When did you become the grown-up in our little twosome?"

"Since you dragged me into adulthood kicking and screaming." With a small smile, Rory pulled a little wrapped box from her pocket and held it out to Willa. "Merry Christmas."

Willa shook her head. "Oh, honey, you didn't have to—"

"You took me in off the streets. You gave me a job and force-fed me morals and honesty and trust." Rory's eyes went misty. "So yes, I'm giving you a present, small as it is."

Willa pulled her in for a hard hug. "I love you, you know."

Rory gave a small, embarrassed laugh. "Well, jeez, you haven't even opened it yet. Maybe you'll hate it."

Willa pulled off the paper and then let out a half laugh, half sob at the sight of the cute little key chain with a bunch of charms, each with a pic of some of her favorite customers' pets. "I love it."

"I'm going home," Rory said softly. "I'm nervous as hell and I might throw up if I think about it too long, but thanks for getting me the ride. Archer called me and said I'm leaving in half an hour. Should be in Tahoe by dawn."

"You'll call me, tell me how it goes?"

"Yes."

Willa gave her a long look.

"Okay, no, I won't call," Rory said. "I hate talking on the phone. But I'll text."

Good enough. Willa hugged her tight. "Still love you."

"Well, if you're going to get mushy . . ." Rory squeezed

her back, clinging for a moment. "Then I suppose I love you too." She pulled back and swiped her nose. "Thought you'd be with Keane tonight."

"Why?"

"Right. Because you're not a thing."

"Okay, fine, I might have been wrong about that before but we're back to not being a thing now. For good."

Rory rolled her eyes so hard that Willa was surprised they didn't fall out of her head. "Because while you love me, you looo-oooo-ooove him."

Willa didn't have the heart to tell her that sometimes love wasn't enough. "I'm not sure it's going to work out."

"Why not?"

"It's . . . complicated," Willa said.

"Complicated as in you got scared that he's not a dog or a cat or a wayward teen that needs taking care until it finds its final home?"

Willa blew out a breath. "Well why don't you tell me what you really think?"

"Sorry." Rory smiled gently. "But he's a good guy, Willa, we all think so. If you can't trust yourself, then maybe you can trust the collective certainty of the people who love and care about you. Don't find him a different permanent home than with you, Willa."

She choked out a laugh. "He's not a dog!"

"Exactly." And with that, Rory kissed her on the cheek and walked away.

Willa turned to the fountain. For months now she'd recklessly tossed coins into this very water, wishing for love. And then, apparently, she'd proceeded to panic when she'd actually gotten what she'd wished for.

"Dammit," she whispered. "Everyone's right."

"Well, of course we are, darlin'."

She nearly jumped out of her skin as she turned and faced Eddie, wearing board shorts and a really ugly Christmas sweater.

He smiled. "So what are we right about?"

"Sometimes I'm too stubborn and obstinate to see reason."

"Sometimes?"

She huffed out a sigh.

He grimaced at the look on her face. "Okay, now see, this is why I never managed to stay married. There's all these landmine discussions and I kept stepping on them and blowing myself up."

"It's not your fault. It's mine." Because of it, she'd walked away from Keane—not because he'd not told her about his house or Petunia, but because she was scared of everything she thought she wanted. Everything that had for once truly been within her grasp and standing right in front of her. "Oh my God." She looked at Eddie. "I've made a terrible mistake. I need a ride."

"Dudette," he said with a slow head shake. "I'd do anything for you, you know that, but they took my license away twenty years ago now."

"They" being the state of California, probably having something to do with the medical marijuana card he had laminated and hanging around his neck.

"It's okay." She slipped him all the cash she had in her pocket—twenty bucks—and a quick hug. "Merry

Christmas," she said before running to the stairs. She dashed into her apartment and grabbed her bag. Then she two-timed it back to the pub and banged on the door.

Sean answered and she pushed past him, rushing to the stage where her best friends in the world were currently fighting over who'd won a bonus round of karaoke—hip-hop style.

Archer was adamant that his rendition of "Ice Ice Baby" beat Spence and Finn's version of "Baby Got Back." Finn was laughing so hard he was on the floor. Elle was sitting on the bar filing her nails listening to something Pru was telling her and nodding in agreement.

They stopped and stared at her, making her realize that she was drenched from the rain and a complete and utter mess.

Inside *and* out.

"So it turns out that I really am too stubborn and obstinate to see reason. And also, I screwed everything up," she added breathlessly. "I need a ride."

They all kept staring at her.

"Now," she said. And then she whirled to the door, knowing she didn't have to wait. They had her back too. Just like she should've known that Keane would have her back. Pushing open the pub door she got to the street and then turned around to see who'd come to drive her so she would know which car or truck to go for.

They were all right there, every last one of them, pulling on jackets as they rushed out the door after her and her heart just about burst out of her chest. "Thanks," she whispered.

Spence pulled her in for a hard hug. "Anything for you," he said against her temple. "You know that."

"Even if I've been really stupid?"

"Especially if," Archer said and tugged on a wet strand of her hair. "Let's go."

"All of us?" For the first time she hesitated. "I'm not sure I need an audience for this."

"Tough," Elle said. "You're family. And family sticks together on Christmas."

Willa's eyes filled. "It's not Christmas yet," she managed.

Spence looked at his phone for the time. "Eleven thirty," he said. "Close enough."

They all piled into Archer's truck because he was the only actual sober one. "Where to?" he asked her.

"Keane's."

He smiled. "No shit. I meant I need an address."

Right. She started to rattle it off and then sat straight up. "We have to go to a tree lot first! He doesn't have a tree, I want to bring him a tree!"

Spence groaned, but Archer didn't blink an eye. And ten minutes later they were all standing in a tree lot, staring at the two trees that were left.

"That one," Pru said, pointing to a very short tree with three branches.

"No, this one," Elle said about a taller but equally sparse tree.

Archer looked at Willa. Then he turned to the guy running the lot. "You got anything else?"

The guy shrugged. "There's one in my trailer. It's slightly used, but it's the best tree on this lot."

"You don't want it?" Willa asked him.

The guy flashed a smile. "Got a hot date with the missus tonight. I'd rather have the fifty bucks."

"Forty," Archer said and paid the guy.

The tree went into the back of his truck and in ten more minutes they were at Keane's house.

Willa still had no idea exactly what she was going to say, only knowing that she had to say something, *anything,* to fix this.

Because she was done running.

When Archer pulled over in front of the house, they all looked at her.

She stared at the house, garnering courage. Thankfully her friends gave her the silence she so desperately needed. When she finally thought maybe she could get out of the truck and not have her legs collapse in anxiety, she opened the door. Turning back, she found the people she loved more than anything all squished in tight together, practically on top of each other, watching her with varying degrees of concern and worry. "I'm okay," she told them, struck anew by how lucky she was to have them in her life. To know she was loved. To believe in herself because they believed in her.

Keane hadn't had any of that and yet he was still one of the most incredible men she'd ever met. He'd never learned to love and yet he was able to feel it enough to tell her.

And she hadn't said anything back. In fact, she'd let

him believe he didn't deserve a second chance, when everyone deserved a second chance. And God, even though she didn't deserve it, she really, really hoped a second chance applied to her too. "Thanks for the ride. I'll talk to you guys tomorrow."

"Oh, we're not going anywhere," Elle said. "We're going to sit here quietly and well behaved—" She broke off to give the guys a long look. "And there will be *no* fart wars while we wait or someone will die."

"Hey, that wasn't my bad last time," Spence said. "I'm not the one who's dairy intolerant."

"Well excuse me," Finn grumbled. "How was I supposed to know the smoothie Pru bought me that night was milk based?"

"He hasn't had any dairy today," Pru told Elle. "He's dairy free."

"You don't have to stay," Willa repeated.

Archer shook his head. They were staying. "Until you tell us you're good," he said, and just like that it became law. "Wave when you're ready for the tree and we'll bring it up."

Okay, then. Willa ran up the steps and knocked. She wasn't sure what she expected but when Keane opened the door, she lost her tongue.

She could tell he was surprised too. His gaze tracked past her to the truck at the curb—and the five faces there, pressed up against a fogged-up window, watching.

"Don't mind them," she said. "There was nothing good on TV tonight."

He almost smiled at that, she could tell. Tucked

under one arm like a football was Petunia, lounging against his strong forearm like she'd been born to do so.

Keane wore only a T-shirt and sweat pants. No shoes. Hair looking like maybe he'd shoved his fingers through it. He seemed tired, wary, and distinctly not happy.

Her fault.

"How long are they going to stay out there?" he asked.

"Until I get my life together." She pulled the door from his grasp and shut it on her friends' collective faces.

"Do they know that might take a while?" Keane asked wryly.

She let out a low laugh and turned to face him, eyes on his face. "You love me?" she asked softly.

"So you *did* hear me." He took her hand with his free one and led her to the kitchen. He set the cat down on the floor near her bowl, and true to form, she waddled over to it and stuck her head into the thing like she'd been starved for the past five weeks.

Keane rolled his eyes, grabbed a clean dish towel, and turned back to Willa, running it over her dripping hair. "You're frozen through," he said, standing close, very close, affecting her breathing. He met her gaze and held it as he dried her off. "You need a hot shower and—"

She wrapped her fingers around his wrists and stilled his movements. "You love me."

He tossed the towel aside and cupped her face. "From the moment you let me into South Bark that first morning and gave me 'tude." He gave a little smile. "And then changed my life with your easy affection, huge heart, and the world's best smile."

"Oh," she breathed, completely undone. Her eyes filled and she snapped her mouth shut for a minute, swallowing hard. "I love you too, Keane." Oh God. She'd never said those words out loud before. She had to bend over for a second, hands on her knees, fighting the sudden dizziness.

Two strong hands lifted her. When she met his gaze, he was smiling a little. "How much did that hurt?" he asked.

She let out a breath. "Not nearly as much as this— I'm sorry I ran off like that. It was just like when you tried to give me your key, I . . . panicked."

"And?"

"And then I blamed you for holding back, but it was all me. I let you in and I fell hard. And then suddenly it was like that bad nightmare of going to school naked. I got scared."

"I know. Come here, Willa." And then instead of waiting for her to do so, he pulled her into his arms. "Are you scared now?"

"No," she said, holding on tight.

"Then have some faith in me to not hurt you."

"I've always have faith in you," she said. "It was the faith in me that took a while."

"This isn't all on you, Willa," he said. "It's on me too. I should've told you about putting the house up for sale. I should've told you about the offers that poured in. But the truth is that you were right all along. I didn't really want to sell."

She stilled and lifted her head to see his face. "So why are you?"

"I'm not." He shook his head. "I rescinded my acceptance of the offer."

She just stared up at him. "Because . . . ?"

"Because this house is no longer just a house to me," he said. "It's my home. And I want it to be yours too." He cupped her face and pressed his forehead to hers. "I'm hoping you want that too. Think you can handle it?"

She slipped her arms around his waist. "There's this incredible man I know. He let me watch him learn that being emotionally closed off didn't work, that it's worth the risk to let someone in."

He smiled. "He sounds smart as hell. Probably he's sexy as hell too, right?"

She laughed and pressed even closer, unable to believe this was really happening. "*So* damn sexy."

He looked deep into her eyes and let his smile fade. "I love you, Willa. I've spent years risking everything for my business, over and over. It's past time to risk my heart for you."

"Does risking that heart include letting me put up a tree?"

"It's a little late for that, I think."

"Actually, it's not." She ran to the front door. Yep, everyone was still curbside in Archer's truck. She waved.

Archer and Spence got out of the car, untied the tree from the truck bed and carried it up the front steps.

Keane blinked.

"Tree delivery service," Spence quipped. "Where do you want it?"

Keane looked at Willa. "Wherever she wants."

"Good answer," Archer murmured as they carted the tree in.

They deposited it in the large front living room. Spence walked out the front door first, Archer behind him. He turned and looked at Willa. "You good?"

She beamed at him.

"Yeah," he said with a barely there smile. "You're good."

And then they were gone.

Keane rubbed a hand over his jaw, staring at the tree, which was only slightly crooked. The topper was Archer's Santa hat.

"The holidays are going to be insane, aren't they?" he asked.

She smiled from the bottom of her heart and took his hand. "Yeah. Scared?"

"Bring it."

With a musical laugh, she leapt into his arms, wrapping herself around him. Then she snuggled in and smiled against his lips. "Mmm. You missed me." She wriggled against him. "Or at least a part of you did."

He entwined his fingers into her hair and kissed her, deep and serious. "All of me," he said. "All of me missed you. All of me needs you in my life. You are my life. We're doing this, Willa. And it's going to be good."

She got anticipatory chills. "Yes, please. We've done it in my kitchen, but not yours . . ."

With a rough laugh, he kissed her again. "You know damn well what I meant. But your idea works too. And after the kitchen, it's the upstairs bathroom. There's a handheld showerhead there that you're going to like." He flashed his wicked grin. "A *lot*."

She slid her hands to his jaw. "Are you sure?"

"Hell yeah. That showerhead's going to rock your world—"

Laughing, she went to kiss him but he stopped her. "I want you to be okay with all of this," he said. "With me."

"I know. And I am. So much. I'm completely yours, Keane."

Her words seemed to light him up from within. "And you'll tell me if it gets to be too much. I don't want you to run—"

She gently covered his mouth with her fingers. "I learned tonight when I thought I'd blown it with you that nothing is ever going to be too much. Now you. You'll let me know if I drive you crazy?"

He laughed. "I love your crazy. I love *you,* Willa. With everything that I am, I love you."

"Oh," she breathed softly. "You're good."

"Give me five minutes in that shower and you'll see how much better than good I really am."

She smiled against his lips. "I haven't given you your Christmas present yet."

"What is it?" he asked.

"Me."

The full-blown smile across his face was brighter than all the lights in the city. "Best present ever," he said and Willa knew that Christmas, not to mention the rest of her life, was never going to be the same again. It was in fact going to be better than her wildest dreams.

Epilogue

#GoodMorningSunshine

On Christmas morning, Keane woke up like he always did, slowly. He took a deep breath and smiled as the scent of Willa's shampoo filled his nostrils. This was because her hair was in his face. In fact, she had shifted in her sleep and was lying half on top of him, using him as her personal body pillow.

The day hadn't even started and already it was his favorite Christmas of all time. It'd only taken four little words—*I love you, Keane*—to make his world complete. But it was so much more than that. It was him realizing that the woman he loved more than anything loved him back every bit as much. It was her being okay with losing herself in him because she knew that she'd always find herself there too. It was her trusting him, believing in him, in *them*.

She was wearing his favorite pj's—absolutely nothing

but her birthday suit—and he slowly ran his hands over all that creamy warm skin he loved so much.

"Hmph," she murmured, not moving an inch.

He stilled, not wanting to wake her all the way, knowing she needed sleep since he'd kept her up most of the night checking off items on their "list."

He'd drawn the Bad Elf fantasy, and in a twist he'd made her the bad elf. The vision of her in nothing but an elf hat and tied to his headboard was going down in history as his all-time favorite, but he was open to topping it.

Still draped over him, Willa wriggled. "Why did you stop?" she asked, eyes still closed, voice groggy.

He went back to stroking her. Every time he stopped, she wriggled and made a noise of discontentment, making him laugh. "Merry Christmas," he murmured in her ear and took her lobe between his teeth.

She sat straight up. "It's Christmas!" she exclaimed as if she'd actually forgotten.

"Yeah," he said, hands on her ass, rocking her into him, loving the gasp that wrenched from her throat. On a mission now, he began to tug her even closer, his gaze locked on his target . . .

"Wait," she gasped, crawling off of him, running naked to her duffel bag on the floor. "I have another present for you."

"Mmm," he said watching as she bent over to rifle through the duffel. "You're giving me a gift right now—"

She grabbed his discarded shirt and pulled it over her head. Then she whirled and ran back to him, jumping on him like a kid on . . . well, Christmas morning. "Open!" she demanded.

The bag was bright red. He peeked inside and pulled out a pair of . . . boxers with eyeballs covered in glasses all over them.

"Interesting," he said.

"Crap!" She snatched back the boxers and stuffed them in the bag again. "Those are for Haley." She ran to her duffel again and came back with another bright red bag, same size as the other.

This time he pulled out a box of joke condoms that said *Size Matters! Think Big!* He laughed and reached for her. "This here's a present that needs to be shown how to use—"

"No, wait!" she said, laughing as she evaded him. "That's Pru's!" And she once again exchanged the bag. This time she peeked into it first and sighed. "Okay, *this* is it."

He took in her shaky smile and the way she was fiddling, and realized she was nervous. Setting the present aside, he sat all the way up, stuffed the pillows behind his back, and then pulled her into his lap. "Better," he said and reached for the present again.

When he pulled out the vintage tape measure, he let out a long breath. "Is this—"

"From the turn of the twentieth century," she said. "It's got a lightweight brass casing with a conversion table on the other side. After you told me about that time you spent working with your uncle and how much you liked his antique tools, this felt like something you might like."

"*Love,*" he said, marveling at it. It was amazing. "Where did you get it?"

"I found it at an antique store on Divisadero Street." She shifted uncomfortably, clearly embarrassed. "It's not much, and I'm not even sure it really works, I just—"

He leaned forward and kissed her to shut her up. Pulling back only a fraction, he held her gaze. "It's perfect. You're perfect."

She bit her lower lip and smiled. "Good. Let's get up. I've got something in my bag for Petunia before she gets picked up—"

"She's not getting picked up."

"She's not?"

"No," he said. "I called Sally and said the cat had to stay because I have a mouse problem."

She choked out a laugh. "You didn't."

"I didn't," he agreed. "I told Sally the cat had to stay because she belonged here in this house, that I'd fallen in love several times over and I needed both my girls here with me."

Willa let out a shaky breath. "I'm not going to get tired of hearing that anytime soon."

"Mew."

They both looked over at Pita sitting in the doorway. "She's demanding sustenance," Keane said.

Willa laughed and slid off him. "I'll go feed her. I'll be right back."

He heard her move into the kitchen. Heard her pad to the bin of cat food and stop.

He knew why. Knew exactly what she'd found. And two seconds later she came racing back into the room, a blur of red hair and soft, sweet skin as she jumped him for the second time that morning.

Straddling him, she beamed down at him, her eyes shimmering brilliantly.

"What?" he asked innocently.

She held out the robin egg blue box. *"Tiffany's?"*

"Are you going to quiz me or open it?"

She slipped the silver ribbon off the box and slowly lifted the lid. Gasped. "Oh my God," she whispered as she gaped at the platinum chain with a *W* encrusted in diamonds. "You remembered about the necklace my mom gave me when I was little." Tears gathered in her eyes as she let him put it around her neck.

This one was most certainly not going to turn her neck green.

"It's beautiful," she said, staring down at it. "It's the most thoughtful gift anyone's ever given me."

"Looks good on you." He pulled her over him and softly caressed her until she pulled back.

"Have you ever made love beneath a Christmas tree?" she murmured.

"No, but I'm in." Catching her against him he rose and then threw her over his shoulder in a fireman's hold, palming a sweet cheek. "I'm all about starting a new tradition."

She was laughing as he carried her to the still undecorated tree and together they crawled beneath it to lie on their backs. Her hand slipped in his as they stared up at the tangle of branches. "To new beginnings," she said.

He came up on an elbow and cupped her face. "Forever, Willa?"

She tugged him over the top of her. "Forever."

Here's an exciting sneak peek at

accidentally on purpose

the next book in
***New York Times* bestselling author
Jill Shalvis's Heartbreaker Bay series,
coming soon from Headline Eternal.**

And look out for Max and Rory's story

one snowy night

a Heartbreaker Bay novella.

#TakeMeToYourFearlessLeader

It was a good thing Elle Wheaton loved being in charge and ordering people around because if it wasn't for the thrill of having both those things in her job description, she absolutely didn't get paid enough to handle all the idiots in her world. "Last night was a disaster," she said.

Her boss, not looking nearly as concerned as she, nodded absently. He was many things and one of them was the owner of the building in which they stood, located in the Cow Hollow district of San Francisco.

A detail he preferred to keep to himself. In fact, only one other person knew his identity, but as the building's general manager, Elle alone handled everything and was always his go-between. The calm, *kickass* go-between, if she said so herself, although what had happened last night had momentarily shaken some of her calm.

"I have faith in you," he said.

She slid him a look. "In other words, 'fix it, Elle, because I don't want to be bothered about it.'"

"Well, and that," he said with a smile.

She refused to be charmed. Yes, they were best friends and yes she loved him, but her love most definitely had limits. "Maybe I should recap the disaster for you," she said. "First, the little lights in every emergency-exit sign in the entire building went out at midnight and then stayed out so that when Mrs. Winslow in 3D went to take her geriatric dog out in the middle of the night, she couldn't find the stairwell. Cut to Blackie then letting loose in the hall just as Mr. Nottingham from 4A—who was sneaking out of his mistress's apartment in 3F—slipped in the mess."

"You can't make this stuff up," he said, still smiling.

Elle crossed her arms. "Mr. Nottingham broke his ankle, requiring an ambulance ride and a possible lawsuit. And you're amused."

"Come on, Elle. You and I both know life sucks golf balls if you let it. Gotta find the fun somewhere." Spence handed her a hot tea. "Here. You look like you're down a quart."

"My life isn't normal."

"Forget normal," he said. "Normal's overrated. Now drink your favorite poison—caffeine."

"Hey, I could survive without it if I needed to," she protested and then paused. "I just can't guarantee anyone else's safety."

"Exactly, so why take chances?"

She smiled but she was still taking what had happened last night personally. She knew everyone in this building, each and every business on the first and second floor, each tenant on the third and fourth floor, and she felt responsible for all of it.

And someone had been hurt on her watch. Unacceptable. "You do realize that the fire system equipment falls under security," she said. "Which means our security company failed us."

Spence's amusement faded. "Elle—"

"No, listen, a year ago now you sought me out for this job, making me your chief CYA. Part of Covering Your Ass means this is my problem to handle as I see fit. And we both know I'm very good at what I do. And what I'm going to do is go discuss this matter with the head of our security company, one pain-in-my-ass Archer Hunt."

Spencer grimaced. "At least let me clear the building before you two go at each other."

"There won't be a fight," she said. "I'm simply doing my job running this building and that includes managing our security company."

"Yes, technically," Spence allowed. "But we both know that Archer answers to no one but himself and he certainly doesn't consider you his boss."

She smiled and mainlined some more tea, the nectar of the Gods as far as she was concerned. "His problem, not mine."

Spence sighed and stood. "He's not going to enjoy you going off on him this early half-cocked, Elle."

"Ask me if I care."

"*I* care," Spence said. "It's too early to help you bury his body."

Elle snorted. Her and Archer's . . . antagonistic relationship was well documented. Archer thought he ran the world, including her.

But no one ran her world except her. "If everyone would just do what they were supposed to and stay out of my way . . ." she said, trailing off because Spence was no longer listening to her. Instead he was staring pensively out the window, prompting her to his side to see what had caught his interest.

A woman stood in front of the fountain courtyard below, staring into the water.

"Oh for God's sake," Elle said. "Would you just ask her out already? What's wrong with you? You've never been shy before. Go work it." She gave him a little nudge. "Hot genius mechanical engineers slash geeks are in right now."

Spence didn't respond and Elle rolled her eyes. "How come men are all idiots?"

This got his attention and he snorted. "Because women don't come with instruction manuals." Pushing away from the window, he eyeballed Elle carefully. "You good now?" he asked. "All murderous urges gone? Because I've gotta go."

"Right," she said with a nod. "Can't let anyone know you're Batman."

When he was gone, Elle finished her tea, applied some lip gloss—for herself, mind you, not for Archer—and left her office, taking her time walking the open hallway. She loved this building and never got tired of admiring the unique architecture of the old place, the corbeled brick and exposed iron trusses, the long picture windows of each unit, the cobblestone courtyard below with the huge fountain where idiots came from all over the city and beyond to toss their money and wish for love.

She was on the second floor, far north corner, from which if she pressed her nose up against her window, and if there wasn't any fog, she could see down the hill to the Marina Green and the bay, and a very tiny slice of the Golden Gate Bridge.

She tried to play it cool, but even after a whole year it was a thrill to live in the heart of San Francisco like this. Although she hadn't grown up far from here, it'd been a world away.

Around her the building was still. It was early so nothing was stirring.

As she passed the stairwell, the door opened and Trudy, the woman in charge of housekeeping services, came through. "Elle," she said in surprise. "Need anything, honey?"

"Nope, I'm good." Good and mad but though she adored Trudy, the woman couldn't keep a secret to save her life. "Just taking in the nice morning."

"Oh, that's a disappointment. I thought maybe you were looking for that hottie with the nice package, the one who runs the investigation firm down the hall."

Elle nearly choked on her tea. "Nice *package?*"

"Well, honey, I'm old, not dead."

Elle watched the woman walk away and shook her head. She moved down the hall and stopped in front of the door with a discreet sign: HUNT INVESTIGATIONS.

The investigative and elite security firm worked cases for criminal investigations and insurance fraud, amongst others, carried by Archer's reputation, no ads or marketing required. Basically they were finders and fixers, independent contractors for hire, and not necessarily tied by the same red tape as the law.

Which worked for Archer. Rules had never been his thing.

She opened the door and let herself into the reception area, which was much bigger than hers. Clean, masculine lines. Large furniture. Wide-open space. A glass partition separated the front from the inner offices.

The check-in counter was empty. The receptionist wasn't in yet; it was too early for Mollie.

But not for the other employees. Past the glass Elle could see part of the inner office. A group of men, five of them, entered from a private entrance. They'd clearly just come back from some sort of job that had required them to be locked and loaded, since they looked like a SWAT team.

Elle literally stopped short. And if she was being honest, her heart stopped too because sweet baby Jesus. The lot of them stood there stripping off weapons and shirts so that all she could see was a mass of mind-blowing bodies, sweaty and tatted and in all varieties of skin colors.

It was a cornucopia of smutty goodness and she couldn't tear her eyes away. In fact, she couldn't speak either, mostly because her tongue had hit the floor. Worse, her feet took advantage of the state of her frozen brain, moving her to the interior door, where she practically pressed her face up against the glass.

Someone must have seen her because they buzzed

her in. They all knew her. After all, her job required her to work closely with the security firm, and therein lay her deepest, darkest problem.

Working closely with Archer Hunt was dangerous in oh so many, many ways, not the least of which was their history, something she did her best to never think about.

She was greeted with a variety of "Hey, Elle" and "Mornin'," and then they all went their separate ways, leaving her alone with their fearless leader.

Archer.

It'd been a long time since they'd let themselves be alone. In fact, she'd always actively sought out ways to *not* be alone with him and given how successful she'd been, she could only figure he'd been doing the same.

Not looking particularly bothered by this unexpected development, Archer met her gaze straight on. He hadn't unloaded his weapons or his shirt and stood there in full utility combat gear, complete with a Glock on one hip, a Taser on the other, and two pistols strapped to his legs. His Army hat was backward on his head. The handle of a butterfly knife stuck out of a pocket in his cargoes, and he had two sets of cuffs and a stun gun strapped to his belt. An urban warrior, wired for sound with a two-way and a Kevlar strapped across his chest and back, telling Elle that wherever they'd been, he hadn't just come back from Disneyland.

She managed to be both horrified and turned on at the same time, but if life had taught her one thing the hard way, it was how to hide her thoughts and emotions. So she carefully rolled up her tongue.

The corner of Archer's mouth quirked, like maybe he could read her mind. But he didn't say a word, instead seeming perfectly content to stand there all badass and wait her out. And she knew from experience that he *could* wait her out until the end of time.

The bastard.

"Long morning already?" she asked, caving and speaking first.

"Long night."

He was big and bad and tough, and he irritated her by just breathing. But when push came to shove, she cared about him and the guys who worked for him. Most of the jobs he took on were routine—civil, corporate, and insurance investigations, surveillance, fraud, corporate background checks—but some weren't routine at all. Forensic investigations, the occasional big-bond bounty hunting, government contract work . . . all with the potential to be life threatening.

The security contract he held on this building was surely tame and mild in comparison and also a favor to his best friend, Spence—and no, it didn't escape her that they shared a best friend. She mostly ignored it. "We have a problem," she said.

He arched a brow, the equivalent of a long-winded query from anyone else.

She rolled her eyes and found herself in a defensive pose, hands on hips. "The emergency exit signs—"

"Already taken care of," he said.

"Okay, but Mr. Nottingham—"

"Also taken care of."

She took a deep, purposefully calming breath. It

was hard to look right at him because he was very tall. At five foot seven, she was nowhere close to petite but even she barely came up to his shoulders. She hated that he had such a height advantage during their arguments. And this was going to be an argument.

"So what happened?" she asked. "Why did the lights go out like that, all at once?"

"Squirrels."

"Excuse me?"

He didn't repeat himself and tired of the macho show, she poked him in the chest with her finger. His pec didn't give at all. *Stupid muscles.* "Listen," she said. "I've got pissed-off tenants, a man in the hospital, and a signed contract from you guaranteeing the safety of the people in this building. So I'm going to need you to do more than stand there all tall, dark, and silently brooding on this one, Archer, and tell me what the hell is going on, preferably using more than one word at a time."

His piercing eyes flashed a disturbingly intense combination of green and light brown, reflecting the fact that he'd seen the worst of the worst and was capable of fighting it with his bare hands. She got that the edge of danger and testosterone coming off him in waves attracted women in droves, but she wasn't one of them.

Or she tried very hard not to be.

She didn't do dangerous men. Nope, only the safe, respectable guy need apply. Not that anyone had applied in a very long time . . .

"You want to be careful how you speak to me, Elle."

The man was impenetrable. A virtual island. And he

didn't like being questioned, she knew that much. But she also knew the only way to deal with him was to hold her own so she just looked at him.

He looked very slightly amused. "Last fall I told you that you had a squirrel colony going on in the roof," he said. "I told you that you needed to hire someone to block off the holes left behind by woodpeckers from the year before or you were going to have problems. You assured me you'd handled it."

"Yes," she said. "Because the landscapers assured me they did."

"Either they blew you off or they didn't do it correctly. An entire colony of squirrels moved into the walls and had a party. Last night they hit the electrical room, where they ate through some wires."

Well, hell. No wonder he was giving her bad 'tude. He was right. This wasn't on him at all.

It was on *her.* "What happened to the squirrels?"

"Probably dead in the walls."

"Are you telling me I killed squirrels?"

This got her a small smile. "What do you think the landscapers would've done?"

"Okay," she said, letting out a long exhale. "Thanks for the explanation." She turned to go.

A hand caught her, fingers wrapping around her elbow and pulling her back around.

"What?" she asked.

This got her another brow arch. When he used his words, his voice was deep, scratchy, and rolled over her like a wave. "Waiting for my apology."

"Sure," she said agreeably. "When hell freezes over." She lifted her chin, grateful for her four-inch heels so she could almost, kind of, not quite look him in the eyes. "I'm in charge of this building, Archer, which means I'm in charge of everything that happens in it. I'm also in charge of everyone who works *for* this building."

He cocked his head, looking amused. "You want to be the boss of me, Elle?" he asked softly.

"I *am* the boss of you."

He smiled and her breath caught. Damn, stupid, sexy smile of his anyway, and he knew it too. And then there was The Body. Yes, she thought of it in capital letters; it deserved the respect. "If you don't want to be walking funny tomorrow," she said, "you'll let me go."

Complete bravado and they both knew it. She'd only been at this job for a year and it'd come as a surprise to her that he'd been in the building at all. An unfortunate coincidence. Before that it'd been years since they'd had any contact, but she still knew enough to get that no one got the better of him.

He did as she asked and let go of her, but not before pausing for a long beat first—just making sure they both knew who was in control here, and it wasn't her.

No one did intimidation like Archer, and in his line of work he could be in a coma and still intimidate everyone in the room.

He had muscles on top of muscles but didn't look beefed up like a body builder. Instead his body seemed lean and seriously badass, with caramel skin that strayed from light to golden to mocha latte depending on what the season was, giving him a look of indeterminable origin.

And sexiness.

It worked for him, allowing him to fit into just about any situation. Handy on the job, she knew. But it annoyed her now. She moved clear, not liking the way her entire body went on a high-level alert in his presence, every inch of her seeming to hum beneath the surface.

It was always a hell of a lot safer to ignore him—and dislike him—from a good distance away.

He waited until she got to the door before he spoke. "I've got a job I need your help on."

"No," she said.

He just looked at her.

Her work was demanding and took up a solid eight hours a day. At night she studied, fighting for her ever-elusive accounting degree. Someday she was going to run her own accounting firm and be badass too, just in a different way than Archer. She was going to be a stable, respectable badass—in great shoes. But in the meantime, she worked herself half into the grave just to keep her head above water.

Problem was, school was expensive, very expensive. As was living in San Francisco. And great shoes. To fund herself, she took the occasional job with Archer when he needed a woman on his investigations. A distraction usually, but sometimes he prevailed on her other skills, skills she'd honed years and years ago when she'd been a street rat.

"It's a challenging job," he said, knowing exactly

how to pique her interest. "Need an ID on a guy, and if it's our man, we need a distraction while we . . . *borrow* his laptop, the one he never lets out of his sight."

"I don't suppose he's the type that you could just walk up to and ask his name," she said.

His mouth quirked in a small smile. "Let's just say I'm not someone who would interest him."

"Who would?"

His gaze slid over her. Slowly. "A hot blonde with legs for days in a short, tight dress," he said.

Heat pooled in her belly and spread outward. Dammit.

"One with the stickiest pickpocket fingers I've ever met."

With a low laugh, she made it to the outer reception area and had just reached for the door when it opened, so that she collided with someone.

The man caught her, keeping her upright. "I'm so sorry," he immediately said. "Are you okay?"

"I'm fine," she said and looked him over.

In his early thirties, he was about her height, medium build, and in a very nice suit. He also had a nice smile, a *kind* smile, and more than a little male interest in his expression. "Mike Cunningham," he said, offering her a hand. "I'm a client of Archer's."

She hesitated for a beat and then let him take her hand. "Elle Wheaton." Then she stepped back from him. "Not a client," she said.

"Ah." He smiled again. "A mysterious woman."

"No," she said. "Just a busy one." She shot one last look at Archer. A mistake because his gaze was inscrutable and on her as always, and she felt her stupid heart do a stupid somersault in her chest.

He came into the front room, moving with his usual liquid grace in spite of being armed for a third-world skirmish. He was quick, light on his feet, and physically strong. But that wasn't what made him so dangerous to her. It was his intelligence. The guy's mind was razor sharp, sometimes dark, and always curious. "Mike," he said, holding the interior door open. "Let's go to my office." He glanced at Elle. "Tonight," he said, clearly certain she'd take the job.

Since she'd never yet figured out how to say no to the hot bastard, she nodded. And for a single beat, the mask fell from his eyes and his golden green gaze warmed as he nodded back.

And then the door shut between them.